THE DEVIL'S DRAIN PIPE

A NUCLEAR WASTE COMEDY

KEITH KIRTS

SYNAPSE—CENTURION
Santa Monica, CA

The Devil's Drainpipe is a work of fiction. All characters and locations are fictitious. Any relation to actual people or places is accidental and coincidental.

SYNAPSE—CENTURION
225 Santa Monica Blvd. Suite 1204
Santa Monica, Ca. 90401

FIRST EDITION

Synapse—Centurion wanted to print this book on American grown hemp paper. We don't want to cut down trees to print our books. Ask your Congressperson why we have to.

Publisher's Cataloging in Publication Data
Kirts, Keith
The Devil's Drainpipe: a Nuclear Waste Comedy
Keith Kirts
p. cm.
1. Fiction 2. Nuclear Waste
3. Humor 4. Religion
LC 93-84180 1993

ISBN 1-882639-01-4

Printed in the United States of America on tree paper

2 4 6 8 10 9 7 5 3 1

For LP

Bon Voyage

ACKNOWLEDGMENTS

Thanks to everyone who has helped with this project. Among them Cindy Maloney, Stephanie Tomita, Elizabeth Porto, Michael Goth, Steve Lapin, Rol Murrow, Rich Hendricks, Karol Rainier, Jim Casteel, Gary Fisher, Mathew Geyer, Harvey Winters and Steve Rosenblatt.

Neil Kellerhouse for typesetting and cover design, and Walberg Design for computer production. Ilene Fogel and Katy O'Harra and the staff at Gemini Graphics for printing. Dan Cytron of Fine Artist's Color & ink for computer output.

Helen Taylor Sheats, who has been an angel over a lot of years to a lot of people. Robert Matthews and Jeff Curry for pushing at the right time.

The night staff at Izzy's Deli for lots of coffee. Also thanks to all the people, relatives, contributors and plants I have known. Without their help this book would not have been possible.

CHAPTER 1

DEEP IS SHALLOW

High on The Devil's Tooth, a mountain east of Pike's Peak in central Colorado, two unlikely companions sat fishing in a mountain stream known as Fawn Brook. A chilly yellow sun cast reflections of craggy snow-capped peaks and many juniper trees onto the clear surface of the water. On the rocky bank, both fishermen leaned comfortably against the bleached roots of a windfallen juniper, each holding a bamboo fishing pole.

One of them, an old, old human wearing white monastic robes and sporting a chest length white beard sat cross-legged, deep in concentration. He stared intently at his red bobber as it drifted slowly away from his friend's green one, leaving an almost invisible wake. The old man's stringy muscles were poised to strike, but as yet he made no move whatsoever.

His companion's eyes also watched the bobber.

Inhuman eyes containing deep wisdom in their wary black depths—the eyes of a yeti, as indeed the creature was. He sat against an adjacent root, holding his bamboo pole with humanoid hands, complete with opposable thumbs. Perfectly relaxed, he seemed, but alert as a wild thing. Greyish fur covered his massive body from head to size 14 feet. The soles of his outstretched feet were heavily calloused. Shaggy grey fur covered the tops of the feet and between the toes, but there was no sign of claws, retractable or otherwise. He wore no clothing, and upon close inspection one could detect worn spots under his arms and on the inside of his trunk-like legs. Curiously, the fur on his heavy skull was thinning tragically, as if fluctuating testosterone levels were working the same magic on the yeti as they do on middle-aged human males.

The yeti, whose name was Montclief, followed the departing red bobber with a mixture of admiration and disgust. The old man was such a lucky fisherman, year after year. Maybe it was the color of his bobber? Maybe the yeti needed a new bobber for himself—a red one. Or he could paint the one he had. Just because it had always been green was no reason to keep it that way.

The red bobber dipped once and still the old man didn't stir. If anything, his fingers relaxed a trifle around the worn cane pole. The first bob of the bobber was usually a feint as the trout mouthed the worm, then spit it out. Next would come the strike. Experience had taught the old fisherman that there was no need for a trout to slash at a worm the way it does at a fly. After all, the worm wasn't going anyplace, just squirming around in the current.

The old man's name was Sri Rainy. Once upon a time in his hell-raising days his name had been Fargo Raisenbe. He wasn't convinced lately that the new name, given to him through a mispronunciation by Pamir Sando, his spiritual Master, was much better. He had been a spiritual guide himself, since Master Sando had sent him forth at age forty to teach the Way. For almost fifty years his life had been dedicated to bringing his disciples, or at least one of them, up to his level—so that he could pass on the mantle, and then seek eternal freedom for himself. That was the duty of a Master, the payback to the Universe for the bounty bestowed on him by his Master. But, by God, his followers *were* a block-headed lot. Year after year, they mistook the unreal for the real and failed to grow. They were filled with false pride, wearing the robes of a seeker as a badge to their mock spirituality rather than as a reminder of their nothingness.

For the first decades, he was patient, wondering why the world kept sending him morons to instruct in the Way; but teaching them nonetheless. More recently he had been forced to face the unpleasant suspicion that maybe he was a bad teacher. Or at least inadequate. His spirit had failed to attract a suitable student; and he was stuck here on this mountain, unable to complete his task. And now there was that strumpet down in town who kept distracting his mind away from serious matters. Gods be damned, he was too old to be a buffoon over a wretched tart, who only wanted to make fun of him while she let the village boys catch her in the pine woods.

Well, at least he had his friend, Montclief—and better, he had a bite. Right, now!

Twitching the pole tip straight up, he set the hook in the trout's mouth. The quiet water exploded as the little fish hit the air, trying to escape the fierce pain in his mouth. Sri Rainy let the willowy bamboo tippet do the work of tiring the fish.

One might wonder how a truly holy man could enjoy inflicting pain on a lesser creature like a fish, but Sri Rainy had answered that question to his satisfaction. Jesus had two disciples who were fishermen, Simon Peter and Andrew. If fishing was compatible with their life, it was certainly okay for him. To say nothing of the miracle of the bread and fishes. Those fish that Jesus himself multiplied must have been alive at some point, or else they would have been called soy/fish cakes or something. Anyway, Rainy had been fishing since he was a boy. Thousands of finny fish had met their karma through the instrument of his hook, and their life protein had then been consecrated to the maintenance of his earthly body. If this was wrong, he was prepared to pay for it on his own karmic wheel. Fishing would certainly not be his most grievous sin.

The little fish tired at last, rolling over on the brook's surface. Sri Rainy hoisted it from the water, a ten inch mountain brown, sparkling radiantly in the weak sunlight.

"Nice one," commented Montclief the yeti, opening the lid of a willow fishing creel.

"Yep. A real scrapper," Rainy said, praising the fish's fighting heart. He unhooked the trout and dropped him into the creel along with two other keepers. Yolanda, Montclief's wife, could do wonders with succulent little trout like this.

*

Sri Rainy's Retreat had been built of field stones entirely by volunteer labor. All real monasteries are built by volunteers; and the Retreat was certainly real, if not altogether effective. On his fiftieth birthday, Rainy had started laying the foundation for the first stone building, alone, on the twenty acres he had acquired from a farmer's bankruptcy sale, near the little town of Pike's Grove, Colorado.

The real estate agent in Brooklyn, armed with several black and white photographs, was probably unaware that the upper reaches of that particular mountain was known as the Devil's Tooth, a colorful local name to describe the grey crag. Had he known, Sri Rainy might have kept looking for a more auspicious site; but he was uninformed. His meager life savings exactly coincided with the asking price for the parcel.

He took that as an omen, and committed himself to Pike's Grove.

The first of his disciples had shown up on the day he began laying the foundation stones, a young bearded drifter named Sam Johnson. Together they hauled and lifted thousands of glacier stones from the fields, fields that were never fit for bountiful farming, and raised the four walls of what was to become the dining hall. Within a month, three more tired nomads were laboring with them. And more came in an endless line down the years.

Those early students had been a great help, Rainy was found of recalling. Devoted and humble, they could work all day and dance the sacred meditation rhythms all night if called upon to do so, and therefore they made great progress. Of course, one by one, they had departed for the city lights. Or had gone to another ashram to further some esoteric side of their learning—leaving Rainy to teach the dregs and the culls that stayed behind.

In the sixties, with the influx of hippie seekers, Rainy's hopes had soared again. Under the influence of the Grand Awakening, the ranks of his students swelled to a hundred or more, and several new buildings were undertaken.

The Retreat currently sported four dormitories, a meeting room, a dining hall and a barnlike exercise hall on a hundred acres of scenic grandeur. But now the permanent residents had dwindled to thirty-five, with a few Hollywood types who came and went as their "creative spirit" moved them. And not one of them was worth a damn. Not really. Perfectly nice people, to be sure. Some of them were even sincere in their lugubrious efforts. But no one of real flair. No fire for knowledge burning hotly. Sri Rainy tried to understand these cycles of learners and followers, knowing it had been the same when he served his Master. Some periods of time were slow and some were filled with rapid learning. The cosmic clock controlled all. But it was very difficult for a teacher to live with the knowledge that his work was unfinished, and that his own days were growing short. At eighty-nine, who could know when the sap would start to weaken? It takes time to raise even a good student to an exalted state. Twenty years was surely the bare minimum. Could he know that he had that much time left? And the seeker he longed for had not appeared.

*

Yolanda made a fuss over the little fish, as she always did. The old man ate hardly anything at the noon meal, so he was no trouble to cook for. And having a guest made Montclief much less gruff. Nevertheless, she worried that Chava, her four year old son, would grow less wary through familiarity with this old one, even though he had never been allowed to meet the ancient yrt in person. Chava was nearly ready to go out on his own. If caution, or respect for the Taboos failed him, Yolanda hated to think what might happen. He was such a gentle child, so unafraid.

The one key taboo of yeti culture—the one thing that was constantly drummed into children from infancy, was to never be seen by yrt star men. It was a survival game. Never be seen and never leave a sign of your passing. Yolanda was all seriousness when she thought of the silly, practical game. In the Atagama Range lived twenty-three yeti families, and there had never been a confirmed sighting by a yrt. And so her people flourished instead of being hunted to extinction.

But Montclief would have his star man friend. No amount of good advice could sway him. She had known he was a deep one when she had married him. Living with a maverick had its trials.

The current success of yetis as a race could be attributed to one simple principle—zero population growth. In a life style with such rigid parameters as theirs, zero growth made perfect sense, of course. No more mountain peaks were being formed for them to live in; and at the Council of Elders, it was agreed not to seek new habitats in the southern ranges. So zero growth kept the status quo as it was. No yeti violated that agreement.

She and Montclief had only the one child. She had agreed to this restriction when they married, because Montclief had another much older son by his first wife, although they seldom saw him. They would have no more children unless, God forbid, something unspeakable should happen.

By strict adherence to the Taboos, the yetis maintained a precarious, but stable community in the high reaches of the world. Their only real worry was the encroaching flatlanders. Every year another cabin or two was built on their domain above the tree line. Why couldn't those yrts just stay down in the heat and bustle, and leave us alone, Yolanda wondered. She thought sadly of little Chava's diminishing future. With every cabin, the survival game became harder to play. To be sure, many of these yrts were driven away by *accidents* made to look natural, but some of them toughed it out.

"That looks delicious," Sri Rainy commented flatteringly, as Yolanda served the trout on the plastic dishes she had stolen from a picnic basket several years ago. The three of them sat on the packed earth cave floor, as always. It was amazing to him how cultured the yetis were, with so little to work with. Yoli, in spite of being six feet five and weighing well over two hundred pounds was one of the most delicate women he had ever known. Woman..? Well, it was certainly difficult to regard her as an animal. Actually, he thought of her as quite beautiful, within and without. He loved to look at the dark mask of fur surrounding her liquid brown eyes. The mask gave her such an alluring look. Sometimes she even wore a wild flower or two in the pure white fur over her ears.

The yeti family was a constant source of wonderment to Rainy. He considered himself sublimely lucky to be allowed to witness their social interaction.

To the best of his knowledge, he was the first man ever so gifted, and the whole friendship mystified and pleased him very much. He thought Montclief was one of the finest people he had ever known—even though he wasn't a person exactly. Or was he? That question drove the old man nuts. And it forced him into town, to the little Carnegie library, where he ordered every title he could find that had anything remotely related to the quest for yetis or abominable snowmen or big feet. After nine years of poring over every published article and book that could be had, he came to the conclusion that he probably knew more about yetis than any man ever had, which wasn't saying a whole lot. Nobody had ever published anything more than speculation. There was not one shred of supportable evidence that yetis existed. No clear photographs, no bones or fossils. Without hard artifacts, the scientific community tended to discount first-hand accounts as figments of a drunken hunter's delusions or perhaps altitude hallucinations. Only he, Sri Rainy, knew different; and he wasn't talking.

The yetis had a spoken language, the sounds of which seemed to disappear into the mountain shadows once the words were uttered, like rain dripping off a ledge. In conformity with many native cultures, they had apparently chosen not to write their words down, not even with pictoglyphs. But they were astonishingly quick-witted. Both Montclief and Yolanda spoke beautiful English, albeit with a mid-western accent, which had caused Sri Rainy's teeth to drop out when he first heard it. Montclief explained this fact pragmatically, saying that only a fool would not speak the major language of the country in which he lived, if only for his own protection.

"Pardon me, honored sir," Montclief had said that morning nine years ago, stepping silently from a clump of alders beside the brook where Rainy was fishing. The gigantic furball had bowed humbly with his immense palms together in a beatific gesture. "I wondered if you could advise me on a spiritual problem

I am having?" he asked, politely. And thereby Montclief had neatly trapped Sri Rainy in the place where he lived.

Too intrigued to be mortally petrified, Sri Rainy had answered the words that sealed a friendship between the two dissimilar beings. "The Great Spirit moves in all things, the waters and the creatures." Those words had come unbidden to his mind when he saw the yeti. Montclief *was* an astounding sight.

Although fully seven feet tall and weighing three hundred pounds, he could move invisibly through the rocks and alpine meadows, not only unseen but unheard as well. An uncanny feat even for a mouse, but for a hulking giant, it bordered on the magical. As their relationship blossomed with time, Montclief confided that he had watched Rainy for several years before convincing himself that it was safe to make contact, in spite of feeling compelled to say hello from the first time he'd seen the old man fishing quietly in a trout stream. The yeti had been so determined to have a human association, that he had followed Rainy to the Retreat where he audited lectures and dance classes on moonless nights, unobserved and unguessed at by Rainy or by any of his students. This was during Montclief's bereavement, when he was half crazy from loss and grief. His first wife had died from complications arising from a fall on a snow field during her second pregnancy. Both the baby girl and Darla had perished in birthing. Montclief was not skilled enough to save them. Darla's mother, who was to attend the birth, had arrived at the cave a week too late.

The question Montclief had asked that day beside Fawn Brook was a complicated sophistry, but also a real question which was causing him moral anguish. "Should one remarry after vowing eternal devotion to another who has died before her years?" he asked, raising his burning eyes to scrutinize Rainy's answer.

➛➚

CHAPTER 2

SHALLOW IS DEEP

Luscious Lotti McCardle had enticed the town drunk into rigging two pulleys: one high on a cedar tree next to the Lodge, and another outside the tiny balcony of her second story bedroom. It took the man a whole day to get the clothesline running smoothly between the two pulleys, just so Lotti could hand wash her dainty undergarments with Woolite in the bathroom sink, then hang them out to flutter dry without running downstairs to the back yard clothesline. The savings in time was enormous since she changed clothes often, and always washed the skimpy bras and bikini panties between wearings. The thought of stepping into underwear a second time without washing it made her skin crawl. Lotti couldn't understand how some women, including her mother, could be such slobs, wearing the same dresses until they practically rotted off. Men were different. If they wanted to wear the same pants and jackets every day, it made sense. Men were slobs to begin with. It was all right for them to smell bad.

Lotti McCardle was one quarter Cherokee Indian, one quarter Australian and one half pure highland Scots. The combination made her restless.

Her brain, which she thought so very clever, was made mostly of clouds and pink cotton candy; but in an eighteen year old woman with jutting breasts and legs that wouldn't quit, success didn't necessarily demand Nikola Tesla upstairs. Already at such a titillatingly young age, Lotti had a shrewd understanding of men. She knew how a hint of sex could wrap any of these local yokels around her little finger—except for Willard Jacks, the county mailman, who acted like she didn't exist. However, she had very big plans for Mr. Dreamboat Willie Jacks. He was going to be her ticket off this mountain and into the beautiful and exciting real world.

To her credit, Lotti was a principled girl. She believed in paying for what she got. Until she could entice Willard to drive her down to Hollywood, California, in his US Mail jeep, she was content to pay for favors from lesser males in the neighborhood—favors such as her revolving clothes line. The coin of her payment was her nubile body. It was a currency in very high esteem out in the pine woods, much to the dismay of the town's old biddies with their clacking tongues.

Her mother, Mary, was thrifty Scots to the bone, and seemed to have no idea in the world how to treat a man. Men don't like stinginess in a woman. Her father, the Cherokee/Aussie dreamer hadn't enjoyed stinginess, Lotti knew that much about him. After he had left her mother to prospect for platinum in Arizona, Mother dear had moved to the farthest outpost of civilization she could find—Pike's Grove. To Lotti's recollection, no man had come visiting more than once, until she herself turned thirteen and started to develop. From then on, several local bachelors showed more than a passing interest in her mother, even to the extent of proposing marriage. Naturally, Mother had said no, wrongly assuming that they wanted her mock Swiss chateau, which was the only solidly built house in town. She also feared for her carefully hoarded savings account. Really, Mother was such a dumb bunny. Lotti couldn't wait to get away from her so that her real life could begin.

She finished wringing out a pair of black crotchless panties that had come airmail from Los Angeles and walked out on her balcony, where she clothespinned them to the line. Now there was a real town! L.A. with palm trees and all those gorgeous hunks. She could be somebody in L.A. People would understand her there.

Her timing was flawless. There, down below in the narrow street was the old holy roller with his scraggy beard. What a geek, she thought, jerking on the clothesline so that it squealed raucously on the pulleys.

Sri Rainy glanced up at the vision of loveliness. The morning sunlight glancing off her naked shoulders and brown hair made rather a halo of sublime brightness around her. He quickly averted his eyes, cursing himself for taking this street against his will, again. His sandaled feet absolutely refused to go to the library along Main Street. They insisted on degrading him daily on Spruce Lane. Damn the girl, and damn my fool urges! His knees felt the accustomed rush of weakness that always hit them when he passed the Lodge. Ludicrous! Absurd!

"Hey, Mortimer Snerd!" Lotti called down to him. All the village children called Sri Rainy by that name, since the first one had stuck him with the label, roughly thirty years ago. As a young girl, Lotti had believed that was his real name, since she was too young to know of the ventriloquist's dummy, who had been so famous in her mother's time. But since the McCardle finances were so intimately tied in with the Retreat, Mommy dear had been quick to correct the girl with a willow switch. "Never call him that," Mary McCardle bellowed, emphasizing her meaning with vicious slashes of the green willow wand.

"I won't, I won't!" the girl promised tearfully, vowing to call the old man *nothing but* Mortimer Snerd when she grew up.

Mary McCardle was not a bad woman in her heart. She even had a Scot's sense of humor, though it seldom showed. She told herself that raising a daughter alone in this hard world demanded that she be very practical. Practicality in this hamlet meant being nice to religious kooks and members of their family, who were visiting the Retreat. Actually, Mary thought the name Mortimer Snerd fitted the old reprobate rather perfectly. His mouth under the white beard seemed to work on a hinge, exactly like a puppet or a ventriloquist dummy's. Mary and most of the townswomen referred to Mortimer Snerd among themselves as the Swami. But it wouldn't do to have her own little girl calling his Holiness a crude name in front of the paying guests.

Seizing opportunity when she first saw it, Mary had purchased the old hunting lodge on land contract from a hunting guide, who had catered to rich sportsmen. He had done quite well with the Lodge before the burg of Pike's Grove sprang up. But with each house and each store, he grew more disgruntled, keeping the dwindling money from hunters and fishermen in his pocket rather than repairing the building. After the purchase agreement was signed, Mary discovered more rehab work than she had imagined possible. She thought that a simple scrubbing with suds and a brush would erase the pipe smoke and dried blood, making the place a fit habitation for tourists; but she quickly learned that there was more to being a hotel keeper than good food and clean rooms. Rotted foundations had to be repaired too, and that took a bank loan with interest to be repaid.

For sixteen years, Mary McCardle had pinched pennies and played hostess to religious fanatics and sightseers who could afford to rent one of Mary's rooms instead of sleeping in the forest, or for reasons of their own choose not to live at the Retreat. Mary's natural Scot's thriftiness was appreciated by most of the guests as a sign of sparse humility, but her daughter knew it was a sign of rampaging miserliness. Mary, far beyond the crass opinions of others, was convinced of the moral correctness of squeezing a penny until it squeaked for mercy.

In any event, the Spruce Lane Lodge, with the fish and gaminess long scoured away, was a fixture in Pike's Grove. Mary had never taken even one tiny step toward discovering if real spirituality might exist at the Retreat. She was, however, bright enough to know that the thin manna of dollars falling on the village resulted only from Sri Rainy. But now, with only thirty students at the Retreat, times were hard for the satellite industries. The local cash registers longed for the hordes of white-robed freaks who brought credit cards with them to The Devil's Tooth. And almost everybody was worried that the old geezer was getting too old. If he cashed in his chips, so would they.

Except Lotti, who cared nothing for cashing chips in Pike's Grove. She just wanted desperately to catch the first jeep out of town, as soon as she had gotten some valuable experience by screwing every man worth screwing on this jerky mountain.

Recovering his sea legs once he was out of sight of the Spruce Lane Lodge, Sri Rainy stepped briskly up the wooden steps of the Carnegie Public Library. That the Carnegie people had seen fit to sponsor a full library in a town so tiny was largely Rainy's doing. Seekers must have access to many different kinds of knowledge, he reasoned. Public education, no matter how work-force oriented it was, had caused modern people to rely on and feel safe with the printed word, so he needed to supply his pupils with books, in addition to oral teachings. By casually mentioning the need of a library to several of his well-connected followers, he was delighted to learn three years later that Pike's Grove had been selected as the site for a county facility. Although the number of books was rated on a per capita basis and would therefore be small, it was a definite improvement over a branch library. There would even be a real librarian.

And there was. Mrs. Esther Olsterholt had been on duty nearly every working day since the library opened twenty odd years ago. She'd been a little haughty at first about the Swami's obsession with yetis, but after the first few books had arrived, Esther had gotten into the spirit of the investigation and had kept her eyes open for any new material. He had joshed her into believing that he had an interest in science fiction, and that yeti research fitted into that category. The science fiction novels he picked up as part of the charade remained unopened on his work table until he returned them.

Before moving into intellectual obscurity in Pike's Grove, Esther had fancied herself a bright young lady. She had a Masters degree in library science from Indiana State, and was hell on wheels with the Dewey Decimal System. Her husband, Ted, had been an ardent lover of the outdoors. When her application for Pike's Grove was accepted, eclipsing the other forty-three applicants, the happy couple had considered themselves about the luckiest people on the face of the globe. But poor Ted had become crippled by spinal meningitis and finally died from the disease at the age of forty-six.

Poor Teddy hadn't been quite right in the head for the last years of his life. The meningitis developed after an avalanche took him for a horrible ride down a mountain slope and trapped him for thirty-six hours. Teddy evidently damaged his head as well as his spine in the fall. He always claimed that there was another occupant in that wild, snowy plummet. A yeti or something like one. And that the awesome beast had eventually pulled him from the snowy grave, and left him in a dazed state to make his way back to the cabin. Of course, no one believed him and there was not a shred of evidence pointing to a yeti or anything else, except a lot of avalanched snow and a twisted spine. Esther herself had not believed the strange story for one minute.

Reasonably enough then, Sri Rainy's sudden interest in yetis had annoyed her at the outset. She assumed incorrectly that he was needling her in that superior way of his. Esther was certainly bright enough to know that the Swami had his long bony fingers in every facet of life in Pike's Grove, but she also knew that without him there would be no library for her to run, and thus no reason to live after Ted's death. Her incorrect assumption was that Rainy was purposely stirring memories of yetis in her. Like most people with whom Sri Rainy came into contact, Esther construed his every action as a volitional effort aimed at furthering his teaching. There was no one else in the library who could be the target of his yeti barbs, so she assumed that he was trying to play with her mind, and she didn't like it even a little bit. Her job, however, was to order books for people, so she smiled bitterly and sent the order off to Denver.

But now, a decade after the first inquiry, Esther was so grateful to the old man. He really was a magician, of that she was certain. Nothing else, except the inquiry into yetis, could have cured her of the loss of faith she had suffered because of her beloved Ted's delusion. Now, not only did she know a great deal about the legends of yetis (and related phenomena) but she had a shining memory of her dear lost Ted. She had even forgiven herself for doubting his word about the avalanche. And it was all thanks to that sublime man, Sri Rainy, who had restored her faith in Ted by forcing her to believe that yetis really might exist. This town owed him more than it could possibly imagine.

After Ted's death, Esther saw no reason to keep the A-frame cabin they had lived in up by Breakup Lake, so named because it was the first of the mountain lakes to break free of ice after the spring thaw. As long as Teddy was alive and vibrant, the solitude of the lake was wonderful; but during his sickness, the long nights became oppressive, and after his passing she had put the cabin up for sale and moved into Mary McCardle's Lodge, where she had been for the past eleven years. There was social life at the Lodge, she had reasoned; and some years, depending on the clientele, this was almost true. Esther lived in a two room suite at the back of the second floor, with a stunning view of the mountains and a Franklin stove for cold nights. One could scarcely say that she was happy like she had been with Ted, but she still had a good job and she got along quite nicely, thank you. Her relationship with Mary had been distant at first, but with the years and lonely winter nights, and the fact that Esther always paid her rent scrupulously on time, a friendship developed. Both women now regarded each other as sisters, and sometimes even more than sisters.

Even though there was no one else in the library, Sri Rainy held a congenial, whispered conversation with Esther, then he left with a science fiction novel under his arm. There was nothing new on yetis, but he hadn't expected that there would be.

During the scant ten minutes he had spent inside, the hazy sunshine had slipped away, and was replaced by a dismal mist which turned to drizzle as he hurried down Main Street. After forty years in the Rockies, he still had not learned to take the weather into account. Sri Rainy set his lips in a sneer and tucked the book into a fold in his robes.

In deference to Sri Rainy, eight-nine years of age need not be dotage for an enlightened man. Once volitional control of the lower energy and voluntary surrender to higher is attained, aging mechanisms with their ever escalating desire to cross-link key molecules of the immune system can be radically inhibited from doing so. Less cross-linking equals reduced disease damage and slower aging. In other words, his juices still flowed.

Although scandalous, in holy history there are many amusing tales of holy men flopping over and kicking their skinny legs in the air when they meet that perfect young tart. Sri Rainy was certainly aware of that somewhat embarrassing lineage. Sufi Masters have an undying penchant for this form of foolishness. Catholic priests succumb in rather high numbers, often selecting boys to dote on so that their oaths aren't technically violated. These were real, dedicated, enlightened (or nearly enlightened) people, who tumbled into the gulf of carnality at advanced ages and made side-show geeks of themselves by wallowing in spermy "love". Wholly inappropriate behavior, he reminded himself, setting off toward the Retreat by way of Main Street. But like guided missiles, his sandals turned onto Spruce Lane forcing his well-preserved body to follow.

He had only just made the turn when a tinkling laugh in his left ear stopped his sandals in their tracks. Repulsive behavior, he snarled at the feet. It was enough to make a saint throw up. But heaping self-condemnation on himself did not unrivet his feet nor strengthen his weakening knees. It was the laugh of Luscious Lotti he had heard, and miraculously she stood on the sidewalk several feet away, having just come out of Hinton's Hardware Store with a four pack of light bulbs in her hand and a square of bubble gum masticating wetly in her mouth.

"Hi, Mortimer," she said. "Been to the library?"

"Yes, actually I have," he said stiffly, showing her the science fiction book as proof. There was nothing he could do or say to relieve his lusting heart without making an utter fool of himself. He could hide behind his kindness or gruffness or holiness with everyone else, but Lotti knew about his weakness and she never let him off the hook. Her eyes gleamed with malicious enjoyment, knowing she could make him be her lapdog anytime she chose to. Rainy did not kid himself, how could he? His heart and lower nature longed to be her slave if only for a day before she tired of the game—or an hour. But his well controlled reason would not let him. He could not offer her baubles in exchange for her favors, even though he knew baubles would work. He could do nothing that might interfere with his high-blown purpose of finding a successor. And to do nothing was worse than to die. His eyes drank her red rouged cheeks and flashing eyes like the last sip of nectar for a dying bee. She wasn't even beautiful in a normal way, but something about her energy pattern and the conformity of her features simply set him ablaze. Good Lord, he thought in wonderment, I don't believe I've ever been this alive before. Blood was literally coursing through his veins. He could feel it like an awakening geyser.

"Why are you staring at me?" the girl asked, all innocence and guile. He knew that nothing was real about her. A sleeping automaton, programmed to exude sex and nothing else. A walking baby factory. A hollow shell filled with fluff. Easily said, old man. So what is it about her that makes you crazy to put your prong deep into the fluff? It had been so easy to say no for the past sixty years. In those sixty years any number of high quality women would have gladly screwed his eyeballs loose, with only a tiny word of encouragement. Why this one?

"I have to be going along," he said as the falling rain pattered harder. Soon he would be wet to the bone, standing on the street gawking at this vision. Not that he cared. And seemingly neither did Lotti. Raindrops caught in her clean hair and sparkled there like diamonds. Lord, she was so incredibly beautiful!

"Would you like to stop over to our house for a cup of tea? I know Mother would be glad to see you."

"Tea..?" he said, suddenly overwhelmed with her generosity. He felt his eyes brimming with tears, and thanked the stars that the rain would wash them away.

"Or coffee. I just mentioned tea because so many of the people out at your place drink herb tea. Or we have beer and wine. Would you rather have a bottle of beer?" she grinned up at him. Her dark eyebrows arched into perfect question marks.

"Tea would be fine," he heard himself say. "Well, let's be going along before you're soaking wet." He took the girl's elbow, ostensibly for support—ostensibly because he just had to touch her and she knew it—and turned her toward the Spruce Lane Lodge.

Electric tingles shot up his fingers where they rested on her warm elbow. Could she feel that? he wondered. Probably not. She was sending, not receiving. The girl had not changed clothes since he saw her on the balcony, fifteen minutes earlier. She still wore the knitted halter top that left her tanned shoulders and midriff exposed and did very little to cover her enchanting breasts. Even though the red fabric was rather close knit, he could see the dark color of her areolas through the tiny squares. His eyes refused his command not to stare. Poor old Sri Rainy shuddered at the open rebellion going on inside him. He jerked his head away to look up at the rain and cedar trees, and got a whiplash of brain pain. The whim that named this street Spruce Lane caused anybody who noticed nature to have instant brain damage. There was not one spruce tree, only cedars.

Thank the Lord for the sanity of wearing heavy muslin robes, he chuckled to himself. There was no way that he could be embarrassed by the engorging of his old, old penis as the hot blood rushed to fill the erectile tissue. It feels fantastically marvelous to be a man, he chortled to himself, well-pleased that this miracle was happening.

"Aren't you cold?" he asked, as they sloshed along. He looked down at Lotti's long, shapely legs. Only a small portion of each leg was clad in wet cut-off Levi's. The Levi's did emphasize the cute roundness of her buttocks, however.

"A little bit," she laughed, charmingly. "Why don't you give me your robes? That way I won't get wet." The girl looked at his dripping white robes. Mocking laughter shone in her blue eyes.

"I didn't think it would rain," he replied, idiotically.

➾ ➽

CHAPTER 3

EMPTY YET INEXHAUSTIBLE

Supervising the cooking at the Retreat was responsible work of the first order. Meals had to taste good to the tongue, be nourishing to body and spirit and stay within a strict budget. For the past three weeks this task had been assigned to Norman Ungerer III, one of the Philadelphia Ungerers. And he did try vigilantly to put out healthful meals, that much could be said for him.

The Retreat was totally self sufficient in regard to menial jobs like cooking, plumbing and gardening. One was expected to lend a hand in exchange for living there — service on the path of enlightenment.

Sri Rainy had given Norman two assistants, Sister Angie and Herb Halperin, both older students, who had actually been in charge of the kitchen until Norman's appointment. These three were assigned permanently, three meals a day, dawn until dusk. Several kitchen helpers rotated daily from the ranks of the resident students to peel potatoes and wash dishes. The helpers generally regarded their turn as drudgery, whereas Norman and his lieutenants felt that food preparation as a high calling.

If Norman could have really supervised, or simply cooked for the thirty-five pupils by himself, the task might have gone smoothly and he might even have felt good about a job well done. But there was a hitch.

Two meals after promoting him from a lowly gardener to Supervising Cook, Sri Rainy had reneged on the supervisor part. Too late. Norman had already gulped down the hook of false pride. Seeing that his fish was firmly hooked, Sri Rainy casually suggested in front of dull-witted Herb and Sister Angie, that it might be interesting for the three of them to form a committee to plan the menus and work out appealing arrangements of food on the plates—all the little things that had made Norman's life a hell since that day. Oh, yes, he was the kitchen supervisor, but he had to barter for agreement from the ghastly duo on every bitching little tiny, teensy, part of the task. One compartment of his mind realized that this was a test, carefully calculated by Sri Rainy to push him along the Path, but the rest of him was being driven stark raving bonkers. No matter what he wanted to serve for breakfast, lunch or dinner—no matter how good it might taste, or how inspired the choice of food groups—Sister Angie always found a way to disagree.

"Always..!!" he shouted aloud. Norman felt at liberty to shout, since he was sitting in the crapper, alone, hiding from his responsibilities. The kitchen help had gotten used to him taking excessively long pit stops, while everyone else confined themselves to a quick elimination so that the outhouse facilities could be used by others and no time would be wasted that could be used purposefully. They even made little pointed jokes about Norman's excess, within his hearing, of course. That was the accepted mode of behavior modification around the Retreat—barbed cattiness.

Norman, naturally, played the same game when someone else's unpleasant manifestations needed a change. He had a keen mind and a sharp tongue of his own. The small faction of students that he counted as friendly laughed uproariously when he cut into a victim. In the safety of a monastic community, where fisticuffs were never resorted to, it was unnecessary to be careful of anyone's feelings. If a sensitive feeling was hurt by an unkind word, that was the injured person's own fault. Why was he holding onto a fantasy of himself? Weak spots should be exposed constantly as the fastest way for growth. Spiritual advancement was the reason every pupil had come to the Retreat, even though they spent most waking moments rebuilding their protective walls.

Sri Rainy, of course, was a master of bludgeoning an inflated ego. He could use a silken touch or his rapier tongue to flay a person, in front of all the other Seekers. Norman adored watching him in action when an errant pupil needed mashing—if that pupil wasn't himself.

Yes, Sri Rainy truly was a wonderful teacher, totally devoid of human passion or compassion. When it came time to push a student up to a new plateau, he could move with stunning accuracy, crushing the poor fellow underfoot like an insect, smashing the atoms of his false ego like an exploding skyrocket. Making him feel like dog dirt. Then propping him up for weeks afterward if need be, until the change had taken place and the student was once again strong. He had the master's touch, no possible doubt about that.

Norman knew how it felt to be picked apart, atom by atom—exposed to the view of all (including himself, of course.) He certainly wasn't looking forward to the next installment. Nobody got off from being targeted. It was bloody painful. That's why they all hid from Sri Rainy like rabbits.

What a bunch of cowards, Norman scoffed, pulling his robe down as he stood up from the outhouse seat. And I'm the most cowardly of the whole bunch.

"The stench of my cowardice can be smelled from here to Burma!" he shouted, poetically. He walked back to the kitchen hoping someone had overheard that pearl of wisdom.

But, of course, to know that you're a coward, and to do something about it are two separate items. Only by eating enough cowardice that it sickens one, can progress be made. And virtually no one is strong enough to eat by themselves. The lifetime of carefully constructed defenses are simply too clever. Tomorrow, the tomorrow defense sighs reasonably. I'll start tomorrow. Really! I will work diligently on this, tomorrow.

So every seeker needs a teacher to bully, push and cajole him into even considering the possibility of change. No real teacher—no real change. Just the chimera—the glossy surface and the white robe covering the same old garbage inside. And who in his right mind would be a teacher, having to deal with sniveling, lying students every day of his life?

Answer—only someone who has to.

"Thank Heavens, you're back," Sister Angie snipped her irritation at Norman Ungerer. "The water heater's gone back on us, again."

"Well, start some water heating in the kettles," Norman said. Dishes had to be washed after the meal. When the water heater started playing games, the procedure was to heat water on the industrial stove top burners. Sister Angie knew that.

"No room," she answered, smugly.

And indeed, a glance at the stove top showed Norman that all the burners were engaged in the preparation of lunch. "And another thing," she crabbed, "I know we agreed, but these potatoes are so tiny. One of them on the plate with that little dab of salad looks stingy. The men will complain."

"They won't complain. There's plenty of bread."

"Why not put two on the men's plates?"

"We don't have extras," Norman snapped. "It's nobody's fault the potato crop is small. There wasn't enough rain. Everybody knows and accepts it."

"I know, but..." she said, wistfully, glancing over at Herb Halperin for support. Herb normally ganged up on Angie's side against Norman. They acted like they were the supreme experts on feeding the masses, but if Sri Rainy hadn't wanted Norman to run the kitchen, he wouldn't have asked him to. Sri Rainy knew who had a head for management, and he wasn't fooled by these two gutter pigs who were just spiritual hangers-on.

"And don't go putting extras on the plates behind my back," Norman commanded Sister Angie, "or there won't be enough for the kitchen help."

She smirked at him, but he knew he'd made his point. She wanted her potato and could be counted upon not to give it away.

*

There was one town drunk in Pike's Grove. The burg was just too small to support more than one public disgrace, although roughly half of the seven hundred inhabitants were closet tipplers. Colorado is famous for its ski runs and rugged mountains, and slightly famous for its alcohol consumption.

Old Tad Foulks, the drunk, had a constitution like iron. His partial disability checks from Viet Nam covered his muscatel tab at Wong's Spot Right Liquor and Laundry, but there wasn't enough left over for food and shelter, so Tad disdained shelter. He lived in the pine woods with the squirrels, foxes and bears, and never shared a drink with them. In the dead of winter, people said he dug himself a snow cave, but that is an unlikely story since he disliked being out of eye contact with Wong's.

His disability was the loss of his pinky finger, which had been neatly blown off by a machine gun bullet in a jungle skirmish. One could scarcely call him disabled, except by drink. To give Tad his due, he was still ruggedly handsome. His face, blasted by booze, sun and wind, was eroded with deep wrinkles and broken capillaries; but somehow the dark walnut skin still seemed healthy. And his bright blue eyes, when he wasn't falling-down drunk, twinkled with a secret merriment as if he was putting one over on the world. He was without doubt an excellent woodsman, the fact that he was still robustly alive proved that much.

Because of his looks, Tad had been the reclamation project of countless earth mothers during his lifetime. Alas, all unsuccessful. A week or two of living under a roof and enjoying the benefits of home cooking, hot water and a mothering woman was as much as he could stand. The price of pussy cut into his freedom more than he could afford. Neither the Alcoholics Anonymous wagon, nor moderate drinking, interested him at all. And even an earth mother likes to see a little progress being made, so eventually he was out the door again.

Still, he had a bit more dignity than a skid-row drunk. And whenever the good people of Pike's Grove needed an object of scorn, they had a built-in bottom rung of the social ladder to wrinkle their noses at.

It was next to unbearable for kind, gentle Sister Angie. Actually, it was unbearable. This task that Sri Rainy had foisted on her was the hardest ever. Before that geek, Norman Fatlip the Third, had complained about the food groupings, her life had been fine.

Until Fatlip had opened his mouth, Sister Angie had run the kitchen for two years of uninterrupted happiness. The meals had been delicious and on time. None of this tripe about not mixing protein with carbohydrates. Where did he get off on that garbage anyway? Studied in college. Big fat wow! Every normal American knows they should eat portions from the five major food groups at every meal. The government spent millions in tax money getting that message across. That's what makes a meal taste good and be nutritious.

Then Big Mouth spouts out his college theory, and suddenly he's in charge. No meat with potatoes. No fruit for dessert. Fruit for snacks or alone without other food. What crap! How about raisin bran, she had asked, or bananas on cornflakes, or raisins on oatmeal? What about cheese and fruit for dessert? Cottage cheese and peaches? What about normal food, centuries old, tried and true?

No. Suddenly, he's in charge and he never even considers that the reason Sri put him in the kitchen was to learn something. Not to always be spouting his mouth. Not to brag about getting the job on his own merits after only a measly two years here. Puffed up with false pride like a toad. Puff, puff, puff. Spout, spout, spout!

Sister Angie, herself, had been living at the Retreat for sixteen years, and never once had she complained about the hard life and the back breaking personal tasks that Sri Rainy had arranged for her. Never one time had she let false pride keep her from giving her utmost to do his bidding. No complaints about the lack of privacy in the freezing stone dorms, or the ice water showers when the water heater broke, or the thousands of personal inconveniences. Never once had she hogged the outhouse like somebody she knew.

Certainly, she was one of Sri's personal favorites, why else would he put her in charge of the kitchen for so long? Preparing the first level food was very responsible work. Not only did the food need to be good, but the vibes of the cooks had to be pure or the food would be subtly poisoned. And she never complained or talked back if Sri should reprimand her for some kitchen procedure that she knew was correct. It wasn't her way to act like she knew everything. Of course, she did stand her ground if she *absolutely knew* she was right, but that was only natural. Sri wanted people to speak up when they were right. And men, even Sri, had to be informed when they were talking on and on about something they just didn't understand.

Yes, Sister Angie felt that she was very close to enlightenment. Surely, it was so. Why else would Sri constantly make his little jokes about her — jokes that cut her to the quick, but at which she laughed gaily, pretending that they bounced off her like water off a duck's back. "Thick as a lump." That was one of his jokes. Her hackles rose just thinking of his mocking voice saying those mean words. Why wouldn't she be angry? There was simply no reason for a person to be that cruel. She never had a bad thought about anyone, not even during her menstrual period when she suffered terribly. Always cheerful, that was her. It made her bristle to even think of those snide, self-righteous words. Thick as a lump, indeed! Another thing that made her bristle was

"Butter Butt." Oh, yes. Yes, indeed. She heard them call her Butter Butt, and snigger about it. Or Sister Butter. Impudent snipes! Who did they think they were, when she sacrificed her whole life, slaving and sweating in the kitchen so they could eat the stinking food—and then they made fun of her!!

CHAPTER 4

FULL BUT EMPTY

"This is quite a lovely old building. It's a pity I never visited before," Sri Rainy said to Lotti's mother, Mary.

The instant he had entered the Lodge, Lotti had run upstairs yelling that she'd be right back with some towels, but so far she hadn't returned, and Rainy was left to make small talk with the mother.

Irritating. What was he doing here, marking time with this husk of a women, dried out by mountain stinginess? He had things to attend to back at the Retreat, and he was missing lunch. This is the way a school boy behaves.

"Yes, the Lodge has been very good to us," Mary McCardle said, chattily. She wasn't quite sure what the dripping wet Swami was doing in her kitchen. He had never visited her before. Any number of envoys had been sent from the Retreat to look in on sick students who were staying at the Lodge, but he never attended them personally. In a flash of insight, Mary knew what she could do to make the great man feel at home. Several years ago, a freaked-out tenant had spent hours framing a small poster of the Swami and had given the result of his work to Mary to hang in the kitchen so she would have good vibes for cooking.

Hanging the picture would have been good for business; but somehow she hadn't thought she'd like the dark magical eyes staring at her back while she stood at the stove. So she had hung the picture in one of the guest bathrooms. Her current bright idea was to get the Swami to sign the poster, since he was here. She hated to think of him passing away, but he *was* old. His autograph on his photo would certainly make it a collector's item.

"Could you wait here for a second," Mary requested sweetly, remembering which bathroom she had hung the picture in.

"Certainly," the old guru answered, assuming Mary was going to check on her malingering daughter.

"I'll just be a minute." She curtsied and scurried up the same flight of stairs where Lotti had gone.

So Rainy was alone with the gurgling tea kettle. He studied its crooked neck, wondering how soon it would whistle, or if it was even a whistling kettle.

Bare feet pattered down the staircase. Rainy knew it was Lotti by the joyousness of the bare heels striking the treads. A ripple of anticipation fluttered in his stomach. The sheer number of body reactions connected to sex was astonishing. Why had he deemed it necessary to put a lid on those natural, heavily loaded reactions after he entered the Way? Actually, this ludicrous scene was almost worth the price of admission in tools for self study. He could apply this new knowledge to his understanding of students' motives. Yes, that was a very pragmatic reason to further his research into Lotti, because after all, he was a teacher before anything else.

Lotti entered the kitchen wearing a pink shortie terrycloth robe which was tied with a matching pink belt. Her dark hair was fluff dried and her legs were blatantly naked up to the hem of the robe. Rainy was sure that she wore nothing under the garment. She smiled devilishly and handed him a soft orange towel.

"You'd better dry off, Mortimer. We wouldn't want you catching a cold." The impish smile continued to play on her full lips. "If you want, I'll throw your robe in the dryer," she offered.

"I'm sure that won't be necessary. It will only get wet again when I leave."

"Don't act like such an old foggy. Of course, you have to get dry. Come upstairs and I'll find you something to wear." Lotti took his hand and led him firmly to the stairwell. Electric contact tingles preempted Rainy's reluctance. He followed along grumbling, but meek as a choir-boy.

On the tortuous stairs, the pink robe rode up with each step, revealing half of each naked, perfectly biteable buttock. Rainy's heart leaped into his mouth and stuck there. The view was awe inspiring. He could hardly constrain his teeth from biting the forbidden fruit.

"Don't stare at me like that," Lotti cautioned, without looking back.

Rainy couldn't even muster a reply. It seemed natural that the girl could read his thoughts, too. Why not? She was obviously a spirit of some kind, or had a spirit helper. And her playful spirit was hurting him—poking fun at him. And yes, hurting him. A pain shot through his liver with every undulation of her butt. What in the world could she gain by flaunting herself so outrageously before an eighty-nine year old man? All he could do was follow those swaying orbs, hoping to further his research. His senses told him that the garden of earthly delights awaited him at the top of the stairs. Some drunken part of him urged the old boy to visit that garden before he died.

At the top of the dark stairs, Rainy found himself sweating and palpitating. It's a wonder that I don't have a coronary or a stroke, he thought. On the flatlands of the upstairs hallway, Lotti's pink robe was back in place covering her rump, but that made little difference to his adrenalized senses.

Lotti's mother darted out of a room, stumbling over herself. "Oh, Mr. Rainy!" she blurted. She swished something behind her back to hide it, then sheepishly pulled it out. A picture of him in a god-awful papier-mache frame.

"Look what I found," said Mary, holding the small poster aloft like it was a cherished heirloom. "I was wondering if you would sign it for me, Sri, now that you've finally paid a visit?"

"Mother, I am trying to get Mortimer into some dry clothes!" Lotti tugged at Rainy's gnarled hand, showing him that she, not her mother, was in charge.

"I'll just takc this downstairs, Your Eminence," Mary McCardle said, gazing fondly at the cherished picture. "When you're dry, will be soon enough. We wouldn't want you to catch a cold. Do you think it will ever stop raining?"

"I hope not," he said, meaning that the crops and the forest needed rain. Each of the women imagined that he meant something far more carnal.

With a smile of disdain at her mother, Lotti led her captured monk into her bedroom.

*

Willard Jacks had been the Pike Township

Postmaster for three and a half years. During the Christmas rush, he hired an assistant, but for the remainder of the year, he and Jolie Spalding handled the job alone. Jolie held down the fort, receiving and sorting mail while he was out on deliveries nine hours every weekday, and longer in bad weather. Most people thought that Jolie was the Postmistress, since she was always at the office; but no, Willard was. The Postmaster, not the Postmistress.

The Post Office bought him a new jeep every four years and by that time he needed one. Some of the mountain roads were simply hideous. His current vehicle was just about used up. Loose rocks had smashed the oil pan twice and cracked the crank case once. Ruts and potholes had destroyed the suspension. Flood water from Fawn Brook had drowned the engine last spring. The plastic side curtains were checked and yellowed from constant refreezing and the radiator was beginning to act up again. Willard had added some radiator gunk this morning, but as the jeep labored up the steep grade above Rickford Meadow, he noticed the heat indicator needle was starting to twiddle again. There was nothing to do but go on—he had a Bean's catalogue for Asa Peters, the old coot who lived up Mudslide Pass, poaching deer and trout all year long, and taking an occasional pot-shot at tourists. Willard was well aware that Mudslide Pass wasn't named by accident and this rain would make the treacherous road down the other side slippery as greased shit, but he was the mailman. He had the mailman credo to live up to, and L.L. Bean needed him on the job.

Willard was considered an imminently eligible bachelor by all the matchmakers in Pike Township, but he never thought seriously about marriage. At thirty-one, he was content with keeping the mail deliveries on schedule, and with his unscheduled visits to several house fraus whom he was boffing while their husbands worked at the saw mill.

His ruling passion, the one that kept him alone in his little cabin most nights, was reading. Willard belonged to three paperback book clubs and took his membership as a privilege. Having a wife around, or even a live-in woman, would infringe on his reading time, of that there was no doubt. And what could a woman do in return? Cook? He already cooked his own venison and beans as well as anyone could, and he ate exactly when he was hungry. Or sex? A mailman on a country route doesn't have to worry about that. Especially a young buck like Willard. Nope, he was content with his life, just the way it was. And in a few months, he'd get the new jeep and then it would be perfect.

He was blissfully unaware that Lotti McCardle was scheming to take him, and more particularly his jeep, to Hollywood. In fact, he was only dimly aware of Lotti at all, since he didn't resort to robbing the cradle.

"Now, Mortimer, get out of that wet rag instantly," Lotti ordered. "What do you call that thing, anyway?"

"A robe, I guess," Sri Rainy said, furrowing his brow. He wasn't exactly sure what to call the cowled gown. His order, the Seekers of the White Light, had no official dress code, and for that matter had no official policy of any kind. There were two ashrams of Seekers in North America and three in Europe. For political and tax purposes, the Order was weakly allied both to the Tasajara Zen community in California and to the Nashqbendi Order of Sufis in Tunis. The Seekers held no regularly scheduled ecumenical councils, although limited visiting of students for purposes of special studies was encouraged. His own teacher, Pamir Sando, had died in 1973, and Rainy thought that perhaps he was the

Elder of the Order now. He hadn't heard from old Carlos Sentori in Trinidad for several years. And now, this minx wanted to know the official name of his robe. It's a robe, what else would you call it?

"It's a robe," he repeated, gently.

"Well, take it off! Cheesh..!"

"It is not my practice to get naked in the presence of young women, my dear."

"Your monkey robe is all wet, and besides you want to, don't you?"

"Yes," he replied, enchanted that she'd called his garment a "monkey robe" to his face. That was the perfect name for it, of course. A monkey robe. Delightful. It had been thirty years since anyone, except Montclief, had had the courage to bait him. "But," he said, "just because I might want to get naked with you, doesn't mean I'm going to. Temporal gratification is not sought after by my Order."

Lotti looked into his eyes with a piquant frown on her rosebud mouth. "Mortimer, are you going to be difficult now that you lured me into the bedroom?"

"I lured you..?"

"Well, didn't you..?"

"Perhaps, I did," he admitted. His knees were quite weak. He sat on the little chair in front of her dressing table, so that the trembling would not prove him a coward.

*

But the two strangest members of the human race currently in Pike Township were the two guys next door to Lotti's room—in Room 9 to be exact. They were geologists, respected men in their field. Dr. Charles Barkley was a graduate of Yale and Dr. Omar Yates had taken his degrees from the University of California at

Berkeley. They were both employed by the Bureau of Lands and Mines, a division of the Department of Agriculture, but they were on loan. The geologists were on the mountain with a mission, as of course, Sri Rainy was also. Neither of these basically good men cared to think deeply on the sinister implications of their mission, which after all was their rice bowl. They were on loan to the Department of Energy and their job was to locate a site to hide or otherwise store all that glowing nuclear waste, which their so called sane government had been manufacturing like crazy for the last twenty five-years.

Other governments all over the world had been making the lethal stuff, too, in cooperation with business men who had the moral and ethical standards of hyenas.

Data from a Lands and Mines satellite had suggested that the granite composition of The Devil's Tooth was a geologically stable environment for the storage vaults, nothing like Mount Saint Helens in Washington, which had blown up not so very long ago. Granite, of course, is formed by molten extrusions pouring from the hot interior of the planet. But hell, that was eons ago. Instability like that could never happen again in Colorado.

Drs. Barkley and Yates were to eyeball the situation, as the saying goes. But the first things they did after renting Rooms 8 and 9 for a month from Mrs. McCardle, was to eyeball little Lotti very thoroughly. At this moment, both men were in Yates' room unpacking their rifles and fishing rods. They had told Mary that they were sportsmen, taking a sporting vacation up here in Paradise. Their own government had suggested that it might be intelligent for them to remain incognito, rather like CIA agents, while they eyeballed the new sites for the deep shafts of hell.

➾ ⇚

CHAPTER 5

CLEAR BUT MURKY

"Well, it wasn't a total lie," Dr. Yates commented, uncomfortably. He was a robustly healthy, dark-haired man in his mid-thirties, who enjoyed rock climbing and was a member of Duck's Unlimited, a conservation club dedicated to purchasing and maintaining wetlands so that future generations would have waterfowl to hunt. "I for one certainly intend to get some fishing in."

"Sure, me too," Dr. Barkley agreed, strategically. "We may as well catch all the trout we can before they start glowing." Both men chuckled. Barkley was slightly the taller of the two and wore a brush cut mustache that matched his longish sun streaked hair. He too enjoyed the outdoors. Geology is, after all, a nature science. Strange that geologists in search of oil and minerals have screwed up so much of nature.

"I guess we won't have to worry about catch and release," Yates joked.

"Hell, no," Charles Barkley rejoined, fingering the split bamboo fly rod, which had been a gift from his grandfather five years ago at Christmas. "I'd say catch and release is a very low priority around here."

Neither man had much faith in the long term safety potential of storing nuclear waste poison, so they joked about it. But the shit had to go someplace. That was a given. Where it was piling up now was very unsafe. Their job was to find a site. History would eventually prove them to be morons, no matter where they put it.

*

"I do not have all day for this, Mortimer dear," Lotti said, tapping her foot impatiently. "The mail comes at 2:30." She couldn't believe that her obvious sex appeal wasn't turning this old monkey into pudding like it did everyone else, except for Willard Jacks. He was just stubbornly sitting there, dripping on her rag rug, which would probably cause the colors to bleed.

"You're dripping on my rug," she scolded.

"Oh, sorry," Rainy apologized, quickly pulling the skirts of the robe onto his skinny lap.

"Well, I'm getting undressed. You can watch," she said, defiantly. Turning her back, she slipped out of the shortie robe and tossed it on the four poster bed. Then she turned back to face him, making her face into the appealing smile of a sex kitten, like the smiles she'd seen in Teen Magazine.

She waited for the visual shock of her perfect body to jolt the old coot into giving her the fawning adoration that she had learned to like very much. Then her conquest. With Mortimer under her belt, she'd be ready to tackle Hollywood. Nobody, even in Hollywood, could be weirder than a famous monkey. How the dickens did he got so famous anyway? Lotti couldn't really imagine why anybody would make a pilgrimage up the mountain to see this old pablum eater, but thousands had since she was a girl. He must have some kind of hidden power. That's what some girls at school told her in the restroom. No female in her right mind could be attracted to Mortimer, but Lotti was perfectly willing to snare some of his power by screwing him. With the boost, she could trap Willard into going to California. Nobody could call Lotti McCardle a dumbbell, no matter how hard they tried.

"Well," she asked, sweetly. "Do you like me?" She noted that his eyes were getting glassy, just like the other men she'd shown herself to.

Rainy cleared his throat. "Of course, I like you," he replied, hoarsely. His mouth was dry. It seemed he actually was catching a cold. He decided to excuse himself gracefully, and return to the Retreat where he could do a health meditation. That would raise his body temperature and throw off the chill. He could do it here, of course; but somehow he didn't think Lotti would appreciate meditating particularly. Her spiritual attributes seemed somewhat overshadowed.

"Well then, hurry up and get in bed before Mother comes back. I want you," she lied.

"Yes, I can see that you do," Rainy responded, ponderously. Impulses inside his renowned mind were skittering back and forth between synapses like a runaway computer. Truthfully, he couldn't remember feeling so amazingly alive. This was exactly what all seekers looked for, the ultimate perfect temptation to hone his will. Maybe he could entice Lotti to invite him here every afternoon. After all these years, he was getting an insight into how the quarks and charms inside his cells danced the cosmic dance. And yes, he longed to join with this young lioness. What an extension of the dance that would be. The thought of coupling made fresh blood rush to his penis, which was already getting more than its fair share. He felt slightly light-headed.

"I told you the mail comes at 2:30," Lotti repeated, pettishly. "Are you going to hurry up or not?"

"How could the mail's arrival possibly have any effect on what we do in your bedroom?" he asked incredulously, regaining a bit of control.

"I always go down to get the mail," she lied again, "in case there's a new magazine or a package for me." The truth was that she always lingered near the mailbox so that she could see Willard Jacks and his magical Jeep; but she didn't think it was quite the time to reveal her California plan to Mortimer. Easing back onto the chenille bedspread, she leaned on an elbow, very aware that she was naked and secretly thrilled at this ultimate brashness. Lotti had never seduced a man in the Lodge before, right under her mother's nose; but why shouldn't she? This was her room, why should she be forced to sneak around in the woods? Her dear mother didn't get pine needles all up her back with crabby old Mrs. Olsterholt. It was disgusting how they made the bed springs squeak and squeal, then the next day acted like nothing had happened. But this old fool was still just sitting there looking at her. She was positive he was aroused, his boner was poking up, making a lump in his monkey robe; so why was he just sitting there? It was mystifying and a little deflating. She was flaunting herself outrageously, and he was just sitting there like a lumpy old toad. Maybe he was a fairy. Of course! All priests are fairies. That's how they keep their stupid vows of chastity.

"Too bad I'm not a boy, huh Mortimer? I bet that would turn you on more."

"What..?"

"Well, don't you have a vow about fooling around with women? You think it's bad or something."

"No," Rainy said, momentarily nonplused. "Our Order has no rules about sexual conduct. Of course, indiscriminate sex is frowned upon; but on the grounds of simplifying social conduct, not because it's morally repugnant. I, myself, have disregarded sexual contact for years as being beside the point on the way to enlightenment. I may well have been wrong."

"Uh, huh," the girl said. Twenty dollar words were not her strong suit. She couldn't even guess at what he meant. That was unfair! He was trying to dodge out of it with big words to keep her from getting his precious sperm vibes. No way! She wanted those vibes!. She turned languorously onto her stomach, displaying her rounded backside to him.

"Maybe you like me better this way?"

"I really should be running along," Rainy sighed. "I'm already late for lunch." He stood up, hoping that his old knees would support him. "Don't get up. I can find my own way downstairs.

Lotti stared at him, not even bothering to keep her mouth from dropping open. This was her first experience with sexual rejection, and it was surprisingly confusing.

"Thank you very much, my dear, for showing an old dog some new tricks. Your loveliness is intoxicating, but I must remain sober, at least for today. I sorely regret leaving, but I must." He twisted the door knob and the door opened. "Give my regards to your mother," he said, shuffling into the hallway, even though millions of his nerve endings screamed at the old fool to stay with Aphrodite.

Once the door was closed, Sri Rainy regained his

composure, which was fortunate, since otherwise he might have fallen down when he bumped into the tall blonde man emerging from the room next door.

"Excuse me," Rainy blurted, catching his balance by grabbing onto the open door of Room 9. "Frightfully stupid of me. I must have been day dreaming."

"My fault, sir," Dr. Charles Barkley apologizing profusely. He eyed the old man's wet bathrobe and beard, and didn't know what to make of them. Did this freak live here? Had he taken a shower with his robe on? "I shouldn't have blundered into the hall like that. I'll be more careful next time. Are you all right?"

"Perfectly," Sri Rainy uttered, with a benevolent smile. "I trust you are, too?"

"Oh, yes. Say, do you live here?"

"Near here."

"Is there a good restaurant in town? We just arrived and wanted to grab a bite of lunch, before we go fishing."

"I don't honestly know," Rainy answered, truthfully. "I never eat in town. I expect Mrs. McCardle could advise you." He tottered on down the hall.

Dr. Barkley looked more closely at Rainy's departing form. His memory had just retrieved a bit of information from a report he'd read about there being a colony of monks on the mountain. This must be one of them. The report stipulated forcefully that the monks were to be left strictly alone—and in the dark as to his mission. It was widely known that religious fanatics could become troublesome. Was this old man spying on them already? Had he been listening at the door?

*

Following Sri Rainy up the street was kind of sad.

The geek had just had his brain jangled loose. He marched straight ahead, aware of nothing except his inner turmoil—not at all proper behavior for a would-be saint. Being a spiritual master is an overrated profession. Of course, it's also underrated for almost the same reasons.

Before a master starts teaching, he's a student with a master of his own. And even though his student life may be fucked up and mind-blisteringly hard, it's bliss because he has no real responsibility except to seek and learn. He's free to fail, he's free to be terrified of the unknown. He's free to delight his master with his stupidity. He's free to overcome his terror and become enlightened. He's free to find his task in life. But once he declares himself a master in his own right, most of the blissful freedom is left behind. What..? We thought enlightened masters were supposed to be free? Ah, yes. Freedom. The chains he frees himself from are the superficial attachments to things, events and people—the very chains that make life worth living.

And with this precious, hard won, freedom comes a life task and students to prod and care for—actually, a complete role reversal. Responsibility. Sober responsibility. It's time to put up or shut up. This does not apply, naturally, to charlatan teachers, nor "get rich quick" TV evangelists. Nobody with more than one Cadillac need apply for sainthood.

And so, Sri Rainy, with his buzzing brain, hustled back through the blustery afternoon to the sober responsibility of the Retreat. And of course, he was late for lunch. And of course, Sister Angie had insisted that everybody wait lunch for him, so that all the pupils were growling with indignation and hunger. It was good for their spiritual growth to have little irritating things go wrong, but it's so hard to remember to be grateful about being jarred out of a rut when you're hungry.

Seeing that lunch hadn't been served, Sri Rainy smiled at the uncomfortable faces waiting in line at the dining hall and walked into the large kitchen. There he found Norman Ungerer, whose face was so red that the veins on his forehead seemed about to pop.

"Why hasn't lunch been served, Norman?" he asked, feigning innocence. Sri Rainy was secretly delighted to have caused this inadvertent chaos. Look at the jaw set on Sister Angie. It's a wonder somebody hadn't mistaken it for lockjaw, and rushed her to the hospital. Yes, appointing the wimp, Ungerer, to run the kitchen was a stroke of genius. A confrontation like this was worth fifty kilowatts of enlightenment to each of them, to say nothing of all the sheep-like students waiting for lunch to be served. He owed Lotti for this. He'd have to be nicer to her in the future. Maybe she was an instrument of his teaching.

"Sister Angie won't let me, Sri Rainy," Norman Ungerer tattled through clenched teeth, so angry that he couldn't speak above a whisper.

"I told you when you accepted the post to make sure the meals were served on time," Rainy chided, chilling the young man with his coldness.

"I know you did, sir," Norman answered in a quavering voice. "What should I have done, choked her senseless, or knocked her out with a frying pan? Those alternatives seem to conflict with the Non-violent Way. Of course, Sister Angie thought nothing of brandishing a carving knife at me."

"We were waiting lunch for you, Sri Rainy," the heavy young woman said, self-righteously. "Shall we serve now?" Her blocky body shifted slightly to hide the butcher knife laying on the stove top beside the pan of potatoes.

Rainy raised his eyes to the cracked ceiling, in mock dismay. "Of course, you should, Sister Angie. Whatever gave you the notion to countermand Mr. Ungerer's orders. He is in charge of the kitchen. Wasn't that clear to you?"

The woman blanched under his criticism. "But, I thought you said the kitchen decisions were to be agreed upon by all three of us?" she said, tremblingly.

"No," Sri Rainy answered, coldly. Turning on his sandal heel, he walked outside. The victorious look of vindication on Norman Ungerer's face almost turned his stomach. What asses they both are, he grumbled to himself, well-pleased none the less. He took his place last in the serving line.

"Well, that's settled," he joked to the throng of students.

They all tittered in response. Sri Rainy was here. Everything, including lunch, would be all right now.

But, of course, lunch wasn't quite all right. The potatoes were tiny and there was only one per plate. The men growled under their breath, as Sister Angie knew they would. In spite of that, everybody was energized in a most amazing manner. Sri Rainy was practically glowing as he sliced his potato into tiny bites and chewed each bite thoroughly.

*

As predicted, the back side of Mudslide Pass was treacherous as a roller coaster. Willard often wondered why the county bothered to maintain this stretch of road at all. One could make a good case for letting it vegetate back to its original state. It didn't go anywhere important anyway, just made a big loop up the mountain and slid down the other side into Pike Township Route 34 before going on into Logan County. About an eighth of the township's highway budget was spent on keeping the rut passable. After a rain or a thaw, boulders and mud always clogged it up. Asa Peters, the only resident at the top, paid no taxes and could have picked up his Bean's catalogue when he came to town on his mule for supplies. He never accepted any other mail, just the L.L. Bean catalogue four times a year. To Willard's knowledge, Asa had never ordered anything from the mail order house, at least he'd never received a package during Willard's tenure.

The road was a joke, actually. Of course, he knew why the township kept it open. For tourism. The saddle of Mudslide Pass was a historical site, complete with its little brass plaque pinned to a huge black granite erratic boulder, which would probably fall into the road someday. Zebulon Pike, the early explorer who had named Pike's Peak, had been standing in the saddle of Mudslide Pass when he first saw the tall white mountain that now bore his name. Some big deal to put up a historical marker about, Willard mused, as the jeep's rear tire hit a small boulder and leaped in the air, causing the jeep to skid horrendously when the wheels reengaged the grease-like mud. Gray granite cliff walls and pine trees slid past sickeningly and the jeep came within a tire's width of plunging over the side, before a white-faced Willard won the fight for control. Sweating coldly, he eased the vehicle back to the right side of the slick road and downshifted into 1st gear. Why hadn't he simply waited for a dry day to deliver the L.L. Bean catalogue? Well, because Willard Jacks was a conscientious mailman. When there was mail to deliver, he delivered it.

Feeling glad to still be alive at the bottom of the mountain, Willard pulled onto Pike Township Route 34 under a canopy of Norway pines, and headed for Pike's Grove. Beautiful country, he decided, like he did every day.

It might be wondered why Willard delivered the mail to the outlying districts before he made the rounds in Pike's Grove. For one thing, that's the way his predecessors had done it. All the sorting procedures and routes were set up that way when he came on board. And then, if anybody in town wanted their mail early, they could stop over to the post office and get it. In a town of seven hundred, it wasn't that big a deal. Everybody had their mail by 3:30. The bank didn't close until four. It all worked out.

Stopping into the one room post office, Willard waved to Jolie, visited the rest room, picked up the mail for the town route, then jumped back in the jeep. He drove to the far side of town and started plugging mailboxes with L.L. Bean catalogues, bills and the odd letter. Willard tried not to pry into the private lives of his route clients, as he called them. But, of course, it was impossible not to know who was getting what kind of mail, who was habitually late with their bills (second and third notices were always pink or orange colored) or who received smut mail in a plain wrapper. Yes, in a remote community like Pike Township, the mailman has his finger on the pulse.

At 2:30, Willard pulled up to the Spruce Lane Lodge, which was usually good for a few surprises. That little teeny-bopper, Lotti McCardle, frequently got packages from Frederick's of Hollywood. It made Willard chuckle. Why would a girl try so hard to be sexy in a burg this tiny? Who was she wearing the stuff for? Her mother? It was laughable.

"Hi, Willard," Lotti sang, stepping out from behind the holly bush where she had been lying in wait. She held out her hand helpfully, so he wouldn't have to bother opening the mailbox.

"Hi, yourself," Willard said. "Going to a party?" The

girl was dolled up in a white blouse with a wide, loose collar. About half the buttons were open. A further glance revealed a black French skirt slit way up the side, dark nylons and red high heels. Quite the little heart throb, he thought. All dressed up and nowhere to go.

"You're all the party I'll ever need, Willard," she said, coyly. "You know that, don't cha?"

"I didn't know you cared," he replied, filling her hand with mail and circulars from the Sears store in Clinton.

"Well, I do," she purred. Her clipped high-country accent wasn't especially seductive, but she didn't know the difference and neither did Willard.

He mentally decided to look her up in five years or so, if she hadn't gotten fat with a swarm of brats by then. "Bet you say that to all the guys," he kidded.

"I do not!" Lotti scolded. She puckered her rosebud mouth in annoyance and glared at him. "Who's been saying that about me?"

"Nobody I know," he laughed easily, and slipped the jeep into gear.

"I was wondering," Lotti wondered aloud, breathlessly stepping up beside the jeep, "if you might like to take a ride with me sometime? I'd do just about anything for a ride in your jeep. I love jeeps. I'll bet you can go just anywhere in this jeep."

"This old thing? I'm lucky to make the routes every day in this antique."

"Don't say that! I love this jeep. I really do."

"Well, you must have a screw loose then," he chuckled.

"Maybe so, but I sure would love to go for a ride with you someday soon. Would you take me on your mail route sometime?"

"Can't do that. Insurance rules. All the kids would want to go, too. Drive me crazy with dinging at me."

"Kids..? You think I'm a kid?" She managed to accidentally bend over so that her blouse bunched open for a quick second.

Willard caught an eyeful. "How old are you, anyway? Fourteen?"

"That's a laugh, Willie Jacks! That's really very funny! I was sixteen last summer."

"Well, I'll be dogged," Willard said. "Too bad I got that insurance rule."

"I'll bet you could take me, if you wanted to. Aren't you curious about the undies I get from Hollywood?"

"Oh, sure. I'm real curious about that, sweetie-pops. Be seeing you." He let out the clutch and rolled on down the street, waving a lazy good-bye.

Lotti stood rooted to the spot watching Willard and his jeep putter down the street. Her eager, conniving mind couldn't get a firm hold on being turned down again. Being ignored twice in one day was impossible, so her nimble little mind did a trick. It told her she was just being friendly. Neighborly. Yes, that was it. And why shouldn't she be neighborly to her mailman and to old Mortimer Snerd? She should. When you're the innkeeper's daughter, you're supposed to be friendly to everyone. That's what her mother was always yammering at her.

➔ ➔

CHAPTER 6

ALIVE BUT NOT LIFE GIVING HOT BUT NOT SUNNY DEAD BUT NOT GONE

Ten thousand years is the projected half-life of the most virulent forms of nuclear waste. These hot, high level wastes are by-products of nuclear reactors and bombs: spent fuel rods, bomb pile waste, reprocessed uranium. Small mountains of this highly hazardous, highly radioactive waste reside in temporary surface storage bins all around the world. Under guard, of course. This is thought to be a gift for our children.

Other mountains of less hazardous hot waste (wipe-down rags, filters, tailings etc.) should neutralize in a much shorter time. About five thousand years. These are thought of as benevolent waste, and are being buried in shallow, unlined, dirt pits. Under guard, of course.

Rather than pursue a sane energy policy, governments decided in the 1950s that they should make this hot bequest to our distant progeny. Senators and Congressmen listened to self-serving advice of scientists and businessmen who wanted to play with this technology, and collect handsome paychecks for fucking up the planet. Senators and Congressmen and Communist party bosses said, Go ahead, boys. The only positive thing one can say on behalf of these scientists is that they probably thought their wonderful colleagues would discover a way to neutralize the hot waste, maybe even reuse it like in a perpetual motion machine; but so far, they haven't. And the small mountains keep growing and glowing.

The problem is not so much how to store it, as how to keep it stored. Nobody knows for sure what all this hot stuff is going to do when it's sealed underground, under guard. Nearly every scientist does agree that the first thousand years is the most dangerous period. It will release tremendous energy during this time, both thermal and radiant.

Scientists agree that keeping these super heated storage chambers safe from water flow is critical, because our children wouldn't want fifty billion rads escaping into their drinking water, let alone their showers. No, that would make our children light up like little glow globes. So the scientists want to protect these piles and piles of hot junk for ten thousand years. After all, some of then do care about their children.

To put things in perspective, five thousand years ago was sort of the time the early Egyptians were building pyramids. Their ancestors are now poking into the giant storage vaults. Just imagine how surprised modern archaeologists would be to find still hot and lethal nuclear waste instead of mummified kings inside the exciting pyramids. It's not an impossible script for our children. In ancient Egypt the pyramid shape might have meant — Stay Out! Danger! Don't Dig Here!! Hot Death! — but the Rosetta Stone was lost. The progeny forgot what a pyramid meant. The warning language was forgotten long before archaeologists got curious and greedy. And the guards went to sleep. They positively just couldn't remember what they were supposed to guard.

This is to say nothing of earthquakes, big meteor strikes, shifting continental plates and mountain eruptions, floods, tidal waves, geysers and plain old nuclear hooliganism. Oh, well. What me worry?

CHAPTER 7

LOOK LEFT LOOK RIGHT

Being alert to something in the wind fits in nicely with our current concepts of wild animal powers. Dogs, for instance, know when an earthquake is coming. Herd animals seem able to predict droughts, forest animals get nervous and run from a forest fire hours before the flames get to them. Is this a heightened power of smelling or hearing, or is it sixth sense, some ability to be in tune with nature? Whatever it is, survivors live to reproduce their species, and no doubt pass that survival trait to their offspring.

Whether or not Montclief and the other yetis could be classified as wild animals with a sixth sense, Montclief himself had been feeling a sense of foreboding since he'd had a disturbing nightmare, and the next day had come upon two normal looking fishermen, fly fishing in the upper pools of Fawn Brook.

Although Barkley and Yates were outdoorsmen, both lacked a sixth sense, so they had no idea that a yeti was watching them from behind a screen of black willows. Troubled by a vague sense of menace, Montclief continued stalking them long after he was bored with their fishing techniques. That they were skillful fly fishermen was quite obvious, but the way they approached the sport was unusual. One or two casts in each pool or riffle, no more, then moving on up the stream. If a trout struck, they played it well, joking and bartering about who had the greater count; but then a quick live release and moving again, until by noon they were in the headwaters where no trout of any size lived. This class of fishermen would know fish habitat, but still they kept meandering uphill, discussing the rock formation. Seemingly, they were much more interested in the faults and fractures of the rock than in fishing. Montclief wondered why that would be?

By midday, they weren't even pretending to fish. Hiking quickly, they reached a sweet spring that bubbled from a mossy rock wall birthing Fawn Brook.

"Well, here it is," Dr. Yates said. "Lower than I thought it would be." His critical eyes scanned the upper reaches of The Devil's Tooth. "Nothing above here but snow run off.

Barkley checked an altimeter on his wrist. "8,500 feet," he said. "The top is 14,000. Plenty of room. We'll have to walk around the mountain to make sure, but it looks perfect."

"I agree," Omar Yates said. "We'll make a circle here at 8,500, but I'm pretty sure this is the top of the aquifer. Nothing else showed up from the satellite."

Barkley chuckled. "My poor damned feet. It must be thirty miles around at this height." He scanned the magnificent view. "What a shame, huh? This place is paradise."

"Everyplace was paradise once," Yates reflected. "But not everyplace has five thousand feet of practically fissureless granite. We'll start here tomorrow. Would you rather go right or left?"

"Left," Dr. Barkley answered. "I always go left around a mountain. I suppose we should hump the tent along."

Montclief listened to all this with great interest, but the only thing he understood for sure was that he'd be here tomorrow to make the hike with the two pseudo-fishermen.

*

Whirling and whirling, like planets twirling around their sun, the dancers swirled around Sri Rainy who was seated in the exact center of the inner circle. The skirts of their robes blossomed softly in the centrifugal force created by the whirling. Eyes fixed gently on up-raised palms, no dizziness. Just awareness of self and the dance inside the whirl. Amazing what the human body is capable of.

Rainy had learned this whirling dervish exercise as a young man on a visit to a Mevlevic dervish center in Turkey, now he taught it to his followers. Not all of the students had reached the abandonment level necessary for whirling. Several students played on drone instruments, accompanying the dancing under the tutelage of Edmund Ragnars, his chief gardener and musician. Keeping true, even time on the drone was critical, otherwise the whirling became ragged and meaningless. Ragnars had attended Juliard music school in his youth, and was an invaluable help to Rainy, in spite of his overblown ego. Talent is a dangerous asset on the Way. But so is no talent. In a sense, every man's cross is equally heavy. Luggage to be born and overcome. Edmund Ragnars was a superb musician, but after twenty odd years, Sri Rainy had no real hope for him. Ragnars was allowed to teach music, since his perfectionism and egoism made an impossible combination for the students to deal with. For the aging musician's own development, Rainy suggested he work in the garden, hoping that the dirt and vegetables would eventually humble his spirit. They wouldn't, of course, but at least it was useful work.

According to the Mevlevis, women were not to whirl

in the inner circle. Instead they joined arms to form an outer circle, swaying gently and moving around the inner whirlers in the counter direction, humming the sweet tune of an Arabic melody blending with and counterpoising the drones.

For Rainy, it was awesome and wonderful to be at the center of the dance. It had been more than a decade since he had taught this movement, the numbers of his students had dwindled until there just weren't physically enough bodies to form the circles. But a year ago, he had felt a deep need to experience the whirling again, and so he had begun teaching the dervish dance to the inadequate number of pupils. And miraculously, students had started coming up the mountain again. The cycles. Who could explain their cause and effect? Certainly not Sri Rainy. He only knew they were.

*

Out in the darkness, Montclief blended with the shadows of a pine thicket to watch the whirling. If he looked a little more human, he would have insisted that Rainy include him in the class, but he didn't look human. He looked like a great strong male yeti, king of the high places. Some joke. King of nothing. Those phony fishermen were planning a mining operation of some kind on top of his mountain. His home. He felt heartsick. Not for himself, but for the future.

Things were so much worse already than the days of his youth. For himself and Yolanda there was no real problem. They could move to another mountain. But there were only so many mountains. One by one they were being encroached by the yrts with their ski jumps and radar dishes and forest service towers. More and more yrts. They never stopped fucking. That must be all they do, fuck, fuck, fuck. More and more puny yrts. The Ancestors had long ago warned against the red yrts, who had no use for the tops of mountains, except the strange ones on their vision quests. But these white yrts wouldn't be satisfied until the whole of the Atagamma was covered with one continuous city. And then what would the sons of Montclief do? Live on the reservations of the Reds and steal sheep? No, someday soon a careless yeti will be shot and die before he can escape. Every yrt who goes on the mountain has a rifle. The big rifles that can stop a grizzly. Someday it will happen, and then the onslaught of trophy hunters will come, hunting us. And we will be forced to kill some. Then they will kill for revenge, and there will be much fucking to make up the numbers, and the females will be sad and happy. Only then will the Council vote to establish treaties with the smooth skin government. Only after enough have been killed.

Then the good life will end. Maybe they will give us one mountain and our very own park ranger to protect us and bring us canned food in the winter deep snow. And the skins will come in the summer with cameras to steal the little life that we have left.

The whirling dance went on and on. The music was foreign to the yeti, yet uplifting in a way he did not understand. It spoke of the stars and the impermanence of earthly things, even great things like the destruction of mountains. But the yeti knew that he did not have business with the stars. He was part of the mountain bones and he could not see a clear way into the future.

Sneaking up to the rough stone wall of the first building that Rainy had built at the Retreat, Montclief lifted a small flower pot from the ground and placed it on a window ledge. This was his signal for Rainy to go fishing the next morning. He seldom used this signal, since the old man went fishing many mornings on his own, always forbidding any of his students to follow him. Montclief hoped the old man would notice the flower pot in his window this night, because the yeti needed to speak with someone who might understand his foreboding.

➾ ⇚

CHAPTER 8

SEEK THE STRAIGHT FROM THE CURVED

As he hurried across the frosty courtyard paving stones toward the kitchen, his old bones seemed to creak in the morning chill. Like most fishermen, Sri Rainy rose well before dawn, but unlike most fishermen who stumble around half asleep making coffee, he had already sat for half an hour of morning meditation in his room, and a shorter guided meditation with the students. Oh, yes, he was a disciplined person; and besides, a teacher can scarcely ask a student to meditate if he is unwilling to do so himself. But unless something special was going on at the Retreat, he went fishing instead of breakfasting with the feebs. Spending his time with Montclief, or even alone, was so much more rewarding than fending off moronic questions early in the morning.

After selecting a couple of hot biscuits from the kitchen, he headed uphill toward the hollow tree at Moss Back Bend where he kept his fishing poles stashed. Montclief didn't eat biscuits, in fact, the yeti was totally self-sufficient. It was such a joy to have a friend who could take care of himself.

Rainy never worried about his fishing gear being stolen. Who would bother to steal two old cane poles in this day and age. Even skid row children used zirconium rods and computerized reels. They wouldn't think of being seen without state of the art equipment. And sure enough, both poles were standing unmolested in the lightning-struck beech tree, which was somehow still growing without a heart. Strong but empty, he mused. Nature was constantly miraculous.

Taking both poles and a rusty creamed corn can which he used as a bait can out of the tree, the old man wondered for the umpteenth time what was so important that Montclief had to post the flower pot signal. Oh, well, he'd know soon enough. Clearing his mind of unneeded thoughts he started upstream. He planned to fish the large upper pool with the undercut bank today. Montclief preferred the upper pools because the dense willow brakes were difficult to penetrate. Most sportsmen wouldn't make the effort.

A hundred yards uphill, he heard Montclief's grunt. It always sounded like the grunt of a warthog, but since there were no warthogs on the mountain, it had to be the yeti. Loosely translated the grunt meant, I'm here. Stop wherever you want to, nobody is around.

The yeti's physical senses were phenomenal. Not once in the ten years they had fished together had another human stumbled upon them. Minutes before an intruder became evident to Rainy, the yeti would disappear into the woods, leaving the old man fishing with two poles. Several autumns ago, Rainy had fished all morning within fifty yards of a deer hunter up in a tree, totally hidden in a camouflage jumpsuit. Sri Rainy had blithely assumed he was alone.

Montclief hadn't appeared that morning. The next time they met, the yeti had told him about the hunter. And several days later down in town, a burly fellow had hailed him as he walked past Hinton's Hardware, asking with a smirk how the fishing was. The fellow had gone into great detail about the trout that the old man had caught. "Lucky no deer had stepped out for a drink of brook water", the hunter had joshed, asininely proud of his own stalking ability. "An old feller like you would probably have heart seizure if a 30.06 cracked practically right in his ear," he laughed.

"Lucky," Sri Rainy had agreed with the man.

But Rainy had his own problems this morning. Before he had seen the flower pot last night, he had half-decided to oversee a few things at the Retreat, then get an early start for the library. By spending a few extra hours in town, he was fairly certain to run into Lotti. He fervently hoped that his idiotic actions yesterday hadn't screwed up his chances with her. What absurd morality had caused him to leave her room? Moronic! Who cares about sexual mores these days? He certainly never had before. Mores change from town to town around the globe. Besides, if she didn't get it from him, she'd get it somewhere else. That much was evident. He was saving her from nothing, just cutting himself out of a superb experience by acting old and crusty. That's the real meaning of *there's no fool like an old fool,* he groused. Who cares if somebody or everybody thought he was acting foolish, at least he'd get his end in. He'd never cared what they thought of him before, why would he be absurd enough to care now when he was going to receive something spectacular? That's settled then, he'd see what Montclief wanted, then go on down to the library. He wondered idly if the yeti knew about his little dalliance. Probably. He seemed to know everything else, why not this? But then, it had happened in town. Montclief seldom went near there, especially in the daytime. Very possibly he didn't know. Well then, it would be Rainy's little secret. No reason to let the cat out of the bag just yet.

Sri Rainy stopped at the edge of a little meadow and turned a rotted log over to find some bait. No reason to climb on up to the high pools, Montclief was already here. They could fish this pool and riffle for awhile, then he could get on to more important matters.

Montclief grunted again and appeared from the same willow tangle that Rainy had just waded through. He bent over the log and picked out a huge handful of white grub worms from the rotten wood. Yeti breakfast, Rainy knew, not bothering to feel revolted. Contenting himself with scooping up a dozen dazed grasshoppers, still too cold and wet to fly, he didn't watch the grub worms disappear into the grey whiskery mouth. Wrapping a piece of aluminum foil over the bait can, Rainy walked over to the brook.

Chewing vigorously, the yeti sat on Rainy's left, nearer the willow brake. With practiced movements, both fishermen unwrapped line from the tips of their cane poles and hooked on a grasshopper. Rainy dropped his line in the fast moving water and waited for his friend to speak about whatever was bothering him.

After a few minutes had passed, the yeti spoke in his soft rumbling voice. "Two men were on the mountain yesterday. They went as high as the Fawn Brook spring. They were studying the mountain's bones. I think they will start mining. I have a bad feeling about this, but I do not know why."

Rainy nodded and kept watching his bobber pulling in the current. "A mining operation would bring people, which would make you and the others uncomfortable. Depending on what kind of mine it is, a few miners would come, or many. It would probably be good for the community, so they will encourage it. I never heard of gold or any precious ore coming from around here."

"They were studying the walls of rock. All their talk was about the fewness of cracks."

"Maybe they want to quarry the granite. That would be much worse for you; but I never heard anybody say this is particularly wonderful granite or even that it was building grade. Maybe it is, I don't know."

"These two acted like fishermen. They were good at fly fishing, but their thought was on the mountain wall. They are coming back today, I will listen more."

"Maybe it's nothing, just a government survey of some kind."

"They are staying at the Lodge of the mother and girl," the yeti reported. "Maybe you will hear something when you go to the library." He paused to watch Rainy's faded red bobber starting to move slowly upstream. I will make a new bobber for myself tomorrow and paint it red, he decided firmly. "It is not a mine that bothers me," Montclief said. "The miners dig until they have what they want, then go away leaving the mountain alone. But I have a bad feeling from these two. That is why I left the signal, to ask you why this is. And when I slept, I had a sweating dream such as I have never had before."

Although he certainly wasn't a foreigner to harbingers of the Spirit or subtle messages that come from who knows where, Sri Rainy was unable to make much of Monclief's statement. He remembered bumping into a strange man when he lurched out of Lotti's room. Maybe that was one of the fishermen. The fellow had seemed pleasant enough, but I was a little discombobulated at the time. Rainy smiled to himself. Given half a chance, he would act much differently today. "You had a bad feeling from the two men you saw?" he asked.

Montclief stared at the red bobber, which wasn't moving now, just hanging twenty feet upstream from where it should have been. "You have a bite," he said, gruffly. This old man was the luckiest fisherman who ever lived. It was unbelievable.

"I know that," Rainy replied, with a deprecating scowl. "I didn't want to break the flow of our conversation."

"So catch the fish. I have a feeling of dread that I can't explain, but the sun came up anyway. I thought to share it with you in hopes that you can find out what these men are here for. I should go now and listen to what they say today." He pulled his line from the water. His hook was bare. The grasshopper had wiggled off. No wonder he wasn't getting any bites. Montclief stood up.

"I have to go, too," Sri Rainy said. He twitched his pole tip and set the hook in the mouth of a ten inch brook trout, which he played for a minute before horsing it out of the water. He gave the fish to Montclief and turned to go. "I'll see what I can find out," he said. "Maybe it's just a geological survey."

*

The world's greatest expert on yetis walked into the empty library. He wondered what his old chum, Esther, would think if she knew that yetis have fears and yearnings just like humans do. An unusual thought struck Sri Rainy, unusual in that he had never thought it before. He wondered if he oughtn't to start writing a book, so that future generations would have a true text on the subject. Perhaps, instead of developing a student to mastery, a book was his life work. Maybe that was the entire reason he'd come to live on the mountain—so he could observe the yeti phenomena and report on it. Yetis, after all, were a fact of life. He even had a suspicion of a theory to explain their existence. More than being a missing link for humanity or even a lost tribe, yetis were the end product of Earth's evolution of the ape species, and a glorious end product they were. Humans, on the other hand, were the descendants of space travelers. But how could he ever get scientific proofs for such a theory, without ruining the splendid freedom of the yeti tribe. He couldn't. Once a book was published, zoologists would arrive en masse on the mountain.

"Morning, Esther," he whispered to the librarian, who sat at her desk cataloging a section of woodland plant booklets.

"Morning yourself," Esther answered, playfully. "I know something that you don't." Her suppressed excitement reminded him of the look that Tiger, one of the cats at the Retreat, got on his face when he caught a sparrow. A few feathers fluttered in mid-air around the librarian.

"I dare say you do," Rainy replied. Was it something about Lotti? Gossip would have traveled at the speed of light, of course. But nothing had really happened. For all anyone knew he had been helping her with a mathematics problem. Unfortunately, Esther lived at the Lodge. He couldn't count on fooling her for long. Maybe he should suggest that Lotti move up to the Retreat. They could get married. That would surprise a few people. "Are you planning to share the secret with me?" he asked.

"There's a major new work about the Sesqwatch coming out in the autumn! I just got the advance notices from the University of California Press." Her thin, liver-spotted hands held a slim pamphlet out to him.

Raising his bushy eyebrows, Rainy took the pamphlet and glanced through a publishers list of new books without seeing why she was so jacked-up.

"It's on page three," Esther chattered.

"Oh, yes." Rainy's eyes focused on *Tales and Myths of the Sesqwatch*. "Sounds like more fantasy," he said, allowing disappointment to show in his voice. Secretly, he was delighted. There would be no conflict with his book.

"They claim the volume is an eye witness account with photographs," Esther insisted. "Read the blurb."

He read:

Noted wildlife photographer, Leslie Winterbothom, has spent ten years researching and collecting

> photographs of Sesqwatch sighting in the Pacific Northwest. This book shows conclusive proof that the legend lives in the remote mountains of Oregon and Washington. 27 photographs and eyewitness accounts. A must read for nature lovers and amateur anthropologists.

"My, my," he said, sounding impressed. "Can we expect that our library budget will stretch enough to order this one?"

"It would be a shame to leave our collection incomplete," Esther whispered, conspiratorially. "Especially since there are so many amateur anthropologists in Pike Township."

"Just what was I thinking," he agreed.

"Great minds run in the same footprints," Esther responded, gaily.

"When might we receive this masterpiece?" he inquired with a chuckle.

"Well, I've already ordered it, so perhaps by Spring."

Esther had heard about Sri Rainy's visit to Mary, and tried diligently not to think the worst of him. She failed at that. In a small town, thinking the worst is a well spring of happiness, since thinking the best of such dull people leads to comatose boredom. Inwardly, she had argued that Sri Rainy was a virtual saint and that nothing untoward could have happened behind the closed door of Lotti's room. But Mary was unconvinced. In the time it took to sip a swallow of the tea that Mary had poured, Esther gave up the defense to speculate on the length of his parts and the staying power of such an old man.

She wished that she had been home for the most exciting event to happen in the Lodge since she moved in; but more than that, now that she knew that Sri Rainy was attracted to town women, she wondered how to lay her own trap for him. All the town women had always speculated on his wild orgies with the empty-headed voluptuous female slave/students, and had felt themselves far superior to those sluts. But now that he had fooled around with Lotti... But bringing up his visit to Lotti would be drastically uncouth of Esther, so she smiled wanly and didn't mention it.

Sri Rainy cleared his throat. "You may have heard that I visited the Lodge yesterday..?"

"Oh, did you..?"

"Yes, that young girl, Lotti, asked me to help her with a mathematics problem." He chuckled to himself.

"Is that so," she simpered, stringing him along.

"I was so rusty that I don't believe I was much help to her. Do you happen to have an algebra book that I could brush up on?"

"Why yes, I'm sure we do." Esther left her desk and wiggled over to the card catalogue, sexy as a Vegas showgirl.

"Have you hurt your back, Mrs. Olsterholt?" Sri Rainy asked in alarm. "You have to be careful about lifting these heavy books." With a smile, Esther opened the first drawer of the card catalogue. A for Algebra and Asshole.

*

It wasn't that he felt disdain or enmity for his students. Not at all. Each one of them was on the Way, even if their progress was at a snail's pace. Some inner dissatisfaction with stock answers had propelled each of them away from a life of comparative ease up to The Devil's Tooth. But the Way was long and coldly merciless. Those it loved were brought to their knees and kept there. None of his current students had an inkling that this was the case, and therefore, Rainy was impatient with them. That was all, impatient. And impatience was a sin. It didn't hasten their progress by one minute, and it slowed his own. Thank goodness, it was an easily seen short-coming. Unlike some of his more devious faults, impatience gave him something to work against daily.

Oh yes, even an enlightened master wages a constant battle against laziness and false pride, all of the seven deadly sins. Human inertia is balanced so that these unlovely traits are always hovering in the hidden corners of awareness, waiting to win the battle. The only real difference between a master and any other human is that a master sees, and is sickened by his own self-deception. Why? Because he looks inside. He doesn't question whether or not he will give in to laziness (just this one more time) because he has long ago convinced his mind to help him fight sloth. He simply fights the never ending battle. In this way he gains mastery of himself, mastery which makes him very human, and detachment which makes him inhuman. Naturally, there's more to it than that, but not much more.

Speaking of self-deception, witness Sri Rainy trucking up the street with an algebra book, which he never intends to read. See him fight the good fight as his heart flutters and he grumbles to himself. Or has he decided to put fighting off until tomorrow? Will he pass this last test, or will he slip back into the mass of frail humanity, giving up all those years of work—beaten by the tart test.

Lotti hadn't been out on her balcony when he had whisked past earlier, pretending to be in such a hurry to get to the library. Her absence had been more distressing than the enlightened master had cared to admit. She was often up there hanging out her lingerie, but not today. Where was she, flirting around town with some ass?

From far down the block, he could see that she still wasn't on the balcony. His heart thumped the disappointment rumba in his skinny rib cage. Perfect tactics, he thought, now she's playing hard to get.

Undaunted, Rainy paused in front of the Lodge, then walked onto the porch. After all, he had Montclief's fishermen to ask questions about. What better place to start than where they were staying? He had forgotten to ask Esther who the fishermen were, so he would make up for lost time by asking Lotti, or her mother if necessary. What was the shrew's name? Mary. Cheapest woman in Colorado. Maybe she'd make him pay for the information. But it would be infinitely better to bypass the mother and go straight to the source. Wasn't Lotti's room next door to the interlopers? Maybe she'd overheard a conversation. Good Lord, maybe she'd seduced them!

He tapped on the substantial hardwood door and stood waiting on weak knees, amazed that at eighty-nine his emotional apparatus had suddenly gone haywire. Perhaps he had a disease or something, like a quick acting leprosy of the nervous system. Ridiculous. He was fine except in close proximity to Lotti. He squared his shoulders.

Mary McCardle pulled the door open. "Good heavens, Swam... I mean, Sri Rainy! I thought I heard somebody knocking. Nobody ever knocks here. They just barge right in like they own the place. Well, well, so you came to pay another visit. Come in, come in. I'll fix a nice cup of tea."

Rainy peered over her shoulder to see if Lotti was hovering around waiting for him. He noticed that Mary was holding the door wide open, so he stepped inside. "Thank you," he said. Lotti was nowhere in sight.

"Before I forget it again, I have to get you to sign that picture. I just know it would mean the world to our guests, and to me, of course. I have it right in the kitchen. Come along now, Mr. Sri."

Rainy followed Mary into the kitchen, grateful to her, but annoyed. Lotti's radiant presence was nowhere in evidence. This was not going to be easy. He should go straight home. If his magnetic powers were working correctly, Lotti would find a way to visit him. But what he did instead, was pull out a chair at the large kitchen table and sit down.

"Yes, that's right, you just sit and rest your weary bones," Mary said, digging in the broom closet where she'd put the framed poster. "You must be exhausted with all the walking and good works you do." She laid the ugly picture reverently on the table in front of him, then whipped a blue ballpoint from her apron and handed it to him.

Rainy studied the younger likeness of himself. One of his former pupils, a rock star named Billy Bad Boy Drummond, had printed it up as a poster to sell in Haight-Ashbury during the 60s. What had possessed him to allow a poster to be made in the first place? But he supposed it had attracted a few students, and money from the poster sales had trickled in for a number of seasons.

"It has glass over it," he said, stating the obvious.

"I noticed that," Mary answered, undeterred. "Maybe we can break out a corner of the glass. That would give you room to sign, wouldn't it?"

"I'm sure you wouldn't want to do that."

"Oh, yes. Just the corner. I'll replace it later." Mary grabbed an aluminum meat tenderizer mallet and advanced on the picture frame.

"Wouldn't it be simpler to unframe it from the back?"

"Oh, no. This will do nicely." The mallet flicked in her hand. Smash! The old glass tinkled merrily, instantly tenderized. Mary shook the shards into the waste basket and handed the poster back to Rainy. "Careful you don't cut yourself," she cautioned.

Rainy was somewhat awed by such direct action. His teacher had been very much like that, all pragmatism and non-attachment. He chuckled and signed his name on the yellowed newsprint. If Mary didn't replace the glass, the poster would crumble to dust in a year or two.

"Is Lotti around today?" he asked, nonchalantly. "I brought an algebra book over to help her with a problem she mentioned yesterday."

"Algebra..?" Mary's wizened red face puckered in wonderment.

"Yes." Rainy said, blandly. "Lotti has a very inquiring mind."

"Since when?"

"I'm sure she inherited the genes from you."

Mary smiled a pleased, sly smile. "Yes, I suppose she did, at that." Her mind flirted back to Lotti's father and as quickly flicked past him when she felt the nettles of abandonment stinging her. "So you think Lotti's a bright girl, do you?" she said. "I suppose you'd know. Myself, I've always favored practicality."

Rainy winced. What was he doing here, wasting time with this old crone? Part of the reason he had sought the monastic life was because he couldn't stand making small talk with imbeciles. It seemed that the less a person had on the ball, the more certain he, or in this case she, was that every word issuing from her mouth was immutable truth. At twenty years of age, Rainy (then Fargo Raisenbe) had been totally intolerant of dullards; but at eighty-nine, he wanted to screw this innkeeper's daughter, so he smiled evenly and asked, "Did you say that Lotti was here?"

"I don't believe she is. She went down to the post office hours ago, and I didn't see her coming back to help with the chores. Let me check."

Going to the foot of the stairs, Mary bellowed at the top of her lungs, "Lotti..!! Somebody here for you!"

Very romantic, Rainy thought, and was relieved when there was no answering shout. Not home. Just as well. His disappointment was bitter, but at least he wouldn't have to mince around the mother in order to get up to Lotti's bedroom. "Well, I guess I'd better be going then," he said, standing up.

"The tea's ready just this minute," insisted Mary.

"Oh, by the way," Rainy said, remembering Montclief's plight in the nick of time. "There are two fishermen living here, aren't there?"

After pouring boiling water into a tea pot and fooling around for some minutes scooping dry tea leaves into a metal tea ball to submerge in the pot, Mary turned her attention back to the monk. "Yes indeed," she said, placing the pot in a tea cosy on the table to steep. "Mr. Barkley and Mr. Yates. And fine gentlemen they are, too. Two weeks cash in advance for two rooms. No doubling up for gentlemen of quality." Seekers always took a double room. She was glad of the chance to insinuate that the Swami's weirdo followers were cheap. Maybe he'd tell them to make a better impression, since the Lodge wasn't full as it used to be in the good old days when she could charge extra for double rooms.

Life is hard for a single mother, he silently reminded himself. "I saw your gentlemen up at Fawn Brook. They seemed like professional men to me. Any idea what they do for a living?"

"I surely don't. They didn't say and I didn't think to ask. Most generally folks will tell me things in conversation; but the gentlemen seemed so keen on the trout fishing, that's all they kept asking about. But, of course, my duties here keep me from being the outdoorsy type, even if I might want to be. Then when they paid cash, I was busy with the receipt. Don't you think, Sri Rainy, that we should all go back to using cash? This credit card business is such a pain to a body."

"I haven't given that problem much thought, Mrs. McCardle. Perhaps I'll just stop up to their room and say hello. It would be nice to have somebody from the outside world to chat with."

"That's what I was thinking myself. But they already went fishing. Said they might camp out overnight and not to worry. Here, your tea's ready." Mary poured tea into her two best china cups and sat down at the table. "Don't burn your tongue, Your Eminence," she said.

Meanwhile, sultry little Lotti had stationed herself in a clump of sighing aspens bordering the post office parking lot. She sat with her back against one of the trees, listening to the mountain breeze whispering through the leaves and branches, and pretending to read a book she had brought along. She wore a short red skirt that showed her legs to good advantage. Lotti knew she had baited the trap to perfection. Willy Jacks would pull into the parking lot to get the mail any minute now, and she'd be waiting there, innocently reading. Totally perfect. Under the skirt she wore a pair of black lace, crotchless panties from Frederick's of Hollywood, which she was sure would turn Willard into jello.

➻ ➼

CHAPTER 9

TO ADHERE IS TO WITHDRAW

TO WITHDRAW IS TO ADHERE

After spending all day trailing the two hiking fishermen, Montclief now lay so close to their tent that he could hear the low snoring coming from inside. The mountain darkness was unbroken by stars. He sensed that rain would begin falling shortly before daybreak.

Every word that the men spoke while they were hiking and after they'd made camp was overheard by the keen ears of the yeti; but all those words didn't make for understanding. He was still left with his unease and no solid reason for feeling it. Most of the day's talking had centered around core boring and isolation chambers and buffer zones. And also wistful lapses into how lovely the mountain was and what a shame to destroy it.

Thinking that they would talk more cohesively of their plans inside the tent, Montclief had sneaked along the shadow of a rock ledge until he was practically touching the nylon tenting. Considerable risk was involved in this maneuver, since one of the men was wearing a large caliber sidearm; but he needed to hear. However, instead of talking, the men had gone to sleep.

When he'd heard enough snoring, Montclief started the trek home. He would return in the predawn rain and maybe encourage an avalanche. Or perhaps he would fake a bear attack. Something had to be done. These two did not belong on his mountain, spreading their rumor of fear.

While Montclief loped toward his cave, Lotti sat on her bed reliving the miraculous events of that day—events that she was totally sure would lead her to Hollywood. It was a kick to be the only person awake in Pike's Grove. Now that she was practically on her way to fame, she felt a nostalgic connection, almost love, for all the dull rustics that she had known all her life. While they slept, getting their full eight hours of invigorating sleep so they could get up at dawn to repeat another day of the same old thing, Lotti watched over them from her lighted bedroom above Spruce Lane.

Today's meeting with Willard and the subsequent jeep ride had been such a déjà vu experience that she had felt compelled to start writing the history of her tumultuous, tortuous journey to stardom into her diary. A record needed to be left for other women of destiny to read and follow. And boys too, for that matter.

The thought of writing a journal had appeared so clearly, while she had been bouncing along Burnt Pine Road in the seat beside Willy Jacks that she knew a journal must be part of fulfilling her quest. Yes, as if by magic, a vision of her diary had appeared—the virginal diary that had been locked in her night stand for two years now. A picture of the leather-bound notebook had simply appeared in her mind! Incredible.

Except for one or two pages which she had filled with childish drivel when she'd first received the book from Esther two Christmases ago, the book was untouched—the absolutely perfect place to record her magic journey. Esther must have guessed the future when she gave the diary to her. And the image of it had appeared like a mind vision right on the jeep's dusty windshield! Not a thought about it—an actual vision! Really incredible. What else could she do but start writing?

And Willy was turning out to be everything that she'd thought he would be. His tall, cool body was simply not troubled at all about the pine needles under his knees. And not ashamed in the least about taking off all his clothes, and hers, instead of just dropping his pants like some people she knew. Lotti had prayed he would be just like that. Like a God. An Adonis. And it had lasted a long time! A really long time. Too long almost, she had almost lost control, it had all been so heavenly. Next time she just might go ahead and lose herself all the way, even though that would be a silly thing to do. No, she probably wouldn't, but the thought was so tempting. A woman can't go around losing control, if she has a high mission; but maybe just one or two little letting-goes wouldn't matter. She'd be extra careful not to let Willy know, then she could just float off on the wings of heaven like she'd been so close to doing today.

Tues. October 12th

Dear Diary,

Today was like the first day of a very big dream. I just know it's going to come true, and now you know it, too. I can just feel it.

W.J. was so ultimately Mr. Cool that I just

had to track him down and turn him into Mr. Begging For It. So as you know, I made THE PLAN. It worked perfect. Mr. Cool never knew what hit him.

I had this little outfit on and he was so overwhelmed with my legs when I just hopped into the shotgun seat of the HOLLYWOOD JEEP when he came out of the post office with the town mail, that he just started the engine. All I said was, "Please take me with you, Willy," and I hiked up the slitted skirt just a little. (It's so slippy anyway that it was practically up to my poonie already.) So he drove us out to Berlinheimer's place for a special delivery letter, and then we went up to the woods on Burnt Pine Road and that's were we did IT.

His thing is nicely large and quite warm. It's uncircumcised and bends a little bit to the left, but believe me that doesn't hurt a thing!!

So on to Phase 2 of THE PLAN. I'll keep you informed about everything. Hollywood here we come!!!

*

Willard Jacks was completely awake and absorbed in *Adirondack Warrior* by Lute Sims, who was probably Willard's favorite science fiction writer, certainly one of his top five. *Adirondack Warrior* was the alternative selection of the Book of the Month Club this month. It was about an Indian brave who goes spacing after he gets picked up by a flying saucer. The book had arrived in today's mail and Willard was a happy guy tonight.

A half-eaten bowl of popcorn and a can of Pepsi sat on the arm of his reading chair. He wasn't dreaming about Lotti, in fact he hadn't thought much about the kid other than to marvel at how surprisingly she had filled out. His body was nicely relaxed as he read, thanks to the twenty minutes spent with her on the edge of Burnt Pine Meadow, but Lotti was just a high school girl. He didn't see any reason to hurt her feelings, but she'd been pretty funny really. Ah heck, she was a nice kid, but if he wanted to get his ashes hauled, really hauled, he certainly wouldn't go looking for Lotti again. His two steady pokes were like tigers in heat. Both Lu Ellen and Fay could really make the fur fly. Actually, he guessed he was a pretty lucky guy.

Taking a sip of soda, he started another chapter, hoping Lotti wouldn't get to be a pain in the butt. She probably wouldn't. Riding in the jeep turned her on more than screwing did anyway.

Yolanda sensed her mate returning home before she actually heard him. She was tired and a little irritable from lack of sleep, but now that he was home she could relax. She took a bowl of elk blood soup from the ice closet and set it to warm near the tiny fire.

Yolanda never slept while Montclief was away, not wanting to miss a distress warning if it came; so the last few days she had gotten little sleep. That was her own choice, of course. He had never asked her to stand watch like a neurotic mother. But Montclief took so many chances. He needed someone to watch over him. Yolanda had started this odd unYeti-like practice right after they were married. She wasn't even sure that he knew, but probably he did. He knew everything else. Since he had never broached the subject, she assumed she had his tacit approval; but she certainly had never gotten a thank you for the sleeplessness.

Montclief entered the cave by a side entrance down a granite chute that left no trail, except an occasional scraped hair, which he made sure that Chava picked clean every three or four days. The front cave mouth entrance was also carefully tended to look unused and forbidding. The yeti spoor kept all animals away, except possibly a grizzly looking for a spot to winter. The careful tending was for the benefit of any lost or not lost yrt. Only they needed to be fooled.

Letting his mind drift back to a warm memory, Montclief thought of the time when he and Darla, his first wife, had shared this cave. One snowy evening, a giant grizzly had wandered in—the two ton beast that the mountain knew as Sigmoid. Montclief had just killed a yearling moose that would last them half the winter, so he and Darla decided to let Sigmoid sleep in the outer cave as their doorman. Killing a grizzly is a lot of trouble, and driving one away is even worse once he's decided to hibernate. So they let him stay, listening to the grunting and snorting of his bear dreams until the quickening of spring sent him on his way down to the meadows for grubs. That was a nice time. His son, Nuk, had been born that spring.

"You're home," Yolanda said, smiling at him. She wanted to be charming, to put him in a good mood; but she saw at a glance that it was a lost cause. He was so sour lately. Darn it, didn't she try every way she could think of to be a perfect mate, and nothing ever worked! And her period was coming up in a couple of days. She had hoped he'd be nice to her tonight, or even rough like he used to be sometimes, because he never seemed to like her during her menstrual days.

"More rain coming," he said, sitting down on a rock ledge.

"Yes, I felt it," she agreed. "Are you hungry?"

"Of course. And it's too warm in here."

"It's only a tiny fire," Yolanda said, defensively. "Just enough to keep the chill off. There's not a drop of smoke."

"We'll have to learn to do without fire. I don't want Chava to grow up soft. Nor should you and I get soft," he said, seriously. "We need to eat raw and sleep cold. Times are not good. We may have to move up range."

Her heart fluttered. Something was wrong. Montclief had never talked about moving before. He loved this mountain, and his relationship with the old man. Something must be terribly wrong. He would never sacrifice his visits with old Rainpuddle, as Yolanda secretly called the old yrt. She rather liked Rainy, even though she knew that her husband's friendship with the holy grandfather set him apart from all the other yetis.

"I'm thinking of calling a meeting of the Council," Montclief said, quietly.

With a sinking feeling, Yolanda served him the warm blood soup, then went into the cold storage room where she hacked a flank steak off the elk carcass. She plopped it on a forked stick and brought it back. "Raw meat on a stick," she said, handing it to him. "The old way. Are you happy, now. Should I put out the fire?"

"Let it burn down," he said, gently. "I'm sorry this had to happen, but we have to get ready for changes. The Old Ways have always served us, it's time to go back to them. At least until I know more."

"What is it...?" she asked. She should have questioned him several days ago, but had assumed he'd tell her if it was important.

"I'm not certain. I had a bad feeling, and a dream of sweating death. So I started following two yrts who came here. They want to change the mountain, somehow. I am wondering if I should kill them. It would be simple, but the future is clouded with mist. I don't even know if killing them would stop it."

"I'll help you, if you want," she volunteered. Twice before she had helped him scare campers who had camped too close to what he considered his territory. Once they had simply pulled down a tent in the middle of a rain storm. The other time it was a small avalanche that obliterated the food cache. It had been fun. He tried to make things fun for her when they had first married.

"I have to think first, Yoli. The answer is well hidden. The old one is trying to find out what they are doing. I will talk to him in the morning; so tonight the yrts will live, as perhaps they should not. They sleep now under a rocky ledge. In the rain, dying would be so easy and so accidental. But the future is too clouded yet."

"Eat your meat," Yolanda said. "It will give you strength. It was a strong elk and a fine hunt."

He grunted and chewed off a bite of the meat.

Montclief had been looking forward to cooked meat and was sorry he'd made such a firm stand on the Old Ways.

Seated in the quite center of the whirling dervish practice, with the students twirling all around him and drone music filling the hole in the Universe, Sri Rainy realized that he'd forgotten to find out anything about the fishermen. He would be meeting Montclief in the morning with nothing to tell him. Maybe he should simply forget to go fishing. No, that would be unconscionable. Oh, drat, he'd have to tramp down into town and try to catch Lotti before she went to bed. Or better yet, he'd ride what's-his-name's bicycle. Ungerer.

He looked for Ungerer in the swirling circle, and not finding him realized that he'd given the twerp to Edmund Ragnars. Turning his head to the left, he saw Mr. Ungerer, owner of a ten speed mountain bike, sawing away on a drone fiddle. The agonized expression on the young man's face suggested that his leg muscles were cramping on him. Too bad. There was still ten minutes to go in this dance. Rainy couldn't cut it short for something trivial like cramped muscles. Eventually Mr. Ten Speed would learn how to sit. Maybe he would discover sainthood in the process.

Rainy sensed a faltering in the flow of the dance and realized in a flash of chagrin that he was the cause. The Dance Master sits at the hub, if his attention falters, as his just had, the whirling goes astray. He cleared his mind of mundane matters and concentrated on a complicated mental counting exercise to keep his sex-crazed mind from wandering again.

Silently as a creeping kitten, Sri Rainy crept through the dark buildings of the Retreat until he came to the ten speed bike that Ungerer kept parked outside the dormitory where he lived. The bike wasn't chained to a tree as it would have been down in the city, so the old monk simply swiped the bike and wheeled it silently out of the compound.

Cold wind whistled around his skinny legs, but prudence caused him to tuck the skirts of his robe around his waist. Rainy remembered that as a boy he had taken many spills because the cuffs of his trousers had gotten caught in the drive chain of his Schwin Strato-cruiser. He certainly didn't want a repeat of those circus tricks on a lonely mountain road. Not with his brittle old bones. Rainy chuckled roguishly as he sped downhill toward town. The cause of the chuckle was the word play that he'd just made up on the concept of his old bones. The word play was his brittle old boner! The thought of seeing Lotti was engorging his old boner something fierce. It was shameful probably, but the cold air whistling up his skirt seemed to be egging it on. Oh, the hell with it, Rainy thought exultantly. This is great! I feel just like a teenager again.

A sudden dark shape leaped out into the road in front of him. What the hell..! He slammed on the foot brakes—but his feet spun backwards on the pedals. For an instant of panic he forgot that the ten speed had hand brakes; then reaching for them, he swerved to avoid the bear or whatever it was.

The startled, bearded face of Tad Foulks, the town drunk, zipped past while Rainy fought for control of the bike. Finally, the brakes caught and the infernal machine slewed to a halt. Rainy cursed himself for forgetting how steep the grade on this hill was. He should know by now, he'd walked it nearly every day for forty years.

"Are you all right?" he called back to Tad Foulks.

"Me..? I'm fine and dandy," Foulks slurred, drunkenly. "Why wouldn't I be? Who is that, Mortimer Snerd..?"

"Yes, it's Mortimer Snerd," Rainy answered. Foulks was harmless. He occasionally begged a meal in the dead of winter, but other than that he never came near the Retreat. And he never called Rainy by the name of Mortimer Snerd when he was begging, only when he was drunk as a skunk.

"Well then, have a nice ride, Mortimer. I thought you was one of those hippie girls, or I wouldn't have stopped you."

"Don't be messing around with any of my women," Rainy warned, even though Foulks was easily twice his size. He really had thought a black bear was on the road when he'd first seen the drunk. "They don't like to to be bothered."

"Hey, I wouldn't bother a fly. Course, if some hippie girl wants to be bothered that's a different story, ain't it? Seems to me like there's more than plenty of them to go around. You're getting too long in the tooth to handle more than one or two a night, ain't you, Mort?"

"I don't handle them at all!" Rainy replied, archedly.

"See..! Plenty to go around, just like I said. You do keep a nice class of women up there, Reverend. Yes, sir, I sure have enjoyed meeting up with a few of them. Searching for free love, ain't they?"

Rainy was too shocked to answer. Had this sodden, filthy drunk really been rendezvousing with the women students? Well, he probably was more exciting than most of the pamby male students who showed up these days. At least he was resourceful enough to live off the land.

"Searching for free love, yes, sir! I'll tell you, Mort, some of those babes could hump the dong off an elephant. I can't hardly stay in the saddle sometimes. But I don't need to tell you that," Tad chuckled, slyly. "You been teaching them techniques all these years, and a mighty fine job you been doing. If you ever need a testimonial, Morty, you just send them reporters to me. I'll tell anybody that you're the greatest teacher that's ever been around here, that's for sure! About the men, now, I can't say. Never go that way, myself; but I 'spect you must do just as good a job with them."

"I'm late already, Mr. Foulks, so I have to be going." Rainy hiked his skirts back up and settled himself on the bike. "Don't be jumping out at people on the road, or you'll cause a serious injury."

"Hey, don't worry about me, Reverend. I never get hurt bad, seems like. And just call me Tad. Old Tad, that's what everybody calls me. This Mr. Foulks stuff makes me think you're talking to my dad." His deep, rumbling laugh sounded like a bear. "And if I was you, I'd get a light on that thing. Yeah, that's it! A light that shines up on your face, so somebody can tell it's you and not one of those hippie girls."

Growling to himself, Rainy pedaled on down the hill. His erection had shriveled during the encounter with drunken Foulks. That was something, at least. He was going to the Lodge to find out about the fisherman, not to seduce a teenager. Doing that would make him no better than Tad Foulks. Had his female disciples really been putting out for a lout like that? Probably. Foulks might have been bragging, but he hadn't been lying. Rainy snorted. If old Foulks hooked up with somebody like Sister Angie, she probably *would* knock him out of the saddle.

The few lighted cabins on the outskirts of town whipped past, then a handful of white clapboard houses. He wheeled into the turn at Spot Right Laundry and Liquor, which was now owned by that Chinese fellow, Wong, who was always courteous, but never actually friendly. He's probably remote because I don't do much business with him. A bottle of brandy for holiday fruitcakes, that was about it. Not much call to dry clean a cassock. That was it! The name he'd been trying to think of the other day with Lotti. Cassock. How could he have forgotten that? Anyway, Wong probably fawned on paying customers, like a Chinese waiter. Now that he thought of it, Pike's Grove was a very strange place for a Chinese to buy a laundry. He surely couldn't be doing a very thriving business.

The Lodge was all lighted up. He counted six

rooms with lights on. That must make Mary nervous, he thought. Lotti's balcony room was lighted, too. Good. He parked the bike inside the hedge so no kids would get the notion of going for a joy ride, and hopped bravely up the steps to the wide porch. Just a quick sashay in and out. Get the background on the fishermen, who probably weren't fiendish at all, but normal miners on a vacation. Montclief was upset by his dream most probably, not by these fellows. But if a little investigation could ease his friend's mind, he was only too glad to do his bit. After knocking on the door, he stepped back to wait. Maybe Lotti would answer it, so he wouldn't have to deal with Mary. Hard to imagine how a nice girl like Lotti had sprung from those cold loins.

The door was pulled open by Esther Olsterholt, whose face brightened instantly when she saw the Swami. Before she recognized her dear friend, she'd been rather frightened of the hooded figure on the porch. She'd thought for a scary second that perhaps it was Death paying a nocturnal visit.

"Sri Rainy..!" she sang. "Well, how nice to see you." She clutched her quilted robe demurely around her thin chest. "If I'd had any idea you'd be paying a visit, I wouldn't be wearing this old thing." It was, in fact, a brand new flower pattern robe from L.L. Bean, just arrived last week, and Esther loved it. She couldn't wait to put it on every evening when she got home from the library.

"No need to dress up for an old recluse like me," Rainy said, charitably, thereby traipsing all over Esther's feelings. "I just came by to collect a little information. I guess gossip would be closer to the truth."

"Gossip? You..? Oh, no, I don't think so. No, indeed." She smiled invitingly.

"Yes, I have to admit to it."

"No need to be shy about seeking out a little warmth and hospitality on a chilly evening, Sri Rainy. Well, come on inside. The stories we hear about the freezing conditions in your stone rooms up at the Retreat are enough to frighten an Eskimo. I'd turn into an ice cube, even in my quilty lounging robe."

"Oh, it's not so bad as all that," Rainy replied, stepping into the comparative warmth of the kitchen. His legs had just about frozen off on the downhill ride. Perhaps he should order a pair of dark sweat pants from L.L. Bean's in case he needed to make any more night rides. Why in hell couldn't Lotti have answered the door instead of this old lady, who in spite of being an old bag was his friend and he had to talk with her. Oh, well, maybe she knew something about the fishermen.

"Esther, I know you wouldn't think of eavesdropping, but perhaps you've overheard something about the two nice gentlemen guests at the Lodge. The fishermen..? I ran into them up on the mountain today and they seemed so pleasant that I thought I'd like to know them better. But I expect they're asleep by now. Fishing is tiring work."

"Won't you step into the sitting room, Sri Rainy, where we can be more comfortable?"

"Didn't know you had a sitting room," he chuckled.

"Well," she simpered, "although I trust you implicitly, it doesn't seem seemly to invite a man up to my room on his first visit; but, of course, if you'd be more comfortable, I suppose it would be all right..."

"No, no. The sitting room is fine."

What had presumably been the get-together room in the old hunting lodge days had shrunk from its former glory. Mary had partitioned the room, so that the edge of the huge unlit stone fireplace nestled snugly into a plaster wall. What was on the other side of the wall, Rainy didn't know. There were no doors in it. Esther sat primly on a nubby fabric covered settee that had obviously been part of the original furnishings.

"What shall we talk about?" she asked, feeling a nervous fluttering under her quilted robe. Sri Rainy was easily twenty years older than she was, so it was silly to get all worked up; but he was the only man who had called on her since Ted had died. Twenty years didn't make that much difference anyway, did it? "Should I ask Mary to light a fire in here? She never does because the flue is stuck or something, but I'm sure it would be all right if she knew you were here."

Rainy's legs were freezing, but he didn't really want to ask Mary to expend a few precious sticks of firewood. Besides, the flue probably was stuck after this many years. To be neighborly, he sat on the other end of the settee, instead of in the wing back chair that looked more comfortable.

"About my fishermen, are they businessmen or what? The fishing was so good, I forgot to ask." He realized to his dismay that he was lying to Esther again. Very strange behavior for someone in his profession.

"Well," she began, wondering if it would be proper to slide closer to him. There hadn't been all this play acting with dear Ted. He'd asked her to go hiking one day at that nice state park back home in Indiana, and after walking for hours in the hot sun, it was natural to go skinny dipping in the lake they found. Nobody was around but some frogs and a cloud of mosquitoes. And after that magical afternoon, there didn't seem any reason to be coy around him. He was an outdoorsman, after all, and a healthy young animal. "Mary was mentioning something about them at dinner tonight," she said, trying to be helpful. "What was it..? Oh, yes. They didn't come back from fishing."

"They didn't..?"

"No, isn't that odd? They weren't here for dinner, and Lotti said nobody answered when she knocked on their door. Mary sent her upstairs to see if they were coming down before everything got cold."

"Lotti said they weren't there?"

"Nobody answered. There was gobs of food left over. Would you like a nice meatloaf sandwich, Sri Rainy. I'd be happy to fix you one, if you're hungry."

"No, no thank you, Esther. I think I'd better consult with Lotti on this question before she goes to sleep." He stood up.

Esther frowned. So that was it. This decrepit old man had the hots for Lotti, just like Mary said! Disgusting. "What's so important about these men?" she asked, innocently.

"Important?" Rainy bluffed. "Who said they were important? I was suddenly extremely curious about what they did for a living. I was..uh, thinking of inviting them to lecture my students, since they were here anyway. That is, if their occupations impact importantly on the outside world." He saw her friendly face looking at him as if she didn't believe a word. "We sometimes invite outside lecturers, you know. So in that sense, I suppose they are important to me. We do try to keep a balanced curriculum." Lies, one after another. It was incredible. Why am I hiding all this? Esther was the one person in town who perhaps could understand, without going to pieces. The fact that I've been lying to her forever doesn't mean I have to lie now. I'll just tell her my pet yeti wants to know. Hell, her husband had yeti experiences. Just because she thought he was crazy, doesn't mean I have to lie. "But since I forgot to ask precisely what they did, I can't invite them, until I do know." He smiled and reached down to touch her hand. "Is that clear?" She looked slightly glazed and he kicked himself for going on so.

"Well, I've never actually met them myself," she said, sweetly.

"Which is why I should speak to Lotti before the child goes to sleep."

"If you wouldn't think badly of me," Esther suggested, slyly. "I do know where Mary keeps the pass key. Would it be unbearably snoopy to enter their rooms? Of course, we'd only be exploring in the interest of your students."

"Unbearably snoopy? No. I think it might be classed as helpful."

"And anyway," she said, trying to make a solid

case for the heinous act of breaking and entering and snooping like a busybody librarian, "anyway, if they're lost on the mountain, somebody will have to go into their room eventually to find out who they are."

"I agree," Rainy said, judiciously. "Once a partner in research, always a partner. Where is the pass key? We won't need to alert Mary, will we?"

CHAPTER 10

LIKE A HAWK SEIZING A RABBIT

The upstairs hallway was lit only by a lone forty watt bulb. Dark, ominous shadows lent authenticity to the stealthy deed as Esther and Sri Rainy tiptoed along.

Suppressing a spate of nervous tittering, Esther tapped the lightest imaginable series of Morse codes on the door to Room 9. Three short taps followed by two more. A mouse would have knocked louder. Then she inserted the key and opened the door. Feeling very unskilled at larceny, Rainy slipped into the dark room behind her and closed the door, thereby shutting out the dim hallway light.

Like frightened blind people, the espionage mission halted beside the bed in almost pitch blackness. A few stray beams filtered through the curtained window from a streetlight, but were much too dim to read anything by.

Neither of them had thought to bring a flashlight. Snapping on the ceiling light would have betrayed their position to the outside world. Rainy chuckled grimly under his breath. It was far from likely that a couple of fishermen on vacation would bring reams of documents related to their jobs anyway. They were up here to forget work for a few days. Damn Montclief and his dream.

"What do we do, now?" he whispered to Esther.

"I don't know. I thought you did," she whispered back, urgently. "What if Mary hears us?"

"Isn't there a Dewey Decimal System for finding incriminating documents?" His attempting at lightening the situation with levity failed miserably. "Where should we look first?"

"Ted always kept his secret things under his socks." His nasty pictures, she meant, but she wouldn't say such a treachery to Sri Rainy. When Ted had gotten sick, one of the first things she did was to get rid of those vile magazines that had mortified her for years. Not that she thought Playboy magazine should be banned. Far from it. She was a librarian and regarded all printed matter as almost sacred; but why did Ted have to read it? It was a slap in her face every time she put his rolled socks away. He knew his precious dirty pictures were gone, too; but he never asked about them, just as he'd never mentioned having them when he was well. But she hadn't wanted Doctor Paulsen to see the smutty things if he had to be called into their home, so she'd burned them one afternoon while Ted was sleeping—carrying them outside with her rubber dish washing gloves so as not to profane her hands. Then she'd peeled the gloves off and burned them, too. What a stench those disgusting smut rags made. They must have been printed with the cheapest inks imaginable.

As his eyes adjusted to the room, Rainy moved carefully to the high-boy dresser. He pulled the top drawer open, causing the old wood to squeal like a rabbit under an owl's talons. Socks, that was all, carefully rolled and placed in a line like good soldiers, but no papers. Not even a sex magazine. Even that would have indicated something about the fisherman, but only socks were in the drawer.

"Socks," he whispered to Esther, who was at his shoulder smelling of lilac talcum powder. He pulled the next drawer out and they both peered in. Underwear. T shirts and Jockey briefs. White. This was getting nowhere. But why would it? He certainly didn't keep his papers and journal in his sock drawer. They were in his desk, where any sane person kept such things. This was stupid! What was he looking for anyway? A wild goose chase based on a yeti's nightmare. It was preposterous. For a wild animal, Montclief was even an extremely poor fisherman.

Swiveling his head to search for a desk, Rainy caught sight of the door cracking open. Light from the hallway spilled into the room. He clutched Esther's arm and they both froze. Caught red-handed. Lord, don't let me be arrested, he prayed. I promise never to do anything like this again!

"Yatesy, can I come in..?" Lotti's sultry whisper drifted into the room. The door opened, revealing—really revealing Luscious Lotti, wearing a see-through red teddy. Illuminated from behind by the hall light, all her charms were on display to Rainy and Esther. Esther caught her breath, like a factory steam whistle.

"Esther..?" Lotti said, rather too loudly. "What are you doing here?" She stamped her foot and started to simper. "And with Mortimer Snerd!" Stepping into the room, she closed the door and flicked on the overhead light, a sixty watter. "Well, Mortimer, what could you possibly be doing in this dark room with Mrs. Olsterholt in her bathrobe? Don't tell me you're teaching her algebra." She laughed, haughtily.

"You wouldn't understand, my dear. And please speak more softly," he begged.

"Try me," Lotti said in her normal voice. She, after all, had nothing to hide. That cute Dr. Yates wasn't in.

"It's rather a private matter."

"I doubt if Mother would understand your private parts..I mean, matters, Mortimer."

"Don't insult Sri Rainy by calling him that disgusting nickname," Ester chimed in.

"You call him Swami, what's the difference?"

Esther gasped. She wished she could crawl under the rug and die of embarrassment, but she settled for taking the offensive. "You little slut, how dare you say that! And how dare you parade around dressed like a call girl!"

"Look who's calling the kettle black," Lotti retorted, justly proud of her debating ability.

A hail storm of tapping hit the door, then the shrill voice of Mary McCardle insinuated itself into the turgid scene.

"Lotti..?! Don't be bothering Dr. Yates! It's time for you to be in bed. Is she disturbing you, Doctor?"

Rainy froze like a statue of Saint Francis of Assisi. Pigeons could have landed on his nose. Esther ducked down behind the bed.

"I ain't bothering him, Mother! We're talking about stuff. He's an interesting man. I'll go to bed in a few minutes."

"All right then. See that you don't make a nuisance of yourself. Are you hungry, Dr. Yates?"

"He fine," Lotti sang out. "They went down to Clinton and had dinner at the Pancake House."

"Well, all right then. I'm setting my alarm for fifteen minutes and you be back in your room before that."

"Yes, Mamma," the nymphette said, delighted at her repartee.

Mary's slippers clipped down the hall and a door shut.

Rainy thawed out. What an outstanding girl Lotti was. His eyes had never left her teddy-clad form. What amazing, succulent young breasts she had. They hung there, pouting at him—the most relevant things he'd seen for ages, maybe ever. They were so....soft looking.

"So what were you pawing through Yatesy's underwear for?" Lotti asked, conspiratorially.

"Um..." answered Mortimer Snerd.

"Sri Rainy wanted to know what his friends did for a living so he could invite them to speak up at the

Retreat." Esther whispered, icily. *Her* motives were clearly beyond reproach. "Since they hadn't returned home, we decided to peek into their room to see if it was worth Sri Rainy's time to plan for them to speak. Does that satisfy your curiosity? I guess we don't have to guess at why you came sneaking in here, do we..?"

"And I guess we don't have to guess why Mortimer is looking at me instead of you, do we?" Lotti gave her curls a saucy bounce.

Glancing over at Sri Rainy, Esther saw that he was indeed staring at Lotti. Worse than that, his penis was poking his cossack out like a pup tent, and he didn't seem to notice.

"Lotti dear," Rainy faltered, "do you happen to know what Mr. Yates does for a living? Perhaps you overheard something?"

"Why didn't you ask me before? Of course, I know. It would have saved you all this breaking and entering like a common criminal."

"I looked for you when I got here; but then Esther was kind enough to suggest this method, and it seemed like a good idea at the time."

"Don't make it sound like I forced you into something," the librarian wheedled. "I was just trying to be helpful."

"Of course, you were, Esther." He turned back to Lotti's teddy. "What does Mr. Yates do, mining engineer or some such?"

"He's a geologist. A doctor."

"Aah, that's what I thought from the way he talked."

"And that's not the half of it. Did he mention the important part?"

"Uh, which important part is that, dear?"

"I'm going back to my room," Esther chirped. She hated Lotti and her perky tits. Only a few years ago, her own breasts had been much better than this slatternly girl's. It wasn't her fault that she was old now, and men no longer wanted her. No, it wasn't her fault, but it made her feel trapped and old and very unhappy. At least she still had her dignity, and she would never let anybody take that away from her. "This has certainly been an unpleasant evening," she snipped.

"Quiet, Mrs. Olsterholt," Rainy hissed. "Go ahead, Lotti, dear."

"What you're looking for is in the suitcase in the closet. Nobody would keep nuclear bomb stuff under their socks. I can't believe how stupid you looked when I caught you. God, it's a riot..!" She burst into a gale of slatternly giggling.

*

The closet door opened with a squeak. Except for the hall door, which had obviously been oiled, it was a very squeaky room. Inside the closet was a Naugahyde suitcase, not cheap and not new either. Lotti opened it deftly. Inside was a blued .357 magnum in a leather holster, which scared Rainy witless. He noticed two rifle cases also standing in the closet, but Lotti disregarded them like they were tree stumps, and zoned in on a cardboard letter case tied with a string. Her nimble little fingers unwrapped the string without breaking or fraying it in the least. Then she opened the packet. "You're not gonna believe what important people I've been talking with," she breathed theatrically, pulling a sheaf of xerox graphs bearing the Department of Agriculture heading. The first few graphs dealt with rock density and faults per mile, which made perfect sense to Rainy. Why not, the guys were geologists. And he probably would have toddled on back to his fishing stream to tell Montclief that all was well, had not Lotti spilled the beans.

"Notice anything strange about those papers?" she inquired, slyly.

"Charts," Rainy replied. "Charts and graphs. Seems fine to me. Perfectly normal. Well ladies, shall we adjourn to a more convivial sphere?"

"They ain't normal, Mortimer. Not at all." Lotti paused for dramatic affect. "Dr. Yates and Dr. Barkley are going to put this burg on the map. We're going to be really important!"

During the course of trysting late last night in both Rooms 8 and 9, Lotti had picked up some fascinating tidbits, and had naturally put her own rational on them. Dr. Barkley being a Yale man would never have volunteered any information to a local poke; but Yates, a rather typical California stud, thought it would be good for his ego to impress the pants off this nympho teeny-bopper, even though her pants were already off and had been for the last hour while she blew his mind with her bottomless sexual appetite. He swore her to silence, of course; then he told her.

Imagine telling Lotti a secret any deeper than the Captain Marvel code word. But she got so excited thinking that Pike's Grove would become a glamorous boom town, that he kept on telling her until he ran out of climaxes.

Then she went next door and milked a few corroborating secrets from the tight-lipped Barkley. She actually had to quit sucking him in mid-stream, and spent a few minutes searching for her chemise, before he suddenly felt that giving away a few government secrets wouldn't condemn him to eternal damnation. No, it would probably be good to unburden his soul. Besides, the cat was already out of the bag. Naturally, he swore her to silence as Yates had; but he couldn't be exactly sure of the solemnity of her oath, since her mouth was full of cock once again.

"They're thinking of opening a mine?" Sri Rainy commented, leafing through a new sheaf of papers. "Yes, I suppose that would be good for the economy."

"Oh, really?" Esther chipped in. A new mine would mean an influx of miners. Maybe life wasn't hopeless yet, after all.

"Although I can't imagine what they think they're going to mine way up here." Rainy said, judiciously. "As far as I know, there's nothing really worth while on the mountain."

"That's exactly it, Mortimer! You are so smart! How did you ever pick up on that?"

"They don't call me Swami for nothing," he joked.

"What exactly did I pick on?"

"Well, I shouldn't tell anybody, but since you already guessed most of it — anyway, you'll find out soon enough. What we've got here is a big mountain with nothing really important about it, just a lot of rock, right?"

"If you say so. I think it's an astoundingly lovely mountain, myself, but go on."

"Sure, it's great, but it's boring as all get out, and all that's up there to help us out financially is a bunch of rock and snow. Well, what if some company like U.S. Engineers comes up here and digs a big hole. They don't ruin the trees or anything. Just dig a big hole inside the mountain, and they hire a lot of local men. Everybody gets a steady paycheck like they always need. Then when the hole is all made, the company brings in all that old nuclear stuff nobody wants anymore, and they just put it down in the hole. Then they cover up the cave entrance and plant trees on it, and everything is great." Lotti noticed that Mortimer Snerd was getting a look of horror on his face, but she blasted right ahead. "And they pay us for years and years to guard the stuff so the Russians don't dig it up and steal it. Get it? We'll always have money up here from now on. Lots of it! This will be like a real city and very important. Pretty great, isn't it? Since we're the ones that are already here, we'll all get rich. Maybe U.S. Engineers will even buy most of the houses at a big profit. Wow, huh?"

Rainy was jolted, no doubt about it. He didn't know what to reply. Montclief's silly dream had been right. Astounding. Unbelievably astounding.

*

Lots of people were roaming around on the mountain tonight, and it wasn't even a full moon. Up near the Retreat, while most everybody was fast asleep, both Sister Angie and Norman Ungerer were out in the dark forest seeking for something other than enlightenment.

Sister Angie was scrambling through a heavily wooded stretch near the road where on Thursday nights she was usually able to find Thaddeus Foulks waiting for her with a bottle of cheap wine. True, he was an animal and a lout, but he had some very good characteristics too, like being a war hero. The worst thing about him, outside of never bathing, was that tonight he hadn't bothered to show up. Most probably he was passed out somewhere. That's why she was searching through the rocks and bracken with a hooded lantern. Her shins were already scraped from not being able to see properly. If she'd known the rotten drunk would play hard to get, she would have worn jeans under her caftan; but they were so much trouble to take off. A robe just slipped up like it was designed for carnal knowledge. Yes, it was a thoroughly practically garment, except that it offered no protection from brambles and sharp rocks.

Unaware that his nemesis, Sister Angie, was scouring the area on a lover's quest, Norman Ungerer was flitting down the dark mountain road like a haunted specter searching for his lost bicycle. He was very pissed that somebody would steal the bike of a pious acolyte, denying him his only means of rapid transportation. Grumbling loudly, he lay the blame on one of several little gremlins from town, who must have sneaked up to the Retreat and snagged the ten speed to impress their felonious cronies. The world was in a sorry state indeed when a holy disciple couldn't even have a bicycle.

Even though he hated the frightening mountain at night, Norman was searching the ditches on both sides of the road hoping against hope that the blackguard had abandoned the bike or had fallen off and cracked his head open. He wanted that bike back! Not only did it give him a certain status at the monastery to possess a new mountain bike, but it also allowed him to go for a ride, now and again to revive his spirit. After all, it looked ridiculous to stay in the outhouse all the time, whereas going for a bike ride was normal. Sometimes he made up a mission like going to town to purchase onions for the kitchen. Since he was in charge, nobody knew except him and Slob-o Angie, who always made sure she blabbed her mouth about where was he going, and where had he been when he got back. Fucking fascist pig. What business was it of hers? She should worry about her own salvation instead of minding everybody else's business.

Norman stepped right along. The night was chilly and he was not dressed all that warmly. What would be wrong with having a light cotton robe for summer and a quilted one for winter? This half cotton and half wool bastard tried to be all things to all people, and failed miserably except on about five days out of the year. He had read about Tibetan monks having quilted clothes for winter, but everybody laughed at him when he mentioned it. If he had decent clothing, then at least he could be comfortable while he suffered toward enlightenment. Norman, of course, had never been bold enough to question Sri Rainy about a quilted burnoose.

His original plan, when anger over the stolen bike had been hot in his veins, was to track the thieves all the way to town, if necessary. But he was freezing, and besides, Norman had a mortal fear of running into a bear. This stretch of road was so desolate. The trees made eerie noises, creaking and moaning in the wind. What was he doing on this stupid mountain, anyway? He was a city boy! It would be different if he had been born on a farm, then he'd know how to protect himself from savage wild cows and bears. He wished with all his heart that he was on a train back to civilization, or even safely in his crummy freezing cell, which at least was safe from bears. What if a hungry bear smelled him and came running out of the woods. God, what would he do? He might fight feebly, but the huge bear would knock him down and bite his head off. He'd seen "Clan of the Cave Bear" with that sexy Darryl Hannah getting stuffed from behind every other scene. The one nice, gentle guy in the movie, the only one Norman could identify with, had gotten his head crunched by a bear. The bear, a huge brute with a shaggy coat just opened his mouth and pawed the nice guy's head in, and crunch! What could poor Norman do against a brute like that? Climb a tree, he thought suddenly! He'd seen Bear Country a long time ago. The little cubs could climb trees like monkeys, but the big mean son-of-a-bitches were too fat from eating grubs and fish. They couldn't get their bulk up a tree. Thank God I saw those films, he rejoiced nervously, because something big was scuffling and snorting in the woods just up ahead.

The hairs on Norman's head stood straight up and quivered. His eyes fixed on a tall, spindly pine tree with limbs low enough for him to climb. He dashed off the road and scrambled over the boulders in the ditch. Panting heavily, he made it to the tree before being devoured. Skinning his arms and knees severely in his cartwheeling fright, he shinnyed up the pine very like a spastic monkey. Locking his legs around a crotch thirty feet about the ground, he stopped to catch his breath. His heart was fibrillating wildly, but he was safe. No bear could get him now. He strained his eyes to see the hulking shape of evil incarnate, but the bear was playing possum now that his snack was safe. All Norman could see was the white crushed limestone road surrounded by inky black woods. I'll stay here until morning, he decided, shifting his legs to gain a better perch. What if I go to sleep and fall? No, I *won't* go to sleep and I won't fall! He heard the bear grunting somewhere down below the tree. In the morning, somebody would come along. Maybe the mailman. Right, the mailman always came about noon. He'd flag the mailman and ride back to the monastery with him. Until then—well, he'd just stay awake. Crashing out of this tree would be horrible. His head would probably land right in the bear's toothy mouth to be crunched like a pear.

Sri Rainy was laboring, at the moment. His grasp of the bicycle's gearing mechanism was feeble at best, and in the darkness his old eyes couldn't make out the numbers on the little chrome gear changer. Consequently his legs were straining mightily to push the bike up a fourteen degree grade in 7th gear. The damned bike had worked so well going into town. Cheap, like all these new fangled things. When was the world going to start building quality products again?

But the real question was what to do about this stunning news? Thank God, Lotti had been forthright while there was still time to take action. But what kind of action? Telling Montclief about it would accomplish nothing. What could a yeti do? Nothing. Get himself killed in some foolish stand, that was about it. No, it was up to him, the spiritual leader of this part of the country. He'd always wondered why fate had led him to this particular mountain. It had never seemed accidental, but he'd never understood the purpose, until now. His duty was clear at last. All the deprivation and training had been leading to this one thing—saving the mountain and the little band of yetis from certain death by nuclear poisoning. He and the Retreat were unimportant. He could move. A spiritual center probably wasn't absolutely critical on this particular peak. But damnit, how dare they destroy the crown of the animal kingdom? It was monstrous! And not knowing about the yetis was no excuse! Some things should be known intuitively, even by governments. When are they going to quit destroying everything that's decent and innocent?

But they've bit off a thorny mouthful this time! Tomorrow he would get a letter writing campaign started. Do they think I'm a weak and helpless old man with no resources? Destroy my work of a lifetime by filling a hole with nuclear madness, for no reason. Just because their energy policies are insane? Greedy bastard energy barons and bomb thugs! Pollute all the oceans and tear down the mountains on a whim, just to hide garbage? I think not! Not this one. They'll get a fight like they never dreamed about in a nightmare. Think they got an old namby, did they?

Rainy was pretty worked up, and it was a good thing, too. The adrenalin gave his old legs that extra push he needed to hump the bike in 7th gear. But finally it became ridiculous to continue on the hideously designed bicycle. He was making no progress. Grousing about Ungerer's stupidity for having a machine like this, he disembarked and began pushing the wheel up the hill. He hadn't pushed the contraption far in the quiet night, when he was surprised to hear what sounded like a whimpering cry for help drifting from the forest. He stopped and listened. Bobcats can often sound like a baby crying, but they don't say quavering words like, "Help me."

That's what this voice was saying. "Help me..! I'm up here!"

"Who is that?!" Rainy shouted out. He thought it was probably Tad Foulks, fallen down drunk. Possibly he had injured himself, but who ever heard of a drunk getting hurt? They don't have bones.

"Help..!" the disembodied voice quavered. "There's a bear over here!"

Rainy might be a doddard, but he wasn't crazy. Those two quavering sentences didn't fit together correctly in the dead of night on a wilderness road. Help. There's a bear over here. The only correct response is—See you later! And gone. But... But Rainy was supposed to be a holy man, wasn't he? He was supposed to answer calls for help, even if it meant taming savage beasts.

Suddenly the forest erupted with trashing and crashing. The bear was coming!

Rainy jumped on the bicycle and ordered his legs to pump. But either terror made them impotent or the gear ratio was still too high for the hill. His forward progress wasn't enough to keep the bike upright. It tipped over, dumping him onto the gravel road.

The bear leaped onto the road, screaming a high pitched scream. Rainy lay on the unyielding gravel, holding the spindly bicycle over his head, prepared to slam the thing into the bear's maw in his last ditch battle. He was surprised to see Sister Angie run screaming past him as fast as her fat legs would go. The bear was after her! Rainy heaved the bike at the black brute with all his strength.

"What the fuck..!!" Tad Foulks roared as he crashed into the ditch beneath the ten speed. Doubtless, he would have stormed out of the ditch and beaten Sri Rainy to within an inch of his life had his head not collided with a large pink granite erratic boulder, which had come from somewhere but certainly not this mountain. At any rate, the erratic rock saved Rainy from a sound thrashing.

"Help me..!" the lonesome voice quavered again. What in holy hell was going on here, Rainy wondered. He watched Sister Angie's flouncing fat buttocks disappear up the road.

"Who is that..?!" he called toward the voice in the night. His own voice was quavering somewhat from exertion, not from fear. For all he knew, he was calling to a ghost out there luring him away from his duty. His duty..? My God, if he was killed, there'd be nobody to stop the nuclear holocaust. He turned to go on his way.

"I'm a person from up at the Retreat," the voice quavered. "Please, help me!"

Rainy stopped. "What was that..?!" he shouted

"It's Norman Ungerer, the head chef! Help me! I'm stuck in a tree..!"

What could Sri Rainy do, he couldn't very well leave that fool Ungerer up in a tree, could he? The old man trudged down into the ditch and up the other side, barking his shins on several sharp rocks concealed in the brush. "Keep talking," Rainy ordered. "I'll find you."

"I'm up here, I'm up here," Norman dithered over and over; and at length the monk actually found the correct tree. Good woodsmanship is something they can't take away from you. And there was pitiful Ungerer way up in the dark branches.

"Come down, boy. I'm much too busy for this."

"Is that you, Sri Rainy?" Norman asked, disbelievingly.

"Of course, it's me. Who else would be out in the woods in the dark of night?"

But his sarcasm was lost on Mr. Ungerer. Up there in the pine, Norman's heart opened and he achieved satori. His teacher had evidently levitated through the night to save him from the bear. He was in the presence of a saint. With a lurch from deep in his soul, he felt his whole being suddenly radiating white light. What a feeling. He had finally come home. Without a thought for his safety or knees, he slid down the rough-barked tree. Landing on his feet in front of Sri Rainy, he immediately prostrated himself and kissed the saint's old Birkenstock sandals.

Rainy kicked him away. "Get up, you moron. Do you know anyone with political clout?" He reached down, grabbed a handful of Ungerer's cowl and hauled the clown to his feet. Strangely, he noticed flickering radiance emanating from the freak's adoring eyes and around his forehead. "Stop that," he growled. "This is no time to fool around. We have important work to do. Follow me. It's a long hike back to the Retreat."

In a very sober trance, Norman Ungerer followed his mentor down into the ditch, then onto the road. Brambles parted for him and rocks moved out of his path. Pulled by a wish to turn his head, he glanced back down in the ditch and saw his beloved bicycle. Agile as a roebuck he leaped into the ditch and retrieved the bike. While down there, he took time to touch the closed eyes of a sleeping, but obviously injured man. Under his gentle fingers, the hurt disappeared. Tad Foulks came out of his coma. His eyes opened to a wondrous sight. A dark angel had touched him and was now leaping away carrying a ten speed bike. Tad sat up and rubbed his eyes. What was he doing in this ditch? He was just home from Viet Nam and all that madness was over. It was time to get on with building his life. He had a degree in poly-sci to get from Colorado U, where he was scheduled to go this fall. No time to be sitting in a ditch. What was this on his face, a beard? How odd. He didn't like beards. Never had.

➙ ➘

CHAPTER 11

TAKE STEPS LIKE A CAT WALKING

Higher up the mountain, terror in the night came visiting the little geodesic tent. The brown eyes of Omar Yates popped wide open as his sleeping brain registered danger out in the dark and woke his body up to deal with it. Omar was suddenly so frightened he forgot he was a scientist. Something very big with rattling claws was snuffing around outside the tent. He jostled his partner.

"I'm awake," Chuck Barkley hissed. He was very glad he hadn't let Yates laugh him out of lugging his .45 automatic along on the trip. It was in his hand now, gripped fiercely, as he struggled to free himself from the mummy type sleeping bag. His only wish was that he'd lugged his rifle along too, and maybe a howitzer.

Whatever was out there was huge and was practically breathing on the tent. Had to be a bear.

Barkley was an excellent outdoorsman. He knew that bears were usually only after food. He'd thought about caching the breakfast bacon and eggs outside, of course; but they were five hundred feet above the treeline and it seemed silly to trot down there with the bacon. And rock caches weren't worth fluff when it came to stopping a bear. If a man could move the rocks for a cache, a bear could tear it down effortlessly.

But far worse, Chuck Barkley had no real faith that the .45 would stop a bear. His .300 Weatherby, made especially for big game was back at the Lodge. What a bright place to leave it. However, deer season hadn't started yet, and Yates thought it would look suspicious to be toting a rifle around.

His mind spun on this one subject—if the bear ripped through the tent, where would he shoot it? Even a black bear's skull is hard as steel, hard enough to flatten a normal lead bullet. Grizzlies were impossible, and judging from the deep growls this was a griz. Sure, the .45 had lots of impact, but would the lead bullet penetrate the skull? Barkley doubted it. A heart shot was the only sensible way to deal with a bear. Maybe the .45 would stop him long enough for them to make a dash to the trees. Why hadn't he slept with his boots on? Only a fool would take his boots off in wild country like this. He fumbled left-handed in the dark for his boots, but where were they? Damnit!

"Maybe we can scare it by banging some pans together," Yatsey whimpered.

"Try it," Barkley whispered back. He had located his boots up by the pillow end of the air mattress, but how they got there was a mystery. He remembered putting them to the side of the mattress so they'd be handy in the morning. No matter, he shoved his feet into the cold boots awkwardly, only using one hand. His right hand was clenched around the pistol and wouldn't let go, even to lace up the boots.

"We left the cooking gear out there," Omar

whimpered, hysterically. "What else is there?"

The behemoth had apparently found the pans, and was banging them around outside, trying to scare himself off. Instead of scaring him, however, the empty pots and pans enraged the beast. He bellowed in anger and swatted one of the pans against a rock. Terrifying sounds in the night, when your only protection is nylon tent material. They couldn't even run out the back because the pop-up tent was sewn all along the bottom. The only exit was in front, virtually under the snarling bear's claws and teeth. Thinking fast, Yatesy's mind landed on his hunting knife. He could easily rip a hole in the back of the tent, crawl through and run like hell. But what good would that do? Big bears are incredibly fast. The thing would pounce on him after a few yards.

"Throw the bacon out," Barkley hissed.

"Where is it?"

"Find it! Throw the whole backpack out. Maybe he smells something he wants."

Locating his pack, Omar crawled to the tent flap and unzipped it. Anyplace, he prayed. Let me be anyplace in the world but here! He pulled the flap open and peeped out—right into the jaws of death. He heaved the pack a few feet outside and fell back on his air mattress, quaking—actually *quaking* with fear. He'd heard of this phenomenon, and now it was happening to him. How interesting. One side of his scientific mind took time to observe the shaking. My body is quivering, he observed, and it won't stop. "Shoot him, Charles," he blurbled through chattering teeth. "He'll kill us!"

"Calm down," Barkley said. "He'll go away. They almost never knock down a tent."

"Shoot him! I'm begging you! Give me the gun and I'll do it." He reached for the gun.

Barkley batted his hand away. "Get hold of yourself! We're not his natural food. If we don't anger him, he'll go away."

"Shoot him! Shoot through the tent. Shoot!! He's right there!"

Omar's panic infected Barkley, as did the rampaging

bear sounds outside. Against everything he'd ever learned about survival in the woods, he fired three rapid shots through the rip-stop nylon. Both men heard them hit. The sound was like a giant hand slapping against a pine plank. Their ears were badly stunned by the .45 report, but not so stunned that they couldn't hear all hell breaking loose outside. The bear screamed like a jet engine. In his agony, he turned and flattened the tent with one swipe, then pounced on it. The wrath of an angry grizzly descended on Omar and Chuck.

Two hundred yards above the campsite, at the top edge of a worm-eaten snowfield, Yolanda flinched when she heard the gun shots and ducked behind a granite outcropping. Both she and Montclief watched the berserk grizzly flipping air mattresses and bodies through the air. Something very strange was going on here. The spirit of the mountain had sent Sigmoid the Great to destroy the invaders. Why Sigmoid? Why not one of the crazies, the tourist bears, who ate rotting fish and garbage by choice.

Howling with grief and rage, the giant red bear took the campsite apart; then dripping a trail of blood he staggered straight up the mountain, the hardest route imaginable—straight toward the two yetis. Lumbering across the middle of the rotting snowfield, leaving a wet red ribbon, he turned his head to stare a mute, incomprehensible stare at Montclief, then limped on up the ravine and disappeared over a ridge.

Montclief looked above his head at the starry sky; but the stars merely twinkled. They gave back no messages or portents. The snowfield where they stood never completely melted. It faced north, and the sun allowed it to live on year after year, melting only partially to feed the spring that was the source of Fawn Brook. Montclief had taken it as an omen that his enemy had deliberately set up camp under the tons of old snow and ice. It seemed clear that he was meant to destroy the menace. But evidently this snowfield had a powerful will to live, or an ally who sent Sigmoid instead.

"I must call a meeting of the Council," he said softly to Yolanda. "These events are beyond my understanding. I think I will invite the old one to attend. I think I have to."

Yoli nodded. She was very frightened, but didn't know why. The mountain was simply protecting itself. It had sent Sigmoid, the dominant bear of the range, to annihilate the invaders. Everything was as it should be. So why was she so cold suddenly, and so afraid?

*

Dawn was cold and carried the threat of rain again. Sri Rainy did his sitting meditation. His mind bubbled with the various pressing horrors that yesterday had presented; but he sat there, trying to let his mind sink to the place of no thought, and at length the cruising thoughts gave up and allowed him to join the cosmic void. It was so peaceful to float on the currents of nothingness that he decided to remain in meditation all day, but a bird landed on his window ledge and made such a racket with its blissful tweeting, that he came back to the world. The image of Montclief flashed through his reactivated mind. He had to make contact with the yeti.

Unwinding his legs from the lotus position, he did a few desultory calisthenics, then went into the main hall to lead the group meditation. Sister Angie was already seated on the right side of the hall. Her eyes were clamped shut in pretended ecstasy. Be generous, he cautioned himself. Maybe she really was trying to meditate instead of faking it. He assumed that faking took up most of her sitting time, since she made such slight progress at losing her self-importance. Being inside her brain must be a real schizophrenic treat. Be generous. If a person sits long enough, something good has to happen if only by osmosis, even to Sister Angie.

Taking his place on the raised cushion in front, he closed his eyes once again and led the group through a quieting the mind exercise; but stray thoughts of how to proceed with saving the mountain kept intruding, keeping him from joining the Void. So after faking it himself for twenty minutes, he ended the meditation and walked stiffly into the kitchen, where he purloined a napkin full of hot biscuits and left for Fawn Brook.

A few paces down the path he was shocked to see Mr. Ungerer sitting in a clump of dewy weeds in the full lotus position, still radiating a weak white light. Wondering what that was all about, he stepped quietly past the youth, deciding to let Ungerer broach the transcendental question when the time was ripe. Trundling on to the fishing pole tree, he found that Montclief's pole was already gone. That was odd. He couldn't remember one time when he hadn't toted both poles.

His legs and shoulders ached from his midnight bike-a-thon. Too bad about the poorly designed bike being damaged. He should apologize to Ungerer about that; but damnit, he'd been protecting himself from a bear. Very peculiar that drunken Foulks had looked like a bear twice in one night. Then the boy had been so spacey after he slid out of the tree. It seemed beside the point to mention how sorry he was about bending the bike frame and breaking out half the spokes against Tad Foulks' head. For the first time since Sri Rainy had known him, the boy hadn't wanted to ask dumb questions about everything under the sun. They'd walked in silence all the way up the gravel road to the Retreat, Ungerer pushing the injured wheel and looking all around with eyes wide in wonderment. Sri Rainy hadn't known what to make of it. Could a nitwit like that jump straight from nitwithood into enlightenment? Maybe so. Rainy himself fixed hot cocoa and cinnamon toast for them both in the Retreat kitchen. Sister Angie wasn't around for once, or he might have invited her, too. What a peculiar night, and now Montclief's fishing pole was missing.

He had never tried to find the yeti, before. Montclief

always found him; but it would test his woodsmanship. He'd probably need to be sharp is he was going to track Yatesy and the other one, Barnsley, all over the mountain, tape recording their nuclear conversations. Oh, yes, he was planning to do that very thing. Hard proof is what Senate Committees want—a smoking gun. Right after he finished with Montclief, he planned to go to Hinton's Hardware and pick up a tape recorder.

Stripping a few frosty crickets from trailside weeds, he eventually stopped at a pool where he thought the yeti might be waiting. An animal as big as Montclief couldn't escape his view if he was really looking for him. But the yeti wasn't here. Too bad, because trout rises were dimpling the pool even this early. He thought about stopping, but he wasn't there to catch fish. He had to find Montclief.

Skirting a jumble of boulders, he was mildly irritated when a tiny stone bounced off his bald noggin. He turned to find the yeti hunkering beside the pool he had just passed, grinning at him—if you could call that a grin.

"Let's fish here," Montclief said. He began unwrapping the line from around the tip of his cane pole.

Rainy scowled and sat on the bank. "Must have walked past you," he conceded grudgingly. He unwrapped his own line and threaded a grasshopper onto the hook.

Carefully unhooking the old green bobber from his line with his gorilla-like fingers, Montclief passed the antique over to Rainy. "Maybe this will change my luck," he said, clipping a tiny red and white plastic bobber to the line. He hooked a grasshopper and dropped it above a likely looking submerged rock.

"New technology," Rainy mused, dropping his own grasshopper nonchalantly beside a surface dimple. "Not as responsive as cork," he commented.

"We'll see," the yeti responded. He was extremely pleased to have put one over on the old fellow, and even more pleased with the color of his new bobber. Red. Like Rainy's. He would hold his own from now on. Whoever heard of a man being able to outfish a yeti? When he was a young whelp under the tutelage of his father, he had spent countless hours submerged in the freezing mountain streams and lakes studying the habits of trout. He knew exactly how and where the big trout lay in wait for the choice nymphs that washed downstream, and how they bullied the smaller trout to maintain the pecking order. With the new bobber, his superior knowledge would assert itself.

They fished in silent concentration in the chilly dawn, both trying to formulate words for the secret they had to tell. The trout seemed uninterested in grasshoppers. Finally, Rainy worked his lips, in the manner that meant he was about to make a pronouncement.

"You were right to be worried about those two men," he said. He lifted his line from the water and dropped the drowned grasshopper higher in the pool, without bothering to put on a fresh one.

"I'm not worried about them now," the yeti answered.

"You should be. Your dream was absolutely right. They want to bring a tragedy to the mountain. Do you know what nuclear waste is?"

Montclief snorted. Rainy thought he heard a note of derision in the snort.

"Those fishermen are dead," said the yeti. His eyes never left the plastic bobber. It was so tiny that the slightest bite would pull it under, but it would create no drag to spook the fish. Montclief had been very interested in the fishing supplies scattered around the obliterated campsite. He'd been surprised to discover the tiny bobber tucked in the corner of a dry fly wallet. Why would a fly man carry a bobber? Could it be that he surreptitiously added a little worm when the fishing was slow.

"Dead? Are you sure?"

"Oh, yes. Yoli and I went in the night to create an avalanche, but before we could do our task, my very old friend, Sigmoid, destroyed them and their camp. He is a fine bear, very old and even tempered; but they foolishly angered him by shooting. Sigmoid is the most honorable of bears. In the end, he defecated on their strips of pig meat without eating any. He went off to heal his wounds or to die. I will look for him to see if I can help. His gesture was purity itself, for one who loves pig meat as much as he does."

"This is terrible!" Rainy said, trembling. "Take me to see them. Maybe they're not dead."

"Of course, Old One. I will take you. But it would be better to let the scavenger spirits have them. In that way the mountain would be placated."

"I don't think you understand," Rainy explained, agitatedly. He stood and twisted the bamboo pole, wrapping the line around the tip. "This will only draw attention to the mountain. An investigation is bound to happen. They'll probably send a team of hunters to kill the bear, and maybe they'll discover you!"

"I see," Montclief replied. "But they won't find me. We covered our tracks quite well."

Rainy's old feet were devastated by the time he limped into the campsite under the snowfield. Birkenstock's may be fine for most things, but trailless mountain hiking is beyond their limits. His toes were bloody from stubbing against rocks and brambles, but when he saw the twisted remains of Drs. Yates and Barkley, he forgot about his feet.

"This is awful," he muttered.

"Yes. Sigmoid was angry," Montclief agreed, without much sympathy. "I will stay here in the rocks, so I don't have to cover my tracks again. Let me know when you're ready to go."

Rainy considered being sick as he toddled over to a mutilated body, but steeled himself and kept going. He had no idea which of the two he was looking at. The hair was blonde and covered with dried blood, the skin was grey. The geologist obviously was dead. Rainy reached into the corpse's hip pocket. Recovering a wallet, he looked at the driver's license. "Foolish to keep a wallet in your hip pocket, Dr. Barkley," he mused, inanely. "Horrible for your back to sit on a bulge like this." He dropped the wallet into the deep pocket of his robe, then inspected the other victim.

"Glory to God!" he yelped excitedly, seeing that this doctor, while horribly twisted and unconscious, was still alive. At least his skin was still pink. "This one's alive!" he yelled to the yeti. "What do we do now?"

*

Lotti was up early this morning. Not worrying about the damp chill in the air, she was hiking her buns over to the post office wearing an off the shoulder marimba blouse, white short shorts and purple platform wedgies. She ran into Tad Foulks sitting on a stump outside Kim Wong's Spot Right Liquor. He was drinking a quart of chocolate milk and eating an x-ray hot dog.

"Hi, Tad," she sang out to her former lover. She thought it was a good idea to be nice to her ex-beaus; heck, Tad could turn into a big man in the boom town. You never know who's going to be somebody. Even Tad.

"You know me?" he asked, looking her up and down.

"Everybody knows you, Tad," she said brightly, supposing his brain cells had done a flip-flop from too much cheap Tokay last night. "It's nice to see you're switching to chocolate milk."

He looked at the milk carton, wondering what she was talking about. "Where's the bus station around here, girlie? I need to be on the next bus to Denver."

"Are you nuts? The bus don't run up here. Snap into it."

"Then how does somebody get to Denver from here? I have to sign up for school."

Lotti did a double take. Of all the surprising things

she'd ever heard, this topped the cake. She put her hands on her swivel hips and stared at him. "You're going to school?" she asked, dubiously.

"Colorado State," he said proudly. "If I can get to Denver."

"College..?" she squeaked.

"Of course, college. I have to sign up early, so the GI Bill checks can get started. Guess I'll have to hitch a ride."

She looked at him incredulously. "Well, if you can get to Clinton, the bus leaves from there. You don't act like you remember who you are. What were you drinking? What's my name?"

Tad looked suspiciously at the cheeky young woman. In Nam, women had been sexy too, dressed in black pajamas or those negligee dresses all the time, but not like this! God, it was great to be back home. "Well," he allowed, "I know who I am just fine, but I'm a little hazy on how I got way up here. I must have pitched a heck of a drunk with my separation pay." The truth was he only had a couple of dollars in his pants pocket. He'd managed to save over two grand in the Nam. Maybe somebody had rolled him while he was passed out in that ditch.

Lotti laughed, delightedly. "You can say that again. A good long drunk. Nobody around here knows what you're like sober."

"You mean, I've been here for awhile?"

"Awhile? Ever since I was a little, little girl. Don't you remember playing hide and seek with us kids in the woods?"

"No," he said, trying to digest what this young woman was telling him. "How old are you?"

"Sixteen and a half. You know that very well, Tad. Don't you recall what we did to celebrate my birthday?"

"No. What did we do?"

"If you don't know, I'm certainly not telling," she said, coyly. "But part of it was putting up my clothesline."

"Are you saying I've been here in this burg for

sixteen years? That's unbelievable."

"Well, yeah. I guess it is, sort of."

"Where do I live? I don't remember. Do I have a job or what?"

"You're the town drunk, Tad," she smiled. "Everybody knows you. Ask anybody."

Old Tad buried his face in his large hands, which were cleaner than Lotti ever recalled. "This is terrible," he lamented. "I have to get down to Denver." He looked up at her suddenly, with a piercing look. "What year is it?" he asked.

*

After he'd done what he could to make Dr. Yates comfortable, and had donned the good Doctor's superb hunting boots, Sri Rainy limped out of the campsite. The left boot bore a slashing claw mark halfway through the fake leather toe cap. After he'd found it, Rainy had searched around for its mate and finally discovered the right boot untouched, twisted in the tenting material. He was glad that the dead man, Barkley, was wearing boots, so at least these weren't dead man's boots. Not that he was superstitious. The boots were a vast improvement over his sandals, in spite of being a size too large. The plan was for him to hike down to the nearest telephone and call Air Rescue, while Montclief remained at the camp to keep foxes and buzzards away, and to nurse the broken Dr. Yates should he regain consciousness. At the sound of an approaching helicopter, he would disappear. The two conspirators agreed to meet the next morning at Fawn Brook to compare notes.

During the hike up the mountain, Rainy had broadened the yeti's horizon with his not very extensive knowledge of the effects of nuclear waste. It had sounded like a horror story to Montclief. No wonder the mountain had rebelled and had sent Sigmoid to take care of business. Montclief now crouched on a flat-topped boulder, moving occasionally to keep the wheeling vultures at bay. At least with the air full of spirit scavengers, the noisy helicopter would find the campsite easily. And yes, it was fortunate that the one fisherman was alive, he conceded. He must have a ferocious spirit to have survived Sigmoid. Like Rainy said, an alive fisherman could testify that he had shot the bear, assuming he lived long enough, and perhaps there wouldn't be a rogue hunt trampling all over the mountain. But how easy it would be to step over to the unconscious man and end it all for him. If such a mutilation ever happened to him, Montclief hoped that another yeti or a cougar would find him and end it quickly. Why would anyone, even a white skin, want to survive in that condition? Montclief wondered casually if shaving off all his facial hair would allow him to pass for a skin? He studied the bloody face there below him. Actually, he'd only have to shave around his eyes and his nose. And his hands. Boots would cover his feet. Nah, it wasn't worth it. And besides, he'd probably look very strange to a real skin.

Halfway down the mountain, Sri Rainy realized he was in a fix. His feet were unused to boots, particularly ones that were a size too big. While they protected his toes from further rock bumping, a blister was rubbing at the back of each heel. And to make matters even more unbearable, his tender toes slipped forward with every step to bung against whatever this new material was they made boots from now. It wasn't leather. He felt like grunting in pain with every step, but refrained, only grunting every third or fourth step. On flat ground the boots would have been fine, except for the heels which he imagined would still blister; but there were precious few flat areas coming down the mountain. So his toes kept sliding down into fake-leather agony.

Stopping at the monastery would do him no good.

He'd always felt that having a telephone would defeat the purpose of an isolated retreat. So he'd have to go to Spot Right Liquor. That was the nearest phone. At least, when he got to the road, he could put his sandals back on. Maybe he should put them on now, and just be careful of the rocks. Good plan, he decided, sitting right down on a tree stump. Blessed relief. Thank God, he'd brought the sandals with him. He'd almost left them in the camp so he could travel lighter.

The first thing he did after standing up again with the boots draped over his shoulder, was to bump his exposed big toe against a sharp spine of granite hidden in a clump of high grass. His yowl of pain reverberated across the woodlands like a bull moose with love sickness. God, it hurt! Rainy stood there with his head raised and every corpuscle in his toe vibrating pain; then he hurried on down the mountain making a special effort to concentrate on where his martyred feet would land.

Mrs. Kim Wong was behind the candy counter of the liquor store when Rainy limped in. Several months ago, she had forcefully demanded to be let out of the slavery of the dry cleaning side. She had just become an American citizen, while Kim himself had not—hence she saw herself as an emancipated woman, at least from dry cleaning solvent and killing heat. Rather than face the ignominy of threatened divorce, Kim gave in. So these days, Mrs. Kim Wong was normally in charge of the liquor and candy counter. Her frugality made Mary McCardle seem almost open-handed.

Rainy realized had a slight problem. He'd been thinking about it for the last half mile before entering the store. The phone outside required money to operate and he, the holy man, disdained to carry crude coinage. Hence the problem.

"Hello, there, Mrs. Wong," Rainy said charmingly,

limping over to her. "How's your garden growing?" The Wongs had a highly touted vegetable garden out back.

"Velly good, velly good," the matriarch replied, bowing and smiling to him. In some Chinese dialects, submissive bowing is translated as: Go fuck yourself, white slime. Sadly, Asians can be racist, too. They just aren't overt about it. "How yourl rovery big garlden?" she asked, obsequiously. The garden which you plant so you don't have to buy anything from us, you tight wallet, the matriarch added to herself.

"Fine," he answered. Establishing rapport by chatting garden talk was a good idea. "Almost harvest time for the potatoes and other tubers."

"Yes," she agreed. "Armost." Mrs. Wong played a guessing game to amuse herself. She always tried to guess what the customer would buy. What did this old skinflint want? A nickels worth of nails like last time? Rather than miss a sale, she had opened a pound cardboard box of nails, which she now wouldn't be able to sell, unless the monk, or another penny pinching devil, wanted some more sometime. "Moll nails?" she asked, hopefully.

"Not today, thanks. I was wondering if I could borrow some money to make a phone call. There's been an emergency up the mountain."

"Some money..?"

"A dime. I forgot to bring money, and it's very important."

"How much interlest you pay?"

"What..?"

"How much interlest you pay foll dime, holy glandfathel..?"

"Look, Mrs. Wong, I know you love to dicker, but this is an emergency. A fisherman was attacked by a bear! I have to call the rescue helicopter."

Her eyes went wide and round. "Yes, you carll! How big bearl?"

"Very big. But you have to lend me a dime. I came straight here from the fisherman without stopping for money."

"I do it," she said, nodding. "How much interlest?"

Foreigners, Sri Rainy grimaced. They all think they're going to get rich, then go home. Instead of stomping out of the store, he smiled patiently, realizing that only pragmatism would work in this situation. After all, it was an emergency. That mauled man needed a doctor. "I'll give you a nickel extra, if you loan me a dime for the call."

Mrs. Kim Wong smiled placidly. "Fifty perlcent perl week," she said with a sigh.

"Fine." He held out his hand. Tomorrow he'd bring fifteen cents when he came to the library. But would he be coming to the library after that embarrassing confrontation with Esther?

Pressing the No Sale key on the cash register, Mrs. Kim Wong pressed a dime into his hand. "Hully," she said.

Sri Rainy glanced down at her like she was crazy, then he realized she meant hurry, so he limped outside to the pay phone. After trying to get a dial tone for several minutes, he dimly remembered hearing that Ma Bell had raised the toll on phone booths. He stuck his head in the door of the liquor store. "How much is a phone call?" he asked.

"Twenty," Mrs. Kim Wong answered, angelically.

"Outrageous," he muttered. "Would you please lend me another dime. Please," he added again, for good measure.

"How much interlest?" she asked, as if bent on a whole new round of negotiations.

"The same as before," he snapped. "Please, hurry. The man is dying!"

"No, moll..!" she squeaked, raising her voice to a high keen.

"What do you mean, no more? The man is dying!!"

"Need moll interlest. You no good lisk! No pay back firlst roan."

Rainy clamped a lid on his blood pressure. "Fine," he said. "I'll give you a dime extra."

"Dime foll this dime, nickre for firlst dime?"

"Yes, I'll pay you tomorrow."

She rang the register again and passed him another dime, smiling as if from a deep wisdom. "Hully, prease. Man die!"

Rainy retraced his bloody steps to the pay phone and made the call to the Fire Rescue helicopter. After giving them directions, he limped down Main Street. He had to find a ride over to Clinton, so he could be at the hospital when Dr. Yates arrived. The hospital would have a real telephone. Now there was a coincidence.

➼ ➼

CHAPTER 12

FUNNY BUT NOT AMUSING

It's funny now things work out, Sri Rainy mused from the back seat of the jeep bound joltingly for Clinton. His lovely Lotti, dressed like a vamp, rode up front chatting like a magpie at Willard Jacks, the mailman, who had consented in view of the emergency to drive Rainy to the hospital. Willard had also lent him twenty bucks out of petty cash from the post office. Beside Rainy in the bouncy rumble seat sat Tad Foulks, with his beard shaved clean and his face and hands scrubbed to a healthy redness. Tad, evidently, had no remembrance of being throttled with a ten speed bike, but he told a strange story about seeing a dark angel last night. An angel which had seemingly changed his life. Tad kept asking Rainy, who he took to be an authority on angels, if entities like that could interact with men. Lotti had insisted that Tad tell the strange tale to Rainy. About all the old man could do in response was nod his head sagely. He was certainly not going to admit his part in the episode, nor would he lie about it either.

Willard, on the other hand, thought the whole story, including Lotti's excited utterances about a nuclear repository on the mountain, had the ring of a sci-fi story. He kept thinking that he'd like to send this crazy scenario to Lute Sims. What a book these crazy characters would make with the Sims touch on them. Willard wondered how the author might present him, the peripheral mailman character. Or would he be a main character? He'd never thought of himself as a central character before, but it was hard to predict how Lute might see the boiling little community with its influx of Hustler Magazines and seed catalogues. Maybe a writer would think the mailman was on the glowing point of a poker, stirring up the fireplace. The lightning rod delivering provocative mail. One never knew how a Lute Sims book was going to permute through its twistings and hairpin turnings. The only problem was that Willard had only a dim idea of how to contact his hero. Write a letter to the publisher? But didn't letters like that just get shit canned? Sure, they did. Lute Sims probably got a thousand such letters per day. Even if he marked it Personal. Even if he sent it Registered, the guy at the publishing company would sign for it, then shit can it.

"I think I'll open a little boutique," Lotti rattled on to Willard. "Don't you think that's a smart idea? I mean, with all the paychecks, people will be needing to buy pretty things for their girlfriends."

Willard grunted, noncommittally. He wasn't convinced that an influx of rowdy construction workers and nuclear waste was a healthy direction for Pike's Grove. It would certainly change things. Being an American, he realized there'd be a raise for the postmaster in a boom town; and, after all, the lethal stuff had to be stored somewhere. And what could he do about it if the Government decided to put the dump up here? Nothing. He did suspect that Lotti's euphoria was slightly misplaced. She was just a kid. On the other hand, he'd better put a down-payment on Berlinheimer's sheep lot to cover his bases. The old man's price would go up when he caught wind of this. Then maybe he could leverage a few acres somewhere else. There was no use being a chump about this boom. If it was coming, it was coming.

In both Omar Yates' and Charles Barkley's wallets was a little yellow card from the Department of Interior, with a name to call in case of emergency. The paramedic in the Fire Rescue helicopter, Long John Hicks, had found Yates' card. On the flight to Clinton, with one corpse and one badly maimed probable vegetable, he had plenty of time to go through both wallets after he sedated Dr. Yates. The sedative was for the off chance that Yates would come out of his coma and start to flail around in the chopper.

The name on the yellow card was Cyrus Jordan, but there was no real person bearing that name. It was a "code name" that lit up red flashing lights all over Washington, D.C. when a trainee admissions nurse at St. Luke's Hospital called the number on the card and asked for Mr. Jordan.

The call in fact had not gone to the Department of Interior, but straight to the Nuclear Regulatory Commission switchboard, where it was routed to the office of Melton Pinkle, director of Land Acquisition. Pinkle, himself, had the yellow cards printed up with Jordan's name on them for distribution to the dozen or so geologists out in the field. That had been six months ago. In the meantime, he had forgotten all about Cyrus Jordan, but he answered the red flashing line. "Pinkle, Acquisitions," he said.

Wilma Dexter, the trainee nurse, asked for Cyrus Jordan.

"Cyrus Jordan..?" Pinkle answered, knowing he'd

heard the name, but not instantly placing it. "Are you sure you have the correct number? This is Acquisitions."

"This is St. Luke's Memorial Hospital in Clinton, Colorado," Wilma said. "We found this number on an emergency card in one of our patient's wallet. It seems official. Is this the Department of Interior in Washington D.C.?" This business, although kind of grisly because of the bear, was pretty thrilling to Wilma. It was her first call to Washington at hospital expense. The call, of course, would be charged to the bear-clawed patient's room, but it made her feel important, like she was part of the government. Although she had voted last election, she'd never exactly felt like a working cog of the government before. She was nineteen, one of the few black people in Clinton.

"Department of Interior..?" Pinkle asked. Then his brain clicked in with the information about this special line, the phone that had never rung before. "Aah, you want Mr. Jordan! I'm so sorry, I thought you said Borden. Ha, ha. Just a minute, Miss. Let me get Mr. Jordan." He removed a handkerchief from his hip pocket and placed it over the mouthpiece, then waited an appropriate length of time before assuming the southern drawl of an imaginary Cyrus Jordan.

During the pause, the mechanical and human ears of information gathering services all over the Chesapeake Bay area waited breathlessly to find out what the hell the NRC was up to. When Pinkle had authorized the auxiliary line, he, of course, did not tell anybody it was a secret line. No one in government would think of waving a red flag by doing that. Nevertheless, phone company employees are not overpaid. Information gathering agencies know this fact, and consider it their patriotic duty to subvert a phone man or two. Consequently, covert taps to the Cyrus Jordan line had been installed on the phone net at FBI Headquarters; over at the Pentagon the Central Intelligence Division had a tap; ditto Langly Field, Virginia which housed the CIA; and straight into the White House basement where the National Security Advisory boys had an ear out. Over on the north shore a

KGB safe house had a tap, even though the KGB was now officially disbanded. The Israeli Secret Service had a line. James Bond's old outfit, the MI-5 had one and so did French Security—and about fifty foreign embassies around town. About the only place that didn't have a tap was the Department of Interior.

"Hello, this is Cyrus Jordan," Pinkle said into the muffled phone, in dulcet southern tones. He knew the handkerchief didn't change his voice much, but what the hell.

Nurse Dexter relayed her story about Dr. Omar Yates being mauled by a bear and being in grave condition. She didn't mention anything about Barkley since she knew nothing. He'd been taken directly to the morgue.

No one listening in on the conversation believed the bear mauling bit, naturally. Calls about bear maulings did not come over secret security lines to the NRC. It was a code of some sort, but what did it mean? And where was Clinton, Colorado? Maybe it was the site of a new missile base that wasn't on their maps? Strange. Pinkle's department wasn't a well known one, nor was Pinkle himself, except to the Japanese and Iranians who were listening. They often had to outbid him at land auctions.

Melton Pinkle didn't put much faith in the bear story either, but why else would a hospital call the emergency number? He had met Dr. Yates once or twice, and he had seemed like a level-headed fellow, except for having that strange Arabian name. Omar. Well, he'd have to do something about it, he supposed. After the nurse rang off, he called his craftiest land negotiator, Dewitt Gefflerhagen, and asked him to fly out to Colorado to look into the matter. This call was also monitored by most of the listening posts around town.

*

Meanwhile, Sri Rainy was also on the telephone. He had conned a nun into letting him make a phone call on the hospital chapel phone. As he punched in the numbers for Los Angeles directory assistance, he felt a smidge guilty at using diocese funds; but this was an important matter. If one of their monasteries was being threatened, they would spare no expense, so why should he? The work had to go on, and there was no sense in using the money he'd borrowed from Willard if he didn't have to. The Pope would understand.

"Operator..? Could you give me the number of William Drummond in Los Angeles, please." While a computer searched for the number, he tried to recall if he and Billy Bad Boy Drummond had parted on amiable terms. He thought so, but Billy had stopped sending money years ago. Ex-students were really such a pain. No matter how ardent they were at the beginning, by the time they left they had manufactured some very good reason for leaving the quest. Usually it was a kind of disdain for the teacher and the teaching. Well, familiarity breeds contempt. He was glad that puny contempt soothed their consciences, because he usually felt throbbing contempt for them from day one. Gad, what a thing to admit. Of course, he didn't, really. They were like little flowers waiting to unfold. Especially Billy Bad Boy Drummond, from whom he now needed a favor.

The telephone computer voice came into his ear with a number. Rainy scratched it down on the margin of a prayer book which was lying on the small telephone table. Since there was no writing pad, he presumed the prayerbook was meant to be used for this purpose, and indeed there were several other numbers on the page he turned to. He eased himself down tiredly onto an uncomfortable straight chair and dialed the number.

"Billy Drummond's exchange," a dewy-voiced operator answered at the other end.

Shit, Rainy thought. An answering service. He'd have to do some fast talking to get Billy's home number from her. "Yes," he said. "I'm sure you don't know me, but I'm Sri Rainy, head of the Seekers of Light Order in Colorado. Billy is an old friend of mine and I'd like very much to talk to him."

There was a momentary silence as if the operator

was distracted, then she said, "If you can leave a number, sir, I'll tell him you called."

"It's very important that I talk to him, if that's at all possible. I'm not at a place where I can be reached easily."

"I could page him, sir."

"Would you do that, please. Thank you so much for your trouble."

"It's no trouble, sir." The line went blank, and Rainy waited.

Billy Drummond had showed up at the Retreat with his rock and roll band in the late 60s, riding high on success and searching for the meaning of life. He had acted like Sri Rainy should be flattered to have him for a student. Perhaps Rainy was, a little, because Billy was very free with his money, even to the extent of financing a new dormitory. But a star of that magnitude didn't really believe he should dirty his hands by doing actual physical construction himself. He was busy with sitting under a tree beside Fawn Brook, waiting for inspiration in the form of a new song about sexual freedom.

Of course, Mammon had to be paid, the band was busy. They'd be gone for months on tour, then stop in for a week expecting special treatment—and getting it from everybody except Rainy. To him, they were just students like everybody else. No, that wasn't quite true. Admit it. The band members were treated like normal students; but Billy *was* special, he glowed with specialness, and a lot of slack was cut for him. To Billy's own detriment.

It was easy to see that Billy was good for business. Sri Rainy became a minor celebrity because Billy was at the Retreat. As a result, the rock and roller was never really pushed or tested fully, and when Billy finally drifted away, Rainy had only himself to thank. Admit the truth, old man. Billy had possibilities and you didn't bring out his best. He was too famous, Rainy growled back at himself. Yes, but he had possibilities and you lost him.

"Hello..?" the sleepy voice of Billy Bad Boy Drummond came into Rainy's ear.

"Hello, Billy. This is Sri Rainy out at the Retreat."

"Hey, Sri..!" Billy responded, warmly. "How you doing, man? You got a phone out there now?" In point of fact, Billy was shocked to hear from Sri Rainy. He'd just been thinking about him the night before, kind of wondering if the old buzzard would let him pay a visit to get his life back on track again. Most of his best tunes had been written up there on the mountain, and he could use a couple of hits right about now. Actually, he needed them badly.

He'd just come from a six weeks stay at Betty Ford's Clinic to help him kick a severe cocaine addiction problem, and his life was in shambles. He hadn't recorded in over two years. His record company was about to sue him, and unless he could get with it, his fans would think he died. And the come-back album needed to be damned good, or why bother. Easy to talk about writing good songs, but he was dried up inside. It was imperative to get back on the good road, that was the only way to make going straight work. Thoughts like that had led him into reveries about Sri Rainy, wondering if it was too late for him to start over.

"No," Sri Rainy chuckled. "We don't have a phone yet."

"I guess you're calling from the liquor store, right?"

"No, Billy, actually from the hospital over in Clinton. I'm glad I was able to get through to you. I need your help rather badly. Do you think you could come up here for a few days?"

Bad Boy's blood ran cold. In the hospital? That was impossible. The old coot wasn't supposed to get sick—ever. That wasn't part of it! What if he was dying? Unfair, unfair!

"Of course, I can come up," he blurted. "Are you all right?"

"I'm fine. Oh, no, I'm not *in* the hospital, I'm visiting someone."

"Phew, that's a relief."

"Yes, I guess it is," Rainy answered, surprised that Billy should seem so concerned. "Well, then can you come up?"

"Anytime, Sri. Anytime! When should I come?"

"How about tomorrow, or as soon as you can."

"Sure, I guess so. Something heavy coming down, huh?"

"Very heavy, Billy. And one more thing, could you ring up any of the old people that you're in touch with. You know, the ones who might still care, and tell them to either come up or drop me a line."

"I've kind of lost contact with almost everybody," Billy apologized.

"Well, do what you can, Billy. And I'll see you soon?"

"I'll make reservations right now, Sri. First flight out. I'm so glad you called. I've been thinking about you a lot."

"Yes. Well, then, I'll see you. Good-bye, Billy." Rainy hung up, not wishing to run up the diocese's phone bill with chit-chat. Who else could he call? It was dumb that he hadn't kept better tabs on his former students. Maybe one of them was a senator or something. That would really help. And he should touch base with Carlo Sentori or whoever was running the International. It was pitiful how he'd let all his ties to the world fall away. Did he think being a hermit was smart? No, he did not, and he was going to repair those bridges in the days to come.

After dropping Tad Foulks off at the Greyhound station, Lotti was a little petulant when Willard insisted he had to get back to Pike's Grove. She had intended to spend the day shopping and having lunch in Clinton.

"Well, what about Mortimer Snerd?" she asked, with a pert bob of her heavy tresses, a bob that was guaranteed to start the heart of a concrete statue.

"What about him?" Willard responded, defensively. "I'm not the community service department. I've got mail to deliver."

"You're cute when you get like that," the girl said, looking deep into his hazel eyes. In view of this exciting nuclear news, Willy Jacks suddenly wasn't her only ticket to stardom. She could easily get one of the miners to take her to California. Construction workers were notorious for moving around. Still, the nuclear storage facility wasn't a sure bet yet. She had learned that much from her mother. When somebody pays the rent, they get the room. She had better keep Willy on the line, just in case. "Well, couldn't we at least stop back at the hospital to see if Mortimer is ready to come home? How would you like to be stranded way over here?"

"I guess so," Willard said, turning the jeep toward St. Luke's. "I didn't know you were a follower of Mortimer's."

"Don't be silly. He's the most famous person in Pike's Grove, that's all. My mother says he brings a lot of business into town, so we have to be nice to him."

"Your mother would know," Willard agreed.

Intelligently, Montclief had slipped away when he heard the helicopter. He watched from a distant tangle of juniper scrub as the rescuers hurried around loading the wrecked bodies; then after the steel bird had departed, he loped up the snow canyon following Sigmoid's track.

His expectations about the bear hunt differed somewhat from Rainy's. He knew there would be an intense hunt for the supposedly berserk bear, whether or not both men died. The white skins couldn't allow a man-killing bear to live. It was clear that the Mountain Spirit had sacrificed Sigmoid to the greater good. Montclief's duty, as he saw it, was to find the bear so that Rainy and the hunting party could be pointed in the right direction. In that way, a kill would be made on the first day, and the hunters would go away satisfied. Or if Sigmoid had already died from his gun shot wounds, the hunting party would find the carcass. Either way the mountain would be saved from total rape, but it would also be known as a dangerous place for yrts. Maybe a few of the hunters would accidentally slip over the edge of a precipice. It could happen so easily. The mountain could become known as enemy territory.

However, in his heart, the yeti knew that winning this small battle meant very little. The aberrant white skins bred like mice. Soon they would overrun the mountain, all the mountains, simply because they had filled up the valleys. It made no sense to Montclief. Why didn't they recognize the elegance of the food chain like a normal species did? Mice bred like mice because their job was to provide food for the larger animals. But nothing hunted bears and cougars. Only bad luck, or bad winters or fire killed them before their natural time, and so The Great Spirit suppressed their birth rate. The yrts, of course, killed them, but not for food.

At the very pinnacle of the food chain, stone men and all colors of star men lived with no built-in breeding control. Only the long cycle of gestation and the helplessness of infants kept skins from producing even faster. Red yrts were somewhat sane, but the others thought that doubling of the breeding pair was legitimate, or even tripling. In fact, this policy would only lead to misery and famine. Had to, and would. The Great Spirit would call a halt at some point. But when? Soon, the yeti prayed. Send a pestilence to decimate the skins before they ruin everything.

Montclief was unaware of the true fragility of the skins. To him they seemed invulnerable, like a swarm of insects. He didn't know about AIDS and didn't really understand atom bombs. He didn't know the skins were poisoning their own foodstuffs so that their immune systems would be weakened, nor that all the water was being poisoned by shortsighted policies of greed. High on the mountain, these things weren't evident. But if they refused to do so themselves, the Great Spirit was more than capable of policing the stupid actions of the skins. Then there really would be misery, and the skins would think of themselves as innocent victims as they died, and died, and died.

When Lotti and Willard woke Sri Rainy from a nap on a couch in the hospital lobby, he seemed eager to go back with them to Pike's Grove—a fact which displeased Lotti so much that her painted toes clenched in the platform wedgies. She had planned to hang around Clinton with Mortimer, who obviously should stay here to talk to Yatsey after he regained consciousness. And it made sense that he'd want to spend the borrowed twenty bucks on her.

"Just let me check on Dr. Yates' condition," Rainy said to Willard. He stood up and stretched his shoulders. All the vertebrae in his back popped, one after another—a really disgusting sound in the quiet lobby. "Then we can go right back. And I really want to thank you for all the trouble you've gone to, Willard. You're a fine man."

The praise tweaked Willard mightily, although he was careful not to show it. If old Mortimer said he was a fine man, then it surely must be true. The old fellow must know his apples and oranges about who was a fine man and who wasn't. That was the job of a priest, after all—being able to tell who was a fine man. And when Mortimer Snerd handed him back the twenty, saying he wouldn't be needing it, Willard was even more pleased. He had chalked that twenty up to a donation to the church out of his own pocket. The petty cash fund wasn't something to play around with.

Lotti did a slow burn as Mortimer trotted off to inquire about Dr. Yates.

"Hello, Governor..!" Melton Pinkle said, with great sincerity. All the listening posts around Washington were again tuned in. It was a rather slow day in the international spy business, so tracking the NRC seemed like a reasonable way to waste the taxpayer's money. "This is Melton Pinkle at the NRC. Just thought I'd give you a call to see how everything is in the Great State of Colorado."

"It's very high," Governor Harold Potts laughed. That was his standard rejoinder to inquiries about his great state. He and Pinkle had met at the Governor's Conference last year in Philadelphia. Gov. Potts assumed the meeting was coincidental, but it wasn't. Pinkle had been in Philadelphia purely on business all the way. A good acquisitions man takes the easiest route to getting what he wants. Friendship with any elected official is a good way to snap up State owned land. A nervous, bribable governor is the best kind of friend. Harold Potts fit the requirements perfectly; but then so did the governors of Nevada, Utah, California and New Mexico, which were also possible sites for the repository. It had been a very fruitful conference for Pinkle. "About a mile up," Harold Potts laughed, completing his little joke.

"Say listen, Governor," Pinkle said, lowering his voice. "Is everything hunky-dory out there?" Lowering the voice worked magic every time.

"Sure, fine," Potts chirped. "Great! Are you getting close to a decision?" Visions of dollar signs flashed through his mind. Not only would Colorado benefit hugely from expanded employment and inter-state nuclear waste shipping, but the purchase price of the mountain would go directly into the general fund. Governor Harold Potts would also benefit hugely. Re:election would be a shoo-in given the superb employment and budgetary figures. To say nothing of the cool half a million buckeroos in a numbered Swiss account—a little fee for greasing the skids. The beauty of it was, there were no skids to grease. Everybody he'd mentioned the repository to was enthusiastic, except those stupid duck stamp people and pinko environmentalists, and they didn't count. If Harold Potts knew anything, he knew where votes were, and those goody-goody Sierra Club fanatics didn't vote worth a pile of piss. He wouldn't even be crossing the NRA gun nuts on this issue. Those freaks were in favor of nukes. They thought everybody should have the right to keep and bear nuclear missiles. It was beautiful. He hoped to hell Pinkle decided to push the deal his way, as promised. What kind of a little gift would help decide the matter? Unfortunately, his spys hadn't been able to turn much up on Pinkle, but the man must have a weakness for something.

"Have you heard about that little trouble we had

over in Clinton?" Melton Pinkle asked the Governor.

"Trouble..? In Clinton, Colorado..?

"Apparently, one of our geologists was almost eaten by one of your grizzly bears."

"You're kidding..?"

"No, Harold. That's the report I got. I didn't know you had a severe bear problem. It wouldn't be right to keep sending my men into a hazardous locale. If you could authenticate this story, I'll hold my report until I hear back from you."

The Governor was righteously shocked. Bears fucking up his re:election! "I most certainly will, Melton. And thanks for thinking of me. I'll get right on it."

The first action he took after hanging up was to call Astrid Horvath, his appointed director of the Forestry Service, to check out this bear bullshit for him.

➾ ⇜

CHAPTER 13

NO UP WITHOUT DOWN NO HARD WITHOUT SOFT

Billy Bad Boy Drummond pulled the sporty red Bronco 4X4 into the Retreat's cobblestone courtyard and parked beside an olive green telephone company repair van. He sat in the Bronco for a minute feeling more solid than he'd felt in ages. The drive from Denver had been gorgeous. There's nothing quite like Colorado in the autumn with the trees changing colors. LA had been hot and smoggy when he'd left, but this...this was like a different solar system. Cuttingly fresh air with all the smells and sounds of nature, and peace. He opened the door and breathed a deep lungful of mountain air as he stepped onto the cobblestones.

A twinge of nostalgia, one of the many he'd felt already this morning, assailed him. Those cobblestones had been a year long project for the whole monastery—part of clearing the fields for easier farming. Everybody went out in the fields to gather the round stones that were laying just everywhere. He remembered pondering deeply about why smooth beach stones were all over the fields at this altitude. A real mystery of the world. Recalling his sense of awe when faced with the insoluble paradox, Bad Boy realized he still didn't know the answer to those stones, even though he'd gotten really interested in geology at the time. Even though he'd read Velikovsky and other thinkers on the subject of how things got where they shouldn't be, nobody's theory totally answered the question for him. A real mystery.

Having gathered two huge piles of stones, a team of workers under Sam Johnson started on one side of the courtyard, and another team supervised by Sri started on the other, pressing the stones carefully into damp mud, always long side down. Billy hadn't really believed the stones would stay in place, but they had. Twenty years later, they still looked great. There. Billy nodded his head significantly, looking down at a ragged line of smaller stones in the middle of the courtyard where the two teams had met. A line of small stones that showed up the glitch of imperfect spacing. A lot of people had said the teams should both start in the middle, but Sri had insisted that if they planned and executed the spacing right, they could start on the outside like the ancient stone masons did, and meet perfectly in the middle. But their concentration hadn't been perfect; and there it was—a ragged line to prove their lack. A sublime road map of lost attention. The old man was so beautiful, always teaching. Twenty years later, here was the story set in stone for anybody to read who knew how.

Billy's anticipation was intense. Since Colorado

Springs, he'd been feeling queasy at the thought of facing the old man. Giant butterflies tickled his stomach. This is silly for a pro like me, he decided. I must have more invested here than I know about. What could Sri possibly want? Why would he call me up like that?

Near the kitchen, he saw a young student with his robe tied around his legs, kneeling beside a ten speed bicycle, trying to repair the spokes in the front wheel. His concentration was total. He'd never even looked up when the red Bronco had pulled in. Billy felt a tremendous surge of respect for the young fellow. I could just stay here, he thought. I could apply myself this time, instead of faking it. I could learn to be like that.

"Excuse me," he said to the bicycle repair man. "Sorry to bother you, but do you know where Sri is?"

With absolute peace and tranquility sparkling in his eyes, Norman Ungerer looked up from the chrome wheel rim at the hippie-looking stranger. "He hasn't come back from fishing yet," Norman said, then turned his attention back to the wheel.

"Looks like you could use a hand with that," Billy said. He had once owned a racing bike, which was more for show than anything else. Just an expensive toy. When it went out of alignment, someone else had fixed it.

"I'd love some help," Norman said, guilelessly. "I'm not much of a mechanic."

"I'm not either," Billy confessed, kneeling on the hard cobblestones beside the bike frame.

Montclief had tracked the great bear for most of yesterday afternoon before coming upon him high on the south shoulder of Mukatee, which the yrts called The Devil's Tooth. He saw the great red lump lying in an alpine meadow, and he knew that Sigmoid had come there to die. A bear bent on survival would have made himself a mud wallow beside a brook. The wet mud would suck the poison out of the wound and keep the flies off. But this meadow was too high for a mud wallow. Sigmoid had either collapsed on his way to somewhere else, or he had chosen this spot for his last battle. Approaching cautiously, Montclief saw that his former cavemate was still alive, but very weak. The bright red lung blood had never stopped dripping out. Because of that, the tracking had been easy. Hunkering down in the tall grass a respectable distance away, Montclief spoke. "There's no water up here, old friend."

The great bear grunted. With an effort he raised his head. His black pig-like eyes stared at the yeti. Then tiredly, he lowered his massive head onto his huge forepaws.

After a time, the yeti rose and left the meadow. Here the bear would be. Here the hunting party would find him.

Montclief related all this to Sri Rainy as they fished the next morning. And he also dropped the anthropological bomb of the century squarely into Rainy's brain pan. There was going to be a Council Meeting of the yetis, and Rainy would be invited. Montclief had already sent word. The caucus was scheduled for three nights from now, and the four of them, Yolanda and Chava included, would leave whenever the bear hunt was concluded. The yeti insisted that Rainy should guide the hunting party, that way there would be no slip up, and the hunters would be off the mountain as rapidly as possible. As an added benefit, Rainy would become something of a hero to the local gunslingers and frightened housewives. Maybe that would be useful in the days to come.

With his head spinning, Rainy hid the fishing poles

in the hollow tree and limped back down the path to the Retreat. One thing was for sure, he'd have to get himself some proper footgear before he tackled those long hikes. Gruesome hikes, actually. Maybe some of the new featherweight boots he'd seen in the Bean catalogue, or better yet those air cushioned high-topped tennies. Now that could be the ticket to real foot comfort. Didn't the Sherpas all wear tennies for their Himalayan trekking expeditions? Correct, they did. Sherpas most certainly knew something about foot comfort. And, if he could catch a ride back over to Clinton, he could get the boots today.

Approaching the Retreat, Rainy experienced great pleasure when he saw not one vehicle, but two, parked in his courtyard. A red jeep wagon and an olive phone company van. Transportation was provided right on schedule. Consider the lilies of the field....

And when he recognized Bad Boy Drummond, with his long hair now streaked with grey, helping the enigmatic Norman Ungerer to fix his cheap bicycle, tightness caught in Rainy's throat. Very intense tightness. It hurt. Words of greeting jammed up in his chest, unwilling to come out, and his eyes misted over. My God, he was actually emotional about seeing his old student. How unusual. Rainy couldn't even remember the last time his throat had lumped up. Maybe he really was getting old and senile.

"Billy..!!" he exclaimed, limping forward to embrace the boy. Who knows why he wanted to embrace him, he'd never done that before either; but in this case it was the wrong thing to do. The toe of his sandal stubbed on a cobblestone. Screaming pain wrenched through his scabbed over toes. His face contorted into a rictus mask.

Both Billy and Norman witnessed the performance, knowing exactly what had happened when the old fellow went rigid. Those cobblestones were killers. Always had been.

Standing up, Billy smiled his commiseration. "Perfect reminder for staying alert, right, Sri? You certainly look awake now!"

Rainy smiled as the pain level in his toe receded to bearable. "Hello, Billy. Nice of you to come up." He patted the rock star paternally on the shoulder instead of hugging him. It had been a good impulse that hadn't been strong enough to survive the moment. And he also wasn't used to being baited by a student—they all treated him with respect. He remembered now that Billy had always insisted on being treated as an equal, with full pecking rights for making jokes. Always the little jokes about awareness and cosmic dildos. It all came back to the front of Rainy's mind. Cosmic dildos. Billy had invented that term to describe any surprising, awakening event. Rainy smiled. Those little jokes which showed a lack of real perception, had put a barrier between Billy and the real thing. Jokes had prevented him from achieving deep realization. And he was still at it. Oh well, he was here, and the task at hand was not cosmic awareness, but shit awareness. Atomic bull crap.

"Yes, I'm awake now," Rainy chuckled. "Rather a fine cosmic dildo, eh? Is that your jeep?"

Norman Ungerer's mouth fell open in a blithering sea of insight. A cosmic dildo! What a genius Sri Rainy was. What a way he had with concepts and words. And how brilliantly funny, too. Enlightenment always had its element of humor, he knew in a flash. What a pleasure to witness him interacting with an older student. He's always so careful with us.

"It's rented, but at your disposal," Billy answered, meaning the Bronco. "What's up, Sri? You planning to have an old home week?"

"Something like that, Billy. Why don't you come into my office, if Mr. Ungerer can make do without you for a few minutes."

Norman smiled to himself at the masterful put-down, pithy but gentle, and went back to the spokes. It was amazing how nice people were being to him lately. That guy, Bill, or Billy as Sri Rainy called him, just came over and started helping. Sri Rainy always said hello now, and even Sister Angie was being nice as pie. It was actually rather amazing.

In a tiny office half the size of his bedroom cell, Sri Rainy kept the records of forty years in a second-hand desk that probably was a bona-fide rustic antique by now. The walls of the room were bare save for a seed catalogue calendar and several small needlework tapestries that had been women's projects over the years. The aforementioned records were woefully spotty. He was always very punctilious about getting names and addresses of entering students, and about noting down arrival dates; but how in Hades was he supposed to keep records up-dated after a student had flown the coop? And to be honest about it, sometimes he wasn't aware that a student had left until months after the fact. They drifted into town for an ice cream bar, and forgot to come back. Of course, a lizard like that wouldn't have the spine to announce he was leaving or even drop a note so the records and the food budget could be squared away.

Rainy pointed Billy into a straight chair next to the desk; then opened the old ledger. He found the name under D for Drummond and jotted in today's date. Billy had checked out in 1976. The Bad Boy had made an issue of leaving, Rainy remembered, that's perhaps why the date was written so boldly. Actually, that was a point in his favor from an accounting point of view. Oh, well, the boy seemed happy to be back.

"So how are you, Billy?" Rainy asked, for openers. "You seem older." After noting Billy's flinch, he added, "Still beautifully young, of course. I just meant you're one of the senior people here now."

Mollified by the senior student bit, Billy related a brief history of his financial trials and dissatisfaction with the life he'd been leading. He skirted the issue of Betty Ford and all the coke. Telling the truth when dealing with a spiritual master was completely necessary, but he didn't want to get kicked out on the first day. Sri had always taken a very dim view of dope. Rightly so, of course. Rightly so.

When Billy paused, Rainy broached the subject of half a million years of radiation contamination on the mountain, and his intended battle with the Nuclear Regulation Commission. He enlisted Billy's help in the crusade, which Billy was delighted to agreed to. After all, a fight against tangible evil is a simpler matter than self-development. Soul searching could wait. Rainy went on to tell him about the bear hunt and his need for new boots, but managed to leave out the part about yetis. No need to alert the world to that issue at present.

Their conversation was interrupted by the telephone installer tapping on the door frame, asking permission to drill a little hole in the wall in order to run the line inside. He had already finished the drop from the pole out by the road and was ready to hook up the phone.

Rainy was annoyed at the thought of a hole in the wall where the cold winter wind could whisk inside, and he was more annoyed at having to pay a phone bill every month. But he needed the contraption, he reminded himself. This was the modern age, and he had to be able to rally his forces. "Can't you just run the cord in over the window sill?" he asked.

"Sure can, sir," Ace Bessemer, the lineman, replied. "Good idea. I was worried about using up all my drill bits on your wall anyway. Won't take a minute and you'll be all hooked up."

Rainy had barely reemphasized his need for new footgear to Billy, and was getting Billy's impressions on the merits of hiking boots versus tennis shoes, when they heard a high-pitched drilling outside the window. Sri Rainy limped swiftly across to the said window and tried to open it. It was firmly stuck as always, so he had to put his back into the effort. He had intended the lineman to open the window.

"Almost got it, Mr. Rainy," Ace yelled into the room. "No sweat. This sill wood is pretty cottony." He meant it was rotten, but saying it was cottony didn't frighten people as much as the word rotten did. The long drill bored through the sill and poked inside, missing Rainy by a foot or so. "Got her," Ace exclaimed, delightedly. "Boy, this is my lucky day. That cottony wood was the second real good thing that happened already today."

"What was the first?" Rainy inquired dryly, knowing he would hear about it anyway.

"I ain't gonna lose my job! They was gonna lay two guys off down to the company because, you know, just about everybody up here has got a phone if they're ever gonna get one. Then we got news of this new mine opening. So they ain't gonna lay Fred and me off just yet, till they find out how soon it's gonna happen. That's about the best news I've had in awhile. Sure would hate to be out of work with winter coming on."

"Good for you," Rainy said. The repository would create jobs, he hadn't thought that part through clearly. The townies would be gulled into loving the project. He had to strike quickly to snuff it before the word got out. Shit, it was already out, who was he kidding? Esther had probably blabbed it all over town. Damn it! "Just put the phone on the desk," he said to Ace Bessemer. "I have to run into Clinton for awhile."

"Sure thing, Mr. Rainy. She'll be done in no time."

*

By the time Billy and Sri Rainy finished at the sporting outfitter in Clinton, quite a crowd of vigilantes had gathered at the Forestry Service office, most notable among them was Governor Harold Potts, out stumping for re:election or something. The Governor had stationed himself in the back of a Forestry Service truck with a portable loud speaker and was angrily venting his outrage against a herd of rabid bears that was making Colorado unsafe for tourism and job producing land development.

A posse of hunters with high powered rifles in the crooks of their arms didn't seem particularly worked up by the Gov's speech. Sri Rainy stopped at the rear of the crowd to catch the drift of the speech. How in hell had old Slick Potts heard about an insignificant bear mauling, let alone found time to marshal his speech writer into pounding out this drivel?

Rainy listened to the ranting for a moment, then leaving Billy to catch the rest of the speech, he tromped into the forestry office in his new pre-broken-in high-tech boots. He had actually coughed up eighty-five bucks for the beauties—well, actually Billy had, but Rainy insisted on paying him back. They were waterproof, breathable, light as a feather yet sturdy, camouflaged and very, very comfortable. The guy at the sporting goods store had thrown in a pair of boot socks for each of them, since Billy had purchased a pair of identical boots for himself. Why Billy needed boots, Rainy didn't know. He wasn't going on any hikes.

Stanley Skaggs, the chief forest ranger, was watching the Governor's speech through the rustic mullioned window, wondering much the same thing that Rainy had—namely what was Governor Potts doing here? It made Stan kind of nervous. He had never voted for Slick, and his job was subject to political pressure, even though until today the Clinton sub-station had been way out of the main stream. He was sure the Governor had picked up the lie twenty minutes ago when they had shaken hands. Stan had said how delighted he was to meet Potts, and that he'd always voted for him. Unless he watched his Ps and Qs, he could be demoted to a fire tower, and he'd had enough of that duty to last ten lifetimes. Stan liked people better than trees, and he was miffed that this bear hunt had fallen to him instead of to Fish and Wildlife where it belonged. That nitwit cunt, Horvath, had somehow gotten her claws into the bear story and wouldn't give it away if there was any chance of getting her picture in the paper, even if it meant getting a bunch of forestry service guys killed. How had she climbed to Head of the Department anyway? She couldn't even give decent head. And what if he couldn't produce the damned bear for her and the Gov? He'd really be up shit's creek. Worse, he didn't know the first thing about organizing a bear hunt. Stan was a fisherman, not a hunter. He'd always detested hunting, although naturally he put on a hearty smile when he talked to hunters.

"Are you Mr. Skaggs?" Sri Rainy asked, pleasantly but firmly. Skaggs' name had come via the sporting goods salesman. Rainy felt that his robe probably looked a little strange with the new boots, but he counted on his reputation to carry him through. Also, he had reported the accident, so that gave him added leverage.

Stan Skaggs turned from the window to survey the skinny old hippie. Not today, he thought. No Jesus freaks demonstrating about saving the bears. Not while the Governor and Astrid were here.

"Yes," he answered, much more politely than he felt. "Can I help you?"

"I'm Sri Rainy from over at Pike's Grove. The one that reported the bear attack."

"Oh, right." Stan face lapsed into a crooked grin. "You were fishing."

"Yes, I fish almost every day."

"There you go. Anybody that fishes is okay in my book. I guess finding them bodies must have been a pretty gory experience."

"It was. Actually, the reason I'm here is to volunteer to help find the bear. He's wounded. I know where he's laid up."

"You do..?" Stan positively beamed his delight.

"I can lead the hunting party right to him. I imagine that would save a lot of senseless bear slaughter, don't you?"

"God, yes. That would be great! Can you leave right away?"

Rainy nodded. "It's a long hike." He squinted at

Stanley Skaggs, taking his measure. "Could I speak freely, Mr. Skaggs. That trigger-happy mob outside scares me. I'd like to take a small party of skilled men up there and get the job done. It's not even bear season, is it?"

"Not for another three weeks. You know exactly where he is?"

"I know where he was at dawn today. He's gut shot, so he won't go far."

"Jeeze. Where was he?" Skaggs looked at Rainy with a layer of new respect.

"I'd rather show you. My students go out in those mountains. I don't want them shot by accident."

"Good point. Say, you're not the old guy that has that Retreat place?"

"I am. Are you a skilled shooter?"

"Me? Hell, no...I mean, heck no. I'm a fisherman."

Rainy smiled. "But you'd know who to bring along?"

"What would you think of choppering in? That hike is going to take up way too much time."

"He's in a high meadow. If we could get close without spooking him, that would be fine with me."

"Say, how'd you like to meet the Governor? What's your name again?" Stan could see promotion feathers sprouting in his cap for a job well done. He'd take Luke and Hy along to do the shooting and skinning. And a photographer. Even his Excellency Potts, if he wanted to go.

"How is poor Dr. Yates?" Rainy inquired. "When he can talk, perhaps he'll absolve the bear from some of the blame, so this scare will blow over. My guess is that the bear was shot before he attacked. He was protecting himself the only way he could."

"Don't even talk to me about bears," Stan shivered. "They scare the crap out of me. Always have."

*

Being left alone in Clinton with hours to kill was exactly what Billy didn't want. It was his own fault, of course, for not leveling with Sri about his coke problem. Sri had simply asked him to wait while he went bear hunting with the Governor; but Sri didn't realize how weak the Bad Boy was. Or might be without supervision.

Being asked to personally wait for the Great Man was a plum beyond description for a real disciple; unfortunately Clinton reminded Billy too much of any anonymous town on any road circuit. The thought of staying alone in a bleak hotel room plunged him instantly back into the deep grooves of his addiction. On the road—how it all had started. Party time.

After ordering the meatloaf lunch special at the Wildwood Cafe, he looked around the restaurant. Every single person he saw, including the ancient henna-haired waitress, looked like a pusher.

After the disquieting lunch, he drove back to the Forestry Service office to listen in on the CB radio, in case there was news of the bear hunt, but the dispatcher wasn't very friendly. The local radio station and several newspaper reporters were bugging the guy for information. Billy was just one more long-haired annoyance. Not much like the glory days. Strange, but not one person had recognized him all day. Refreshing really, except that Billy discovered he was used to being somebody. In L.A. he was still well known wherever he went. These people were out of it. He hadn't busted his ass touring all over hell, singing his throat raw, to be a nobody.

Wandering outside, Billy thought he might sit under a tree and catch a nap; but several clusters of local thrill seekers were hanging around to catch a glimpse of the Governor when he returned. The Bad Boy could tell that every one of those assholes was itching to get him high, just like always. Every greasy pocket was bulging full of crack. But no thanks, fuckers. He hadn't spent 44 days in Betty Ford's hell, just to make some shit-kicking street pusher wealthy.

Fuck no. He was stronger than this weak little urge. This giant, gargantuan, strangling urge to get high on anything! Fuck Sri Rainy. What am I doing up here, waiting for him? Am I some kind of valet? Fuck no!

"No..!" Billy screamed to himself, tearing the door of the 4X4 open and jumping in. He rolled the windows up, locked both doors and belted himself in. Turning the FM radio up full blast, he kicked the truck into gear and roared out of the Forestry Service parking lot. Once on the main road, he drove full bore back toward the Retreat. That kid! He had to get back there and help that kid fix his fucking bicycle!

CHAPTER 14

THAT BRAVE MEN EVERYWHERE CAN PROLONG THEIR YEARS

Two helicopters hurtled across the noon sky flying through high mountain valleys—carefully skirting the treacherous wind conditions of the peaks. One chopper was Forest Service green, the other National Guard desert camouflage.

Sri Rainy sat up front beside the Forest Service pilot so he could see the meadow where he'd "found" the bear; but even in that choice seat he was beginning to feel queasy. The pilot, introduced to him as Whitey Ralph, seemed to take great pleasure in making unexpected power dives to check out points of interest down below. Rainy's stomach, which on the ground had always been made of cast iron due to his diet of basic brown rice and vegetables, did a dipsy-doodle with each freefall. After forty years of being more or less in control of his daily life, including not ever flying, he detested being trapped and subject to the whims of a gung-ho sky jockey.

"We're not at the right mountain yet," he protested feebly after each new plunge.

"Just checking it out," Whitey replied, happily unruffled, pointing out rock formations or a stand of budworm ridden trees to the folks in back of the chopper. Two of them, Skaggs and the woman, Astrid Horvath, were Whitey's immediate supervisors, and he wanted to look competent for them. The other two members of the party were the expert hunters, Luke Grodin and Hy Many Blankets. Grodin was a burly, rough-bearded Anglo. Many Blankets was a full-blood Eastern Kiowa. Both wore old red checked wool shirts. Grodin's bushy head was covered with a Denver Bronco's cap. The Indian kept his longish black hair back with a red bandanna headband. Apparently, they eschewed the camouflage so much in vogue with modern hunters. Both men had made a point of eyeing Rainy's new boots before crawling back to the tail with their rifles and back packs.

"All this diving is confusing my sense of direction," Rainy whined, thinking that might shame a practical man like Whitey Ralph into discontinuing his daredevil acrobatics.

"Just sit tight and enjoy, Reverend," Whitey chuckled. "I know more or less where we're going." He pushed the joy stick sharply forward and dived downward. "There they are..!" he shouted, turning his head to make sure his bosses were looking out their windows. "Dall's sheep. That's the flock I was telling you about!" He pulled out of the dive and skimmed over a flock of bounding mountain sheep, scaring the life out of the timid creatures.

Rainy's stomach made a queasy orbit. "If I throw

up, I'm going to aim it at you," he hissed, peevishly.

"I wouldn't do that, Reverend. Stick your head out the window. I mean it."

"Cut the bullshit, Whitey, and get us to the bear," ordered the mannish voice of Astrid Horvath. "If you want to work for a Park and Recreation tour, I can arrange that."

"Yes, ma'am," Whitey said, clamping his lips together so he wouldn't make one of the obscene retorts that he was famous for.

"The Governor is a busy man," Astrid explained. As a skilled administrator, she knew the value of explaining her position when it became necessary to crack the whip. An explanation took the sting out. She tried always to blame the whipping onto a powerful man, such as the Governor.

"Yes, ma'am," Whitey replied. "Bearing straight for The Devil's Tooth Mountain." Indians and yetis called the craggy peak Mukatee. Mukatee meant Flame of Spirit, not Devil's Tooth.

Hy Many Blankets sitting in the back seat knew the mountain's real name. He thought it was peculiar, but understandable that the bear would head for a sacred mountain to die on. It was probably an omen that this bear was a spirit messenger. He might not be easy to kill. And Rainy, the old holy man of the white-eyes was guiding the hunt. Another peculiar omen. The Kiowa people knew the old long beard, and while they had little direct contact with him, they thought he might be the ultimate contradiction—a real, white holy man. And he, Hy Many Blankets, newly elected war chief, had been hand picked to do the killing. A very peculiar, omen filled, helicopter ride.

In the second chopper, Colorado One, rode Governor Potts and his crew of three cronies and four newsmen, plus Dewitt Gefflerhagen. A party atmosphere, aided by several jugs of Wild Turkey fire water, pervaded the modified Huey gunship, which was flown by Major Freddy McCullem of the Colorado National Guard, who was cold sober. McCullem loved to fly, but occasionally he wondered why he kept volunteering to play nursemaid to a bunch of drunks. He was wondering exactly that today—and judging from the erratic flying of Whitey Ralph, he concluded that Whitey was also in his cups. Hopefully, Whitey the Geek wouldn't put them up against the side of a mountain.

In the back of the Huey sat Pinkle's #1 snitch from the Nuclear Regulatory Commission. A blander looking fellow than Dewitt Gefflerhagen had never been born. He was so bald and unobtrusive that Governor Potts found it easy to suck up to him, even to the extent of regarding him as a confident. Pinkle's man was obviously sold on Colorado. Gefflerhagen pretended to take a hit of the bottle every time it was passed to him, but in point of fact, very little whiskey passed his tonsils. No one seemed to notice.

Beside Gefflerhagen sat Tag Pritchard, the political reporter for the Denver Post, who was one surprised dude to be going along on a grizzly hunt. Tag assumed that Gefflerhagen was a taxidermist, since the Governor kept blabbing to the little man about having a bear skin rug made.

Governor Potts was justly proud of his major brainstorm of the day. He would have a grizzly skin rug made from this horrid bear and would present it to Pinkle, not as a bribe, of course, but as a lavish and expensive gift from the Mile High State.

Dewitt Gefflerhagen thought a bearskin rug was about the most ridiculous bribe he'd ever heard of. Pinkle would loath it. What he wanted was part of the pay-off money from the numbered Swiss account. About one third, actually. But Potts didn't seem real swift on the up-take as to how government business was done. It was Gefflerhagen's primary job to explain it to him.

*

Both helicopters circled The Devil's Tooth

Mountain, starting near the top as Rainy suggested. He had just realized that he would look very foolish if the bear had moved, or hid himself in a cave or something. The only information he possessed was the route Montclief had taken from the bottom, and the yeti's description of a red-brown hump in the middle of a high, south-facing meadow. He had stupidly forgotten to ask for a description of landmarks surrounding the correct meadow. The need to cover his lack of knowledge loomed rather large.

"All these meadows look the same from up here," he said, lightly. "There's a good size brook at the bottom of the mountain that meanders up hill, or actually downhill. The meadow I'm looking for is above the spring that feeds that brook."

Whitey Ralph didn't bother to digest that information. He turned his head to Skaggs and Astrid Horvath. Unfortunately, Stan had never set foot on The Devil's Tooth, and therefore was no help. Neither was Astrid.

Astrid Horvath, after graduating with a Masters of Forestry Conservation from Michigan State, had worked eleven months in a forestry tower on Pike's Peak, where she had briefly known Stan Skaggs. When her promotions started coming, she'd spent the rest of her career in Denver.

Stanley swiveled in his seat for a pow-wow. The hunters might know the brook that the old man wanted to find, but both men had their eyeballs glued to the side windows. "Let me see the map," Stan said to Whitey. "We'll find him. How's the gas?"

"Two hours, a little less." He passed a worn map book back to Skaggs.

The copter whumped across the face of The Devil's Tooth. Rainy strained his eyes, but saw nothing that could be remotely interpreted as a dead bear.

"Hey ya," Hy Many Blanket's soft voice snorted from the back seat. "There he is."

"Where..?" Whitey called.

"Down there. Go left. Middle of dry meadow."

"Oh, yeah. Got ya. Christ! Oh, sorry, Reverend... Looks just like a big red rock, don't he.

"That's all right," Rainy answered, absolving Whitey of taking the son of the Lord's name in vain. He felt vast relief. Montclief was an amazing person. The meadow and the bear were exactly as he'd described them.

Both choppers landed at the downwind edge of the meadow a quarter of a mile away from the bear. The two hunters jumped out with their rifles and began their stalk. Astrid insisted that the rest of the party stay near the aircraft and keep quiet, which was fine with Rainy. He'd been about to suggest that he would only be in the way now that his job as a spotter was done.

But drunks have a hard time contenting themselves to missing out on action—and governors are difficult to control in their own states. After a few minutes of terse, excited whispering with his staff photographers and newsmen, Slick Potts decided it was in the best interest of his constituents for him to tag along after the hunters, in case they needed help. Somebody would have to sit on the dead bear to hold it down for the photographers, and he intended to be that brave man on the six o'clock news, saving his voters from the bear menace. Astrid watched helplessly as the Governor, three aides, two political stringers and two photographers with their video cameras and Nikons bouncing merrily on their L.L. Bean camera vests waded through the knee high brown grass at a brisk clip.

Nudging Skaggs rather bossily, Astrid hissed, "Stop them."

It was obvious to Stan Skaggs that he wasn't going one step closer to a live, wounded griz than he already was. If Slick Potts wanted to be mauled, that was his business. "He's the Governor," Stan answered, hoping that response was self explanatory.

"Get the guns," she ordered. Both of them, as well

as Whitey Ralph had brought deer rifles along just in case. One, naturally, didn't go hunting without a gun.

"We're not going to shoot the Gov, are we?" Stan attempted a joke as Whitey hopped into the cockpit for the artillery. Answering the weak joke was beneath Astrid's dignity, so she stared acidly at the departing Governor's party, which after all was under her care. If he got hurt, her head would tumble.

Whitey emerged with three rifles and distributed them. After quickly loading up, Astrid, Whitey and a very sick looking Stan Skaggs hurried after the Governor. They at least were wearing their Forest Service uniforms and hunting boots, whereas the Governor's group was dressed for a shopping mall appearance.

Which left Sri Rainy in the company of National Guard Major Freddy McCullem, and Dewitt Gefflerhagen. Rainy thought it might be a good idea to reboard his chopper in case the bear decided to charge in his direction, but Gefflerhagen seemed bent on starting a conversation.

"So are you a priest or something?" Dewitt asked in his interested, friendly manner.

It wouldn't have been polite, nor would it have shown much bravery for Rainy to hop back into his seat and shut the door; so he stayed on the ground, skillfully ducking the amiable, bald fiend's attempts to interrogate him.

Billy Drummond, bad boy on the run, had gained a hold on himself by the time he reached Pike's Grove. He felt pretty foolish, but stronger than he remembered being in years. He'd actually beaten a major dope craving all by himself. It was great! Just like they'd told him at Betty Ford. When a big one comes, as it surely will if you're out in the world doing your thing, run like mad. But run toward something good. And he'd done it! Somehow he'd remembered at the critical point.

God, it was fabulous! That kid, Norm, had saved him. The only reason he felt at all foolish was that Sri Rainy was expecting him to wait in Clinton. The old boy would probably be honked if his taxi service was AWOL.

Pulling to a stop in front of Wong's Spot Right Liquor, he felt actually perky as he bounced over to the pay phone and used his telephone credit card to put a call through to the Forestry Service. He explained who he was to the harried dispatcher and learned to his relief that Sri hadn't come back yet.

At the precise instance that Billy hung up the phone and turned to his truck, Lotti McCardle waltzed out of the liquor store licking on an orange Dreamsicle. What a coincidence.

She wore a Parisian hooker outfit today. Short black skirt, provocative red short sleeved sweater, black hose and spike heels. A long French silk scarf (red, white and green) was wrapped around her neck. To top the outfit off, she wore a green beret.

"Billy Drummond..!" she cried. "Hi! Remember me?"

Billy definitely didn't remember this fox. He had no clue. But she knew him. So, he wasn't completely forgotten by the younger generation, even up here. Great. He had known the Rolling Stone article was wrong about that.

"Hi," he answered, smiling at her. "How's the Dreamsicle?"

Lotti held out the ice cream bar to him. "Want a lick?"

Billy hesitated. Before AIDS and herpes he would have simply stuck out his tongue and swapped spit with this fox, and probably would have balled her in his dressing room. But now he hesitated.

Lotti shrugged and licked it slowly, showing her pink tongue.

"Do you think boy scouts are still doing blood brother ceremonies since AIDS?" he asked, with a wink.

"Search me. I don't have AIDS, do you?" She had no idea if she had it or not, and tried never to think about the possibility.

"No, I don't," Billy replied, quickly. He also hadn't been tested. He might have picked the disease up from some doper girl. He'd never been interested in boys, but he certainly couldn't be accused of leading a modest life. Sharing needles had been cool for awhile there. Thank God, he hadn't gotten hooked on heroin.

But Betty Ford probably did an AIDS test on him, now that he thought of it. Wouldn't they have told him, if he had the disease? Why was he so dumb about checking up on his health? Damnit, these stupid diseases had certainly slowed the love child movement down to a crawl. Somehow that wasn't fair. "Let me have a lick of that," he said, brashly sticking out his tongue.

Lotti held out the Dreamsicle. "Don't you remember me?" she asked again, flashing her best eye twinkle. Seeing his confused look, she said, "I'm Lotti. You stayed with us when I was little. Lotti McCardle, over at the Lodge."

"Oh, my God! Cute, little Lotti?" She preened as he stared deeply at her face. Billy had stayed at the Spruce Lane Lodge several times when all the rooms at the Retreat were filled. It had been a gas. He and the band had driven the stingy landlady crazy. "Of course, I remember you, but you're supposed to still be a little girl. What happened? You grew up."

"Do you think I'm pretty now, Billy?" she asked, innocently twirling around so he got a good flash of black nylons.

"Adorable. Pretty as a model," he said, honestly. "Do you still live at the Lodge?"

Lotti frowned adorably. "Where else? You know Mother. She'll never leave here. Is that your Bronco?"

"Hey, listen Lotti, I have to run over to Clinton and pick up Sri Rainy. Want to ride along?" If nothing else, Billy had a high self-preservation coefficient. Having Lotti chattering girl talk would hopefully keep him from flipping out again.

"Is he over there again?" the girl asked, incredulously. "I was just there with him yesterday. How's the guy?"

"What guy?" Billy stuck his tongue out for another lick.

"The guy at the hospital, who else?"

"I don't know about that," Billy answered, wiping his mouth with the back of his hand. "Sri went on a bear hunt. Can you picture him going hunting after all those years of preaching peace and love?"

Lotti laughed adorably, making sure her pert breasts jiggled provocatively in cadence with her mirth.

Both Luke Grodin and Hy Many Blankets had lots of experience with grizzlies, enough experience not to trust a wounded griz under any condition until they were personally sure he was dead. This one, a huge boar, sure looked dead from a hundred yards away. He was humped up in the middle of the meadow, a place where no live bear was likely to be. Nor a dead one, either. He hadn't moved since they started the stalk. But a bear being smack in the center of the meadow was mighty strange, they agreed in whispers. And the way he was lying gave them a poor angle for a heart shot, through layers of fat. Therefore, they hadn't tried any make-sure shots, although they were within range for the coup de grace.

The unique ceremonial placement—dead center in the meadow, convinced Hy Many Blankets that this was indeed a spirit bear carrying big medicine. He planned to take the great heart and liver back with him today. No one would object to that. White people didn't understand Bear Grandfather Power; but the wilting tribe of Kiowas, who lived to the west of Clinton, could certainly use some spirit guide power—any power for that matter. Winter was coming, and once again they would probably be dependent on hand-outs of canned goods and thin blankets. The hunter knew that the grizzly's skin and claws, although needed for the full Bear Spirit Dance, would most likely be spoken for; but at least, he'd get the heart—even if he had to walk back with it. Or if he could kill the bear himself, that would be even stronger medicine. Maybe he'd ask Big Luke to hold off until he had a chance to count coup. That was it, he'd count coup on the griz, alive or dead. How could anybody know for sure? It was still an act of bravery.

Since he was now the Secret War Chief of the tribe, stances had to be taken, even if there were no witnesses who counted. Hey ya, The Great Spirit and his bear messenger would witness it, and Hy Many Blankets would sing the tale of bravery. Then everybody would eat a bite of heart meat cooked the traditional way, and he would have provided strong meat for his people.

"Think he's dead?" Many Blankets asked, softly. They were both bent at the waist, stalking quietly from down wind, but at fifty yards any bear would have heard them by now.

"Maybe," Grodin whispered back.

"Mind if I run in and count coup on him?"

That surprised Big Luke right down to his size 12s. He knew all Indians were crazy, but he'd always thought Hy Many Blankets had his shit pretty well together. What was this counting coup business? Did he want to scalp the bear or what? That was insane.

"Run that past me again, Chief," Big Luke whispered.

"You know, I run in and tap his nose, then jump out of the way. It's very powerful," Hy added stubbornly, seeing that Big Luke was underimpressed.

"You want to touch a wounded griz on the nose? Are you nuts?"

"I'll use my rifle to touch him. It's a ritual show of bravery. Very good for the bear's spirit. And for me."

"What am I supposed to do?"

"Just watch."

"What if he gets you?"

"He won't. This bear is a spirit messenger waiting to die for my people."

Big Luke mulled that over. Pretty spacy, but if this crazy Indian had gone to the trouble of asking, he probably meant to pull the stunt. "Just supposing he grabs you?" Luke asked, slowly. "Am I free to shoot then, or what? We wouldn't want him to get away, with all these people watching."

"Shoot him fast," the Secret War Chief answered, chuckling nervously. He was committed now. He'd been half hoping that Grodin wouldn't let him try it. The saliva leached out of his mouth. In a deer skin pouch under his shirt was a little round power stone. He should get the stone out and put it in his mouth. Nuts, there should be members of the People here with him, so he didn't feel such a fool; but there was only Big Luke and that asshole Governor, who hated Indians, and was making a huge racket a couple hundred yards back. Well, at least Luke was a fine hunter. His word would be believed, if it came to that.

Motioning Luke to stop, Hy Many Blankets removed his jacket and shirt, then he untied his hunting boots and took them off, too. Smiling a go-to-hell smile at Big Luke, he quieted himself with a quick, silent hunting prayer, then catapulted toward the Great Bear's hump.

Flying across the dead grass, Hy Many Blankets felt power surging up his legs. Warm autumn wind whipped his black hair. It was beautiful. From now on, he would live traditional all the way. Let his hair grow and braid it. Build a tee-pee. Get a permit for buffalo, and keep getting them until he had enough skins for a real tee-pee. Sell his jeep and get a couple of horses.

The great bear hump grew large, filling his field of view like tunnel vision. His secret war cry leaped unbidden from his lips like a wail from the beyond, inflicting sudden terror on his enemies. The bear loomed in front of him like a dark red mountain. The great head lay quietly, but the black beady eyes watching him were very much alive. Hy Many Blankets swung his rifle in a warrior's arc, tapping the great head—counting coup. Actually, he bonked Sigmoid between the ears with the sharp front sight.

Instead of dying in peace in his favorite meadow, Sigmoid suddenly found himself under attack. Pain whacked though his head. He lurched stiffly to his feet, roaring his challenge and swiping at his pitiful attacker. The sharp claws connected with flesh, and the inflicter of headaches sailed through the air. Rapid thunder cracked—fresh pain tore through his chest knocking him down in a cloud of torn grass and dirt, bursting his mighty heart. Blood gushed into his mouth. Mighty Sigmoid sighed a bubbling sigh, fell over on his side and died in the autumn sunshine. His spirit sailed through the air to join the Great Mystic Bear. Harmony ruled all.

"Never seen nothing like that!" Big Luke observed to himself. He hadn't seen the bear's spirit, but the Indian's dance with death had been plenty weird. Charging up to the bear, he snapped off a quick shot through the eye into the brain, and loped across the field to where Hy Many Blankets lay twisted and bleeding. "You are one crazy, crazy Indian," Luke said, feeling irrationally proud of his friend.

The War Chief was conscious and his eyes were gleaming. Four deep slashes scoured his chest, seeping blood. His right pectoral muscle seemed torn loose, and his right arm was broken, but his spirit was gleaming brightly. The rifle which he'd used for a coup stick was nowhere in sight. "The bear wasn't dead," Hy said, stating the obvious.

"He's dead now, Chief," Luke answered. "Just lay there quiet like. We'll get you patched up. It don't look real serious." Luke had seen a first aid kit in the chopper, and naturally the chopper would air lift them to the hospital. All in all, they were in much better shape than they would be with an accident on a normal hunt.

Luke noticed the Governor and his party running drunkenly up to the bear. Cameras started clicking. Fucking creeps. If he didn't need the money, he'd never work for government agencies. He kind of wished the bear would revive and eat the creepos; but of course, it wouldn't. Look at Potts sitting on the bear's head. Fucking moron. And here came the Forest Service, toadying after the Governor.

"Hey, Skaggs..!!" he roared. "Get the chopper over here pronto. The Chief got raked!" He waved the rifle over his head to attract attention.

Astrid and Stan Skaggs were too busy kissing ass and posing to be bothered with what the hunter was bellowing from way over there. But one of the photographers, Jackie Sims, broke free from the pack and trotted over to Big Luke.

"Could we get you to pose with the Governor for a shot or two," the blonde kid asked, officiously. Then he caught sight of all the blood. He looked green for a second or two, then keeled right over in a dead faint.

Luke scoffed at the weakling, then fired his rifle into the air. That would get some attention. He planned to kick up some dust beside the Gov with his next shot, but luckily a lot of white faces turned in his direction.

"Get the choppers over here!" he bellowed. "We got a wounded man!" He saw the boss lady say something to asshole Whitey, then the pilot took off running for the helicopter. The whole party left the bear and chugged over to Big Luke. "Stay back," Luke shouted, threateningly. "Give him room to breathe. It looks worse than it is! If he don't bleed to death, he'll be fine."

"Did you shoot Jackie?" Tag Prichard asked, eyeing the fallen body of his comrade in newsprint.

It would be hard to say which of the two men were more skilled at giving misleading information. Sri

Rainy was an actual Master at it. Too much information short circuits a student; therefore a teacher has to withhold the vital secrets until the student has almost reached masterhood himself. And of course, the same tight-mouthed rule applied doubly to the idly curious and to the media. Sri Rainy, therefore, was not a media darling. He didn't drive a Cadillac, and he had never looked for converts. Converts searched for him.

Dewitt Gefflerhagen served a slightly darker lord, but his negotiation skills were developed to a remarkable degree. Hence, in the ten minutes the two men spent together beside the helicopters, they developed a healthy respect for the other's austerity and singleness of purpose in blanketing any revealing facts. Neither had learned anything of consequence, except that here was an emissary of the opposition, a worthy adversary. And both girded themselves to flay the other.

Their companion, Major Freddy McCullem, wasn't even aware that a battle was taking place. He thought these two kindly older gentlemen were having a nice chat, maybe about philosophy, in which he had no particular interest. If it didn't fly, it was beneath Freddy's notice.

"Are you a priest or something like that," Geff had asked casually, approaching Rainy obliquely. Long experience and a yearly memo at the NRC had taught him that religious leaders can be stubborn SOBs when backed into a corner. If this was who he thought, the nut with the cruddy non-affiliated monastery near the proposed site, Geff had no intention of backing him into a tight place. He was going to blow the old kook out of the water, way before any public fight got started. The NRC was going to suggest that the Interior Department requisition all the land on that side of the mountain for a small national park. Let the old fart fight rabid campers and RV freaks over that issue. Then, if at some time in the future, the park started to glow, the NRC could shut it down in the interest of national safety. In the event that the dump site was located somewhere else, normal grazing permits would be issued to selected ranchers and the rich would get a little richer.

"No, I'm a bear hunting guide," Rainy responded with a sly grin. "Done pretty good, don't you think? Are you one of the reporters?"

"Yes, I am," Dewitt lied. Well, it wasn't quite a lie. He could have passed a polygraph with it. He was going to report back to Melton Pinkle.

"Which one of them people is the atom bomb man?" Rainy asked. He had allowed himself to slip into a twangy Rocky Mountain drawl, believing it would make him seem more innocuous, in spite of his white robe and long white beard.

"Beg pardon?" Geff answered in his native Indiana nasal twang which he had never bothered to lay a veneer over.

Rainy was sure he was talking to the culprit, Astrid's description had been very complete when she described the man to Whitey. A geeky bird that you wouldn't trust with a puppy, she had said. "The Forest Service lady said there was an atom bomb person in the other helicopter. Which one is he?"

"No idea," Gefflerhagen answered. "First I heard of it."

So they twanged back and forth until they saw Whitey Ralph running full tilt toward them, waving his rifle. Figuring the grizzly was after him, both our brave adversaries jumped back in their respective helicopters—which put Rainy in the thick of the action and left Gefflerhagen out in the cold. Whitey jumped in the cockpit, and whipped the whirly up in the air. Then he flew it across the meadow and landed next to the wounded Indian. Governor Potts was waving his arms like a air traffic controller, while flashbulbs popped.

CHAPTER 15

SMALL LOSS, SMALL GAIN GREAT LOSS, GREAT GAIN

Lotti very definitely did not think of herself as an opportunist. She always paid in advance. Everything she'd ever gotten was the result of hard work and good management skills. Meeting Billy Bad Boy Drummond so accidentally had been far from easy.

First, she'd recognized him driving Mortimer through town in his flashy red Bronco; then when she saw the 4X4 stopping at Kim Wong's place, it took a dedicated effort on her part to run downstairs, slip back through the woods and cut across Wong's garden so she could enter by the rear door. Then the investment of her capital for the Dreamsicle, so that she could saunter out the front door licking it and be so surprised to see Billy. Surprisingly, he'd had the gall to call her an opportunist on the way to Clinton, after she'd given him a superb blow job. All she'd done was casually mentioned that she might like to go to Hollywood with him. If that was opportunism, she'd like to know what capitalism was all about?

Billy, of course, hadn't meant to be insulting. He was feeling fine. He'd always enjoyed having groupies crawling all over him. And to be perfectly candid, in the music business if you weren't an opportunist, you didn't get very far. So it had been a brotherly comment, one opportunist to another; but the girl had taken it wrong and had scooched up against the passenger door where she sat pouting.

"I don't think that's very nice, Billy," she whined. The red 4X4 cruised into the outskirts of Clinton, past the lumber yard and Highway Department garage.

Billy hardly ever felt like talking after sex. He wished that Lotti had climaxed, so she would quit sulking. He hated that. Over the years, hundreds of teeny-bopper girls had sworn that they climaxed while going down on him. The excitement of being with him was too much for them. Yeah, well, he'd never exactly believed that, and it certainly hadn't happened to Lotti. About all he wanted to do was pull in under the trees at the Forestry Service place and catch a half hour of shut-eye to replenish himself. "Don't pout," he suggested. "Hike up your skirt and play with yourself. That might entertain you until I come back to life."

"I most certainly will not!" she screeched. "You're disgusting! Mother was right about you." She'd never had a man make such a repulsive demand. What was wrong with him fucking her. That's what she wanted. Then she'd have Billy Bad Boy where she wanted him. Playing with herself in front of somebody was too icky. Oh, no, definitely not! No way, Jose!

"Take it easy, I'm not trying to offend you." Christ, this was the last mountain girl he was picking up. Civilized women from now on, or nothing. He'd probably said that "playing with yourself" line to five hundred women when he didn't feel like talking. They either thought it was a joke or they wanted to do it anyway. Nobody had ever been angry before, ever. And damnit, he wasn't up here to chase quail. What had he been thinking about?

Frumping around in the seat to show her displeasure continued to seem like a good idea, so Lotti thrashed her hip up against the door a few times. The cold shoulder always made men take notice. Making sure her legs were displayed to best advantage, she turned her face away from Billy—just in time to see Mortimer Snerd stepping from a helicopter in the hospital parking lot, his white robe billowing in the chopper wash. "Oh, my God," she yelped. "There's Mortimer!"

Billy slammed on the brakes and swung into the hospital driveway. He parked as close to the chopper as possible, watching a couple of orderlies unloading a dark-haired man onto a rolling stretcher cart. Sri Rainy hadn't seen the 4X4 yet.

"What's going on?" Lotti asked, craning her neck to see. Since they were at the hospital, anyway, she decided to run inside and check on Omar Yates' condition. If he was better, maybe he'd give her the latest low-down on the new mine, so she could plan her future. But Jiminy Crickets, Billy Bad Boy was a guaranteed ride to L.A., even if he was weird. She hated to throw that away, unless the boom town was a sure thing. Darn it, why had Billy turned out to be such a rat? She was positive that one, or maybe several of the handsome, muscular miners would be easier to twist around her finger.

"Mortimer..!" she yelled out the window. When the old geeko turned to look, she was delighted to see his mouth drop open in surprise. "I'm running in to check on Yatesy..!" she shouted at the monk, popping out of the truck and sprinting up the concrete walkway in her spike heels.

Billy climbed out of the truck, too. No naps here. That would mean no nap at all until bedtime. Sri was a little rigid about naps.

Sri Rainy approached Billy with a quizzical frown

on his face. "You found me," he stated.

"Like you always said, there are no accidents. I would have probably driven right past, if that girl hadn't seen you."

"Lotti," Rainy replied, trying vainly to disguise the jealousy in his voice. What the hell was Lotti doing with Billy Drummond. It certainly hadn't taken the crooner long to snag her. But why was she in Clinton? On the copter ride back, he'd been thinking about how to entice Lotti's help with his anti-nuke campaign. She would be perfect for the media—and a very bad enemy. And, though it stabbed him to admit it, he would get a lot more volunteer help with her on his side.

"Where did you find Lotti?" he asked, casually. His acid jealousy would have to be swallowed. No wonder lust was one of the Seven Deadlies. And beyond that, it was ridiculous for an ninety year old to be jealous of a child, no matter how much she played around. She couldn't help it. Simple biology was taking her for a ride. Maybe this affiliation with Billy would work to his advantage. If she bonded with Billy, it would put her in the right camp. Instead of being jealous, he should encourage their friendship, no matter how much it shrank his gonads.

"She's a strange one," Billy smiled, having no inkling of the bout that Sri was fighting. "I knew her when she was little, but she's sure not little now. What happened with that guy on the stretcher?"

Rainy could still smell the Indian's blood in his nostrils. The chopper ride had been redolent with the sweet, wet smell. He was extremely grateful to be back on solid ground. The hunt had been a remarkable experience, and he was proud of his stomach for sticking with him during the emergency. It had been touch and go all the way back. Being reminded of one's weakness, now and then, is remarkably useful. Nevertheless, he planned never, ever, to board another aircraft in this lifetime.

"There was a hunting accident," he reported to Billy. "It seems the man wasn't too badly hurt. How nice that you were waiting here for me."

Sri Rainy had plenty of reason to be proud of himself. Everything that he had set out to accomplish had been done, and perhaps more. The bear had been found and killed. Even during the hectic rescue operation, Rainy had made a point of showing the clotted gunshot wound in the grizzly's side to a reporter and a photographer. To stupidly blunder on that bullet hole had been a neat acting feat. And while posing for a photograph beside the bear with Governor Potts, he had found out who the man, Gefflerhagen, was—an agent from the devil, just as he had suspected. Yes, a very good day's work, and now he had to get back to the Retreat and start telephoning.

"Let's be going then," Sri Rainy said, stamping his new boots on the pavement. They were good boots. He felt very anchored wearing them. "Nice boots, don't you think?" he asked Billy.

"Very nice," Billy Bad Boy replied. "Shouldn't we wait for Lotti. I brought her over from Pike's Grove. I'd hate to leave her stranded."

Rainy was a couple of facts short of being able to figure that out, so he nodded his head sagely as both men walked toward the hospital lobby.

"I'm his sister," Lotti pleaded with the young, black nurse at the visitor's desk. She had already been informed that Dr. Yates was still in critical condition and could receive no visitors, but Lotti was not a girl who believed in being told no by a hotel clerk. She was well acquainted with the dodges of hotel employees, and a hospital was just a glorified hotel with sick guests instead of vacationers. "I came all the way from Des Moines to see him. Omar will be mad, if you won't let me say hello."

"I don't believe he has regained consciousness, Miss," the young nurse said, uncertainly. "Your brother must be very popular in Washington, D.C. There's been a string of visitors for him."

"Yes," Lotti lied. "He's a very important man. I'll just sit in his room until he wakes up. I'm sure he wants me there. What is his room number?"

Wilma Dexter tapped the eraser end of her pencil against her small white teeth. Mr. Gefflerhagen from Washington had left specific instructions that Dr. Yates wasn't to be disturbed; but surely family members took precedence over that. On the other hand, hospital rules had to be enforced. This job was no lark. Wilma had thought she'd be helping people, but what she mainly seemed to be doing all day long was keeping people from doing what they wanted to; and to be honest about it, she thought they were right most of the time.

"We have a strict visitor policy that only two visitors are allowed in the room at once. Your mother and father are already up with your brother. If you'd care to wait in the visitor's lounge, I could send word up that you're here. That's the best I can do until one of them comes down."

Drat, Lotti fumed. She turned away from the nurse to think up the proper response. Her sharp eye caught sight of Mortimer Snerd and that jerk, Billy, coming through the glass doors. "There's my husband," she said to the nurse. "Tell Mamma and Daddy, we'll get a bite to eat and come back later." She turned from the counter and clacked across the tiled lobby on her high heels. Sidling between Mortimer and Billy, she turned them both around and headed them back out of the door. "Yatesy's condition is still critical," she explained to Mortimer. "They won't let him have visitors yet."

"That's too bad," Rainy growled, feeling his carnivorous manhood start to grow alive again. The child's delicate touch on his elbow excited him unbearably. "I wanted to tell the chap that his grizzly is dead."

"Well, another day, Mortimer. What's for lunch? Isn't that darling little lunch place with the patio just around the corner?"

*

To Sri Rainy's surprise, a fair number of his former students were already involved in the anti-nuclear movement. Not only was every person he called delighted to hear from him, but most were genuinely shocked to learn that the mountain was under siege.

He got a little nervous when person after person volunteered to come up to the Retreat to get the campaign started. Where would he put them all? Well, that was Billy's worry. He'd be handling all the logistics during Rainy's upcoming trip with the yetis.

Rainy had to chuckle when he thought of that. He'd told everybody he was going on a cleansing meditation by himself, something he'd been meaning to do for years. He would be back when he was purified and ready to deal with the power structure. Meanwhile, Billy would be in charge. True, it was a small lie. If he wasn't purified by now, he wasn't likely to make any noticeable new strides in that direction. And he wasn't prepared to tell the world about the yetis just now. Why couldn't civilization leave him alone for a decade of so, then he'd have something of import to say. But, of course, only this crisis had spurred Montclief to include a human's input into the decisions of his clan's future.

And yes, it was risky to leave Billy in charge, but there was nobody more qualified. How badly could he screw things up in only a week or two, even at his worst? All the students, both old and new, were a little in awe of the singer, so they probably wouldn't give him a ration of shit in such a short time. And even if they did, well, Billy might make some spiritual progress, which was the whole point anyway. Actually, it was almost gratifying to see Billy taking hold of the situation. He was planning an open air rock concert with his band to raise funds and alert the nearby community to the danger. A letter writing campaign had already been organized, and Rainy had noticed a general lessening of bickering among the women whenever Billy was around. Yes, it was fine. Sri Rainy thought he might be able to stay away as long as two weeks if he needed to.

The only slightly odd spot in all of this bizarre configuration was that young Norman Ungerer and his bicycle had disappeared. He hadn't been at this morning's meditation or at lunch. Apparently, he had flown the coop. Rainy probably wouldn't have thought anything of it, except that Billy kept asking about the strange young fellow. Apparently, they'd hit it off the morning of Billy's arrival, and Billy had planned to anchor one of the new teams with Ungerer.

But without Norman Ungerer the kitchen was working much smoother now. Sister Angie was even putting out some very good meals, geared toward getting favorable attention from the rock star.

All in all, things were moving along splendidly. If he could only be sure of enlisting the townspeople in the cause. It was impossible to conceive of anyone being moronic enough to believe that billions of rads would be a good next door neighbor, but apparently some of them believed that. Perhaps it would be a smart idea, he thought, to mosey into town. Maybe he could change a few minds at this early stage, before opinions became set in granite. And maybe he'd stop by to tell Mrs. McCardle how her boarder, Dr. Yates, was progressing. Lotti would possibly be there. She was certainly a peculiar girl. Difficult to get a reading on. He'd been so sure she would want to help with the letter writing; but after Billy bought a fancy lunch for her, she'd announced that she was looking forward to the construction workers who would work at the mine. The mine! She thought it was going to be a silver mine or something. And neither he nor Billy could dissuade her from that notion. Well, he'd have another shot at it, if she was home.

*

After obliquely explaining the exact nature of the appropriate gifting process to Governor Slick Potts, twice, Dewitt Gefflerhagen had caught the first plane back to Washington D.C. He reported to his boss, Melton Pinkle, on his successful mission and on the cast of characters surrounding the "Pike's Peak Folly" as Pinkle jokingly called it. The joke was, if the NRC had planned to put a nuclear repository inside Pike's Peak, most American citizens would have been up in arms; but since the site was one mountain away, nobody gave a damn.

Still chuckling at Pinkle's wit, Geff sat at his tidy desk and made a phone call to his opposite number at the Interior Department. Geff was a firm believer in the National Park System. In fact, if the whole country could be nationalized, then leased back to farmers and housing managers, this entire myth of private ownership could be put to rest.

It was laughable really. To his knowledge, there had never been one case of a private owner standing in the way of a government program, no matter how hard the peon tried to hold on to his miserable acreage. So why not call it like it was? Visionaries like Mel Pinkle and himself shouldn't have to play the charade of negotiating, which took up so much time and energy that might have been used more constructively.

*

Young women like Lotti are not so uncommon, if you think about it. Remember that her father had flown off shortly after her birth, leaving the girl with no male role model and no feeling that a man would stick with her unless she was more alluring than her mother had been. Not an uncommon feeling, one might presume.

And in every little burg around the country, isn't there always one girl who is more stunning and more daring then the rest, and doesn't she have the opportunity to pick and choose among the available studs? Aren't the boundaries of her choices far wider then her sisters'—fenced in only by her imagination and her luck? And aren't these beauties often regarded as fickle and heartless because they sift through the possibilities that life provides? Enough said. There is one in every town, in every graduating high school class. And the straight and narrow life is no less difficult for these rare beauties than it is for their lesser endowed sisters. They just have more possibilities, and not always enough moxy to make the right choices.

Poor little Lotti, who nobody should blame for being overwhelmed by her possibilities, was washing her Frederick's of Hollywood undies and hanging them, one at a time on the squeaky pulley clothesline which needed repairing again, when Sri Rainy just happened to amble under her balcony in his new hunting boots and robe. She saw him sniffing around under the balcony and was momentarily revolted, before she remembered that thanks to her guiding star she was still a virgin with the old wizard. Thank God, she had rebuffed him. Her skin crawled at the thought of his ancient smelly beard touching her. What had she been thinking of to lead him on? Mortimer Snerd was the worst stick in the mud of anyone she knew. What a dead end! Who does he think he's fooling? However, a perverse side of her nature decided to tease him, just for practice.

"Hey, Mortimer..!" she yelled out the window.

Rainy looked up at the balcony, pretending to be startled at seeing Lotti in her black lacy slip. He waved his bony hand. "Hi," he called back. "Are you busy?"

Lotti snorted to herself. God, she was getting clever at knowing how men would react. "Could you climb that tree, please Mortimer, and fix my pulley?"

"What's wrong with it?" he asked, looking up at the limbless cedar tree. Even a monkey would have trouble climbing that one.

"It squeaks and it's kind of sticky when you pull on it. Tad Foulks fixed it for me last time, but he's not around anymore."

"Do you have a ladder?"

"A ladder?" she laughed, haughtily. "Tad didn't

need one. Never mind, I'll do it myself." She ducked off the balcony and trotted downstairs, thinking that this was Mortimer's last chance. If he wasn't willing to climb a simple tree for her, she was never going to give him any sweet treat, which he so obviously wanted.

And sure enough, there he was just standing beside the big cedar tree, looking up at the pulley, but making no effort to climb the tree.

"You're so lame, Mortimer. I'll do it myself, but don't come around here anymore sniffing after me." She showed him the tin of 3-in-1 oil that she'd picked up on her way through the kitchen. He made no move to take the tin from her, so she stuck the flat little can between her teeth and started shinnying up the rough bark—which of course caught on the silky material of her slip, causing it to ride way up over her rump as she climbed. What a view Sri Rainy had. He thought for sure his veins would explode from the rush of blood as he watched the naked buns and hairy slit hump their way up the tree.

Wedging herself over a substantial limb like Tad had done, Lotti took the oil can from her teeth and doused the rusty pulley. Then she dropped the tin without warning, hoping to conk Mortimer's bald dome with it. Nuts, it missed him. "Bombs away!" she giggled, after the slim tin landed at his feet. "And stop watching me. That's not part of our deal from now on."

Crestfallen, Rainy lied recklessly. "I'm not watching. I'm merely trying to act as a safety net for you, in case you fall."

"You are watching me, and I don't like it!" she retorted, rather too loudly. Look at him squirm, she thought maliciously.

"If you would dress more chastely, you wouldn't have the trouble of thinking men were watching you, when they're only trying to help."

"The way I dress is the way I am, buster?" she quipped. "It's me. I don't tell you how to dress, and you don't tell me!"

"I wasn't telling you, I was making an

observation," he said, looking up directly between her legs. Stunningly gorgeous. His eyes wouldn't disengage from the dark V with the little folds of pink peeking out.

"Go away," she said, bluntly. "I can get down very nicely without your help, you old lech." She unwound her leg from the crotch of the tree and inched her way down the trunk. "Go away! I mean it."

"Fine," he replied, hanging his head in shame. His feet in the camo boots began moseying toward the street. The rest of him was in tatters. The mighty warrior, who had determined to take on the entire nuclear power and defense industries, was unmanned by a brash young girl with a brash young twat. It wasn't fair. But the camouflage boots kept moving until they reached the pavement of Spruce Lane, then turned left for their trudge up the mountain to the Retreat.

But the journey was not uncontested. Rounding the corner across from Kim Wong's Spot Right Liquor and Dry Cleaning, he was waylaid by the furious bundle of energy known as Mrs. Wong, bursting out of the Liquor Store door in her flip-flops.

"Why you no pay me rike plomise?!" she squealed.

My Lord, I forgot all about the stupid thirty-five cents, he realized. "I'm terribly sorry, Mrs. Wong. In all the excitement, I forgot your money."

"Folgot..?" She knew all about people who forgot. Nobody ever "forgets", they simply don't pay.

"I'm sorry. I'll have someone bring it in tomorrow. Thirty-five cents, right?"

"Light. You sule you bling? You no tlick me?"

"No, Mrs. Wong. I no trick you. We're neighbors. I'll have someone bring it tomorrow for sure." He bowed his head gravely.

Mrs. Wong, who was well versed on what a bow meant under these circumstances, bowed back three quick, low, dirty bows that would have shamed the Emperor himself.

But Rainy didn't seem to notice the insult. He just shambled on up the hill, looking very sad and old.

*

No fire burned in the cave, and after sundown it was cold. Unless Yoli missed her guess, this winter was going to be a lot less fun than any time in recent memory.

As a girl she had gone through a fireless winter in her father's cave, and she'd been cold all the time. Even though a gentle person, her father had insisted on practicing unheated conditions, so that everyone in his family would know that the Old Ways were perfectly livable; but after that year they'd always had fire. Yoli wondered now if that winter had been due to some emergency that her parents kept from the two girls. She would ask her mother at the Council. It seemed strange for a yeti family to keep something like that from the children, but maybe they had. Even though her parents didn't take the reckless chances that Montclief did, they were far from stiff. She remembered endless games and laughter in their big cave behind Winutchiwan. Maybe it was just that three females occupied it, and here there was only one. One was not enough. She might ask her mother about that, too.

It would be so good to see normal yetis again and be preoccupied with normal things, instead of always wondering what yrts were going to do. At least with no fire, her fur would grow thick and luxurious. She was sure to get many compliments on that. Maybe a childless bachelor would find her attractive. She loved Montclief, but there were so many buts. He was an extraordinarily fine provider and wise in every way, and just, and on and on. But she was young and she wanted to fool around and have other kinds of fun. He was so strict about fooling around, even after she'd explained so demurely that she was sure a certain bitter root potion would solve any problem that might come up. Her father had certainly not behaved so strictly about the taboos, and her mother was always happy, even though she perhaps talked too much. Maybe Yoli had chosen wrong. Of course, Chava was learning things from Montclief that few yeti youngsters would know, but she prayed he wouldn't grow up to be as cold-hearted as his father. Or as his half brother, Nuk, who lived wifeless far to the north.

But, of course, she had gained vast prestige by marrying Montclief. And they had been happy in the beginning.

Little Chava lay sleeping on an elk skin in the warmest nook of the cave. At least there was no draft to give the child a cold. Tomorrow he would have a full day. Montclief planned to let him lead the party the whole way, but Yolanda had her doubts. True, he was big for his age and strong, and he ran down rabbits at will, and had even killed two yearling deer single handedly; but he was only four years old. Montclief undoubtedly planned a slow pace in deference to the old one; but if any trouble occurred, Yoli planned to snatch up the baby and run to safety. She knew that would incur muttering and the cold shoulder from Montclief, but what was new about that? Four years old was too young to be tested with an eighty mile hike. This whole trip was stupid. The old grandfather could hardly walk eighty feet in those floppy sandals.

She wished Montclief would come home from wherever he was. When he left the cave, he had said he was going out to consult the omens. It was a little late for that, Yoli thought. He'd already called up the Council and invited old Rainpuddle, thereby putting everything at risk. Frumping down on her elk skin, she wondered why life couldn't be good and simple like it used to be? And why did she have to be smack in the middle of all the trouble? She would have to take sides at the Council, and she didn't know yet which side she would stand on. Why couldn't Montclief stay home on this night of all nights? His large body threw off a lot of heat. The cave was noticeably warmer when he was in it. And she might want to talk to him about the several things that were bothering her.

CHAPTER 16

DEFLECT A THOUSAND POUNDS WITH FIVE OUNCES

What is life really all about, Sri Rainy found himself wondering in the pre-dawn mist as he trudged up the mountain with his bedroll and the haversack of food on his back. He'd certainly thought he had known what his job in life was, but this past week had pushed him past that comfortable stability. That was good, he reminded himself, marching along toward his rendezvous with Montclief. Stultification is death. All real action is out on the cutting edge, but what did any of this—from Lotti to nuclear dumps to yetis—have to do with developing a successor to take his place in the Order? He couldn't get a meaningful handle on it, but it must be connected. After all, he had been given the mantle of leadership. The things that were happening to him must relate in some way to the continuity of the lineage. Wouldn't the laws of the world want to keep a true teaching in good working condition?

But maybe not. Maybe everything was in flux. Look at Tibet. Thousand of years of passing the dorje on from one master to the next generation. But not now. The Dalai Lama was doing his best to keep the tradition alive in Nepal, but for how long? The world had turned on that long established Buddhist Order.

The Seekers of Truth were less than two hundred years old. You'd think it would still be a viable, youthful teaching capable of spawning masters for generations to come. Unless the world was tired of all teachings for some reason. Or perhaps his interpretation of the Seekers' message had stumbled from the true path. Maybe so. It was conceivable.

Although he had scrupulously obeyed the tenets of poverty and self-sufficiency, maybe his spirit was dim. In truth, he had always wondered about that. How was a person to know, really? In moments of certainty during meditation, he knew he was on the right path for himself. He was a Seeker and had been taught by an enlightened master; but maybe he wasn't the stuff that great teachers are made from. Holders of the Light. Passers of the Flame. How was a person to know, except by seeing the light fully kindled in the being of a student? And he never had, had he? He didn't know—that was the annoying truth. He simply wasn't sure. And without that sure knowing, what right did he have to the mantle? And yet he was certain that he himself had been enlightened. Pamir Sando couldn't have been mistaken.

What if I wasted it all at the last minute on that girl, who had no chance at anything meaningful? No chance, and I knew it. But I kept on smelling after her, and let the Ungerer boy slip away. That's the tragedy. That's why you're a fake. After all these years, that's the kind of Seekers' master you turned out to be. A blind idiot, chasing skirts, leaving that boy to wait, like there was plenty of time at his critical point. But there is no time to delay at the crucial moment, only action. That's the rule. What if Pamir had let me flounder through that awful confusing time alone? It's no wonder that the boy had set out on his own. God knows where he is, and you're the biggest fool of your generation. He was sent to you, and you failed. Failed the Order and the future.

Yes, Sri Rainy wasn't altogether pleased with his recent conduct as he shuffled up the path beside Fawn Brook. And in addition, he didn't actually know where he was going. Montclief was supposed to find him when the coast was clear. Already, he'd walked far past his usual fishing areas. Looking around at the new and rather awesome landscape, Rainy thought it was a shame that he'd gotten out of the habit of exploring. It had been twenty years since he'd ventured this far afield.

When he first moved to the mountain, he'd taken a number of overnight trips, and in doing so had gotten a feel for the country where he'd chosen to live. But eventually the overnighters had dwindled to day trips and then just to fishing. Well, he'd been busy. A monastery doesn't run itself. But gosh, it was good to get out again. Refreshing. If he had kept up the practice of exploring, maybe he wouldn't have made so many stupid mistakes. But no use whipping himself over missed opportunities. He was out here now, heading toward something that no human had ever witnessed—no human even conceived that this was within the realm of the witnessable. No matter what his failings, he was a fortunate man. His spirits lifted with the new yellow sun. He felt hugely grateful to be afforded this opportunity.

A small green pine cone plunked onto the dirt three paces in front of him, quickening his mood of expectation. Since there were no pine trees overhead, he took this to be Montclief's signal. Often, the yeti would plink a pebble off his shoulder or hat. Rainy would plink a pebble off his shoulder or hat. Rainy glanced around, but instead of Montclief, a smaller version stuck his tawny head out from behind a jumble of rocks and motioned timidly with his furry hand. The small yeti looked almost cherubic. He even smiled shyly as he motioned again for Rainy to follow.

The fact that yetis came in various sizes made sense after the old fellow wrapped his brain around it. Just because Montclief and Yolanda were gigantic, didn't preclude there being short ones. He trucked up the hill after the fluffy brownish yeti, who purposely slowed himself down to stay in view, but made no effort to walk near Rainy.

After a few hundred yards, the guide stopped in an open clump of aspens and turned to wait. Rainy walked up, putting on his friendliest face and said a few words of greeting in Yetiese. Instead of answering, the guide twisted his head rather proudly to the left and out stepped Montclief, who returned the greeting. Yolanda stepped out beside her husband. She smiled briefly.

"This little one is my son," Montclief said, consciously gruff. "His name is, Chava, four winters old. He will guide us."

A surprised Sri Rainy turned to look at Chava. "Pleased to meet you, Chava," he said. A yeti child. How remarkable. He'd never realized that Montclief had a child. Where had the boy been hiding when he'd eaten dinner with them in the cave?

Montclief presented the old man to Chava. "His name is Rainy," said Montclief.

"Hello," said Chava very quietly, forming the English word as he'd been coached. He took a backward step toward his mother.

So the four of them journeyed laterally across the mountain, through majestic scenery, staying well away from any man-made paths. Rainy hadn't given much thought to how far they would walk or how long it might take. The yetis carried no baggage of any kind, and Chava set an unhurried pace. Rainy found he was surprising. Montclief had invited him, it was up to the yeti to make sure he arrived in one piece. But as the sun passed the midpoint and they still hadn't stopped to eat anything, only to drink from the brooks they passed, Rainy felt weakness creeping up from his empty stomach.

"When do we stop for lunch?" he inquired.

"Whenever the Spirit provides food," Montclief replied. "I'm hungry myself. Maybe you make too much noise, scare food away."

"You mean we don't eat until you catch some game?" That was a disconcerting thought. What if no game showed up? He could share his supplies with the yetis, but somehow he didn't think biscuits and canned beans would go all that far. He also had a sack of brown rice and a sauce pan for boiling, but that was for the evening meal when there was a fire. Being a fairly good woodsman, he had hoped to find some arrowhead potatoes or other wild aquatic tubers to augment his diet, and nuts and berries; but so far none of those things had presented themselves. He certainly wasn't going to eat grubs. He supposed they'd camp near a brook, and for that happy event, he'd brought a hand line and a few hooks. Fish he ate, of course; but he hadn't eaten flesh since, well, since a long time, and he wasn't going to further damage his karma by starting now. Losing track of Ungerer was the last wrong thing he was going to do, ever.

"I have biscuits and beans," Rainy offered. "We could share them."

"Thank you, but we are living the Old Way this winter," replied Montclief. "Are you tired? Do you need to rest?"

"No. I'm just hungry." Actually, Rainy was surprised that he wasn't bone weary. The hiking of the previous few days must have hardened him up some, and his feet were fine in the new boots.

"Chava is hunting for us on the journey," Montclief stated. "We should go on for a few more miles, then stop for the evening hunting."

"If we stop near a stream, I'll try for some fish," Rainy said, salivating. A few succulent trout roasting on a spit would be a superb finish to a perfect day.

*

The post office had been humming all afternoon, but now most of the humming noise was coming from the adding machine inside Willard Jacks' head. Yesterday he'd put a hefty down payment on a sixty acre parcel that old man Berlinheimer wanted to get rid of, and this morning he'd given two hundred dollars earnest money to Carl Shirtser to hold his rundown place up above Rickford Meadow until they could draw up the papers. At two-thirty he had an appointment at the Bank of Colorado in Clinton to arrange for both loans. Since his credit rating and employment record were excellent, and he'd gone to high school with the loan officer, he expected no trouble with the financing. It was only a hundred and thirty acres total, and his scheme to get the forestry service to replant it with quick growing white pine was almost foolproof. No matter what happened with the rumored repository, this was a good deal for him. The trees would be planted for watershed management, a free service according to the bulletin he'd posted on the office bulletin board several months ago. Even though white pine limbs were a little weak for holding ornaments, he could harvest them at Christmas when they were big enough. Folks in Denver wouldn't know the difference. Or he could wait until the trees matured, and log them for pulp. Either way he'd own a totally renewable resource. The payments on both places would be easily manageable on his salary, that's how good of a deal he'd gotten. Both farmers had been glad to get shut of their poor grazing land at a very cheap price. Old man Berlinheimer had needed the cash for his new false teeth and only ran a few sheep in the field anyway.

And then if this nuclear storage panned out, and the town did boom, he'd be fixed for life. Wealthy by forty. Maybe he'd take a trip back East and meet Lute Sims, then he could really tell him a couple of ideas for stories. Like this bear mauling saga. Everybody thought it was a bear doing all the damage; but what if it was a space alien in a grizzly suit trying to protect his fragile alien colony on top of the mountain? What a zinger of a story. The only person in the whole five state area who catches wind of the real culprit is the local mailman, who is independently wealthy and only stays on as the route man because it gives him a chance to drive around his county chatting with everybody—and getting pussy. No, maybe better leave out the pussy part. Willard wasn't sure how that would look in print. Maybe it was giving too much away about the fraternity of mail carriers.

*

More and more people kept arriving at the Retreat through the morning and into the afternoon, crying happily and embracing old friends, before getting down to work. Although delighted to get the help, Billy Bad Boy Drummond realized he was going to be short of his original estimates on virtually everything, from food to toilet tissue, envelopes and postage stamps. He also realized that the Retreat exchequer was pitifully inadequate. It didn't take a genius to figure that out, he'd already coughed up about two grand of his own limited funds in only three days. Sri really did live by his vow of poverty, but that didn't help much in time of crisis. At this rate, Billy wouldn't have a bank account by next week.

That was a disquieting thought. All that money he'd put up his nose. What a waste! And these people all thought he was well-heeled. This was going to get embarrassing very soon unless he could think of embarrassing very soon unless he could think of something. Sure, he could record an album, but the payoff from that would be months down the pike since he already owed Black Jack Records an album on his old contract. How could he get an advance on a new contract? Why had he been so stupid about business? One moron move after another, culminating with Edgar Buck overdosing. That took the cake. All those years when Edgar was his manager, Billy had pissed and moaned about him being a shark; then the instant he died, the great Bad Boy got so shook up he wouldn't talk to the billions of agents and personal managers who swarmed around salivating for his account. And as of today, a year later, he still hadn't hired anybody. Bright, really bright. Now when he needed somebody to cut him an advance, he didn't have a manager to do it. Beautiful. They'd laugh him out of town if he tried to negotiate for himself. So who did he know among all those sharks and reptiles who might understand anything that was going on up here? Nobody. Okay then, who could get him the biggest advance?

Maybe Sammy Gorsuch? Sammy was always hounding him with promises of how much he could do. Of course, Sammy was a loathsome scum, but he probably could get a deal with A&M. He had them in his pocket, at least that what he always boasted. He'd have Sammy set up a live recording session for the concert up here. A live album was always a smart idea. That would take care of his contract with Black Jack. Then Sammy would cut him a new deal with either A&M or somebody else. Great! He was thinking clearly again. This mountain was always fabulous for getting his shit together. If he could find time to slip down to the river with his guitar, maybe he could write some new songs. The only problem was when. These people kept him hopping every minute. Things were never so frantic in the old days. He'd never remotely recognized it before, but Sri must be an organizational whiz.

Two teams of letter writers were hard at it, typing and hand writing demands to Representatives and an evening activity group of letter writing, which would go on after dinner every night that Sri was away in meditation. Billy figured that they could inundate the Congressional Committee members of Energy and Natural Resources, making enough noise to start the ball rolling. If he could somehow get a national hook-up on his rock concert, that might also be very effective. He could make a plea for everybody to write their congressman. Obviously, rock and rollers were intelligent enough to be scared of nuclear waste. If a countrywide letter barrage could happen, that would certainly turn the tide and make them choose another site for the dump.

But two teams of letter writers didn't seem like much. Billy wished he could come up with a way to put more people on the task, now that all these ex-students had shown up. But they were also the cause of the snafu. He'd had to triple the gardening crew so that the harvest could get done quickly. Damnit, they needed the food, and they also needed the ten man maintenance crew that was fixing up the old dorm which hadn't been used in eight or nine years. Even cheap paint cost a fortune, and the small amount of lumber and tar paper he'd authorized to repair the roof was out of sight. Clinton Lumber and Supply had a monopoly, and milked it to death. Maybe he'd swallow his pride after dinner and announce that the Retreat needed money. That sounded simple, but none of these people appeared to have struck it rich in their years out in the real world. You'd think that at least one of them would have volunteered to kick in a few bucks, but so far that hadn't happened. They were all ecstatic to be here, hugging everybody in sight in an orgy of reunioning, and eager to give up their time in a good cause—but no dinero. Well, they could kick in enough to cover their own food. They'd have to buy food down on the flat land, they could buy it here, too.

And he wished that Sister Angie in the kitchen would stop stalking him like a cow in heat. He didn't want to rebuff her and have her sabotage the meals, but the thought of stuffing her made him slightly nauseous. He was beginning to understand that a vow of abstinence could be useful; but damn, he hated to make a big deal over a vow, because a couple of these cuties were immanently plugable, if he ever found time.

*

Since it was the evening of the third Tuesday of the month, there was a meeting at the Cooperative Grange Hall out on Highway 34. In a town with no movie theaters, no YMCA and no all night donut shop, a Co-op Meeting is often mistaken for a social event. The three women from the Spruce Lane Lodge thought it was their civic duty to be there, especially since Esther Olsterholt had the prestigious post of 1st Secretary, in charge of the notes. Esther's clear reading voice could hardly suppress its excitement each month until Tim Waters, the Co-op president, got through shaking hands and flirting long enough to call the meeting to order and request her to read the minutes of the previous meeting. Then after primly opening her typewritten notes, which showed everyone how conscientious and literate she was, her lilting speaking voice began recalling the deathless drivel they'd been arguing about last month—and which they had rehashed all month in their kitchens and would again rehash tonight, so that Esther could once more take it down in shorthand and recall it to them next month. Endless primary topics of conversation were: Grazing Rights Leases On Public Land, which poor ranchers couldn't get a fair share of; Government Price Supports, which poor farmers and ranchers didn't have enough acreage in production to get much of; Tourism And The Lack Of from Mary McCardle; and Social Events at the two churches and the rural high school. It was pretty exciting fare, and most folks left the meeting hot under the collar.

Esther was in good voice tonight. The minutes of the previous meeting had gone well, with no cat-calls for reading blunders. They loved to have their little jokes at the librarian's expense, but not tonight, thank you. Tim Waters then opened the meeting to new business, and Esther's ballpoint got ready to write. Randy Hinton, from over at the hardware store, popped up first like he always did for his spot of free advertising.

"Well, in light of the griz mauling epidemic," Hinton began. His salespitch always started with a current topic. "And since no house around here can be too safe from marauding bears, Hinton's decided to put high powered rifle shells on sale right up to the first day of deer season." He went on to detail the specials on bear loads, apparently unconscious of the fact that he put ammunition on sale every year at this time, so he could turn his stock over before it ossified.

Mary hopped up brightly for her monthly tourism speech, in which she always exhorted the township to put on a pumpkin festival or Easter egg festival—anything to get some tourists to drive up the mountain. Mary, herself, was pretty disgusted that the bear had been killed so soon. She hadn't even gotten an overnighter from all the excitement. True, she still had two rooms filled with hunting and fishing equipment rented to the two mauled doctors. She was keeping in daily contact with the hospital in Clinton about Dr. Yates' condition. If he recovered, she felt sure he'd be able to pay for the rooms, if not she supposed she'd have to bill the estates of both doctors. Toward that end, she had started a special ledger for the two rooms, including cleaning and telephone toll charges to the hospital.

"As some of you may know," Mary began, tight-lipped, "we should really start thinking about a welcoming committee for this new mine. Lord knows, a project like that would certainly be a boon to our tourism industry, and we should encourage them in any way possible."

The ensuing two hour discussion featured rumors and wild speculation based on those rumors, starring slinky young Lotti as the key witness for the future. Under heavy cross-questioning by the local worthies, Mary appeared often in a supporting role to give corroborating testimony, and even Esther herself, made a lengthy cameo appearance to detail the documents she'd seen in Dr. Yates' room with Lotti and Sri Rainy. This last bit of reportage was accomplished with nobody questioning the eyewitnesses very closely as to how they happened to arrive at the main venue. Around ten-fifteen, the meeting broke up, having ground the gossip into a very fine, digestible powder. Only Esther's spiral shorthand book prevented the meeting from going far into the night. When she announced the lamentable fact that the book was filled, Tim Waters shouted his willingness to hear a motion for adjournment rather than have the war lost for want of a loose nail (or in this case a note pad.) Esther's writing hand was beginning to cramp up, anyway. During the milling around which followed, she was able to mention her poor cramped hand thirty times or so, and to milk out an equal number of sympathetic responses. All in all, it was a very gratifying evening, and a follow-up meeting was unanimously agreed to for two nights hence.

Somehow or other, Sri Rainy had failed to bring his ground cloth along on the hike. As a consequence, the cold and damp was already leeching up through the quilting of his sleeping bag. Although he had scraped out hip and shoulder depressions in the loamy soil under a pine thicket, and he was currently almost comfortable, the old camper felt sure that before morning he would be stiff and freezing. Perhaps he'd catch pneumonia and die on this little expedition. That would serve him right for forgetting the ground cloth.

After hard hiking all day, dinner around the campfire should logically be a cheerful affair with the smells of roasting meat and trout, and it was eventually. But first, Rainy got to experience a yeti marriage squabble.

Montclief had apparently laid down some kind of rule about no fires for the duration of the uneasiness over the nuclear dump. Yolanda seemed to think that was a silly idea, and so did Rainy for obvious reasons. The argument was very quaint, actually. Rainy enjoyed it extremely from a sociological point of view, and it also reminded him of the somewhat daily bickering that his parents had indulged in all his life before he left home.

His parents no longer bickered, of course. Years ago, they had passed into a better realm, or a worse one, or at least different. Or perhaps to nowhere at all. Rainy felt that he should have a better idea of how things transpired after death, but he simply didn't know. He'd spent practically his whole life reading about and investigating phenomena that purported to offer explanations. The problem was that so many of the theories and eye witness accounts differed radically. Realistically, how was he supposed to know what happened at death, until he died himself? Then all the students who expected answers from him would, no doubt, be left in the same lurch he'd always been in—no answers, and no access to friends who had died. No way of knowing for sure what it was all about.

Well, he'd find out the real facts soon, as soon as this up-coming bout of pneumonia settled in his lungs and killed him. Perfect. And he couldn't even blame anybody but himself for forgetting the ground cloth. He'd had it laid out on his bed, then walked out the door without it. Slippages like that filled him with such chagrin that he knew it must be time to quit this charade of being a teacher. A mind was supposed to stay razor sharp well past a hundred years unless chemical imbalances impaired its functioning. Reluctantly, he acknowledged that such an imbalance might be causing him to forget things. Possibly he'd always had it, and Pamir hadn't noticed the deficiency when he insisted that Rainy was prepared to go forth and teach the Way of Seeking Truth. Quite possibly Pamir had been a fake, too. Strange that he'd waited sixty years to think those thoughts, but better late than never, he supposed. Or maybe a fever was setting in?

At any rate, the spat between Montclief and Yolanda had ended with a small fire being kindled by Yolanda, while Chava went out hunting. The little campfire burned cheerily, practically smoke free. Rainy had set his brown rice to cooking, then he and Montclief stepped down to the tiny brook, and with crude fishing gear caught a nice mess of native cut throats. That had made the day's hike well worth while. The little beauties were so eager to bite that Rainy was sure this clear brook had never been fished in, or certainly not for a very long time.

By the time they had a nice stringer of fish threaded on a willow switch, Chava had returned with five rabbits, three snowshoe hares and two cotton tails. Yolanda had gathered a peck or so of pine nuts and was roasting them in a reflector oven made with three flat stones. All in all, it was a meal fit for a king. And although Montclief groused about the stink they were putting up for anyone to smell within two hundred miles, he ate the cooked rabbit and fish with undisguised pleasure. In fact, everything was fabulous until Rainy discovered that he'd forgotten his ground cloth.

*

Hy Many Blankets had insisted on being home in time for the feast. So his cousin, Buddy Wolf, had driven Hy's pickup over to the hospital and Hy had signed himself out, in spite of the condescending frown of the head nurse.

Even if he were dying, which Hy wasn't, no Kiowa brave would miss the chance to sing his song of counting coup on brother grizzly, nor miss the once in a lifetime opportunity of being the big warrior at a ceremonial Bear Heart feast. Staying in the hospital, even though it was paid for by the hated Forest Service, would miss him his chance to see the women's eyes glow in his direction, and the other men's grudging envy at his hunting bravery. So he signed his name, and leaning on Buddy Wolf's shoulder, he maintained his proud bearing as they walked out to the parking lot, even though he was in quite a bit of blinding pain.

When the wounds healed, Hy decided to go shirtless the rest of his life, weather permitting, so that the claw scars of honor could be seen by all. Maybe he would even rip off the bandages tomorrow during his song and show the fresh wounds complete with two hundred and six stitches. No, that probably wasn't a smart idea. If his chest muscle came unpegged, he'd have to endure old Two Eagles chanting over him for a couple of hours, pecking at him with a mummified eagle claw, before anyone would drive him back to the hospital. When the wounds were healed would be the right time to show off the scars. He could draw another crowd. Even kids would leave their pathetic TV sets to see that.

After discussing how bumpy it would be to recline in the back of the pickup, which was where Hy had thought he'd ride home in glory, Hy let Buddy help him into the cab. Sitting proudly erect, he crossed his arms—the good one over the broken one in the plaster cast—across his chest to hold himself together. Even then the bumpy ride was a trial of bravery, since the pickup's suspension was none too good. Hy had been meaning to get that fixed. Oh well, he could still be dignified by gritting his teeth against the pain as they jounced up the rutted road to Willow Mesa Camp, as it was called.

Willow Mesa Camp was an smallish section of bare rocky tumbleweed desert, on the far west side of

Mukatee, or The Devil's Tooth. In 1949, the government had built an encampment for the tribe on the worthless land. A dozen clapboard houses. All the buildings had deteriorated into shacks over the years. Hey ya, it was home, and they didn't have to pay rent. The grandfathers had made a huge mistake in leasing their family reservation land for ninety-nine years to that big grazing outfit. But what was done was done, even under duress. They wouldn't get their own land back for 58 more years. That was a short time in the history of the Eastern Kiowa Nation. Maybe the Bear Heart Ceremonial would keep them strong at Willow Mesa.

Buddy Wolf and two other men had taken a pack horse up to the dry meadow and packed out the heart and as much meat as they could carry. Buddy said the meat was still okay, even though the skin and head were missing. The bear meat would begin boiling at dawn in the traditional way, so it would be tender by the end of the dance. Well, not totally traditional, none of the women remembered how to weave water-tight baskets, so they would use aluminum cooking pots. But they would heat rocks in a fire, then tong the hot rocks into the cauldrons. They would do their best to get the ceremony right. Hy Many Blankets felt sure the Great Spirit would overlook that small infraction. He had been guided to the bear so the Ceremonial could take place, hadn't he?

The pickup bounced to a stop in front of the clapboard shack belonging to Hy and Bettita Many Blankets. He noticed that another pane of glass had been broken out of the front window in his absence. Damn those kids. Why couldn't they be out hunting, instead of always playing their stupid football. White man's football in the autumn, baseball in spring and summer. Broken windows all year long with never an offer to fix them. And in between breaking windows, they watched TV. Hey ya, one more thing for him to repair before winter. Next year he'd have a teepee with no windows to break. Delivering that news to chunky

Bettita would be better than any TV show. He climbed carefully out of the pickup, surprised that no one had run out of the house to greet him. Bettita would probably divorce him if he insisted on living in a teepee. Oh, well. Maybe the Great Spirit would provide him with a thin new wife who was interested in living traditionally. Someone had to keep the Old Ways before it was too late.

CHAPTER 17

TO LIFT UP ONE MUST FIRST UPROOT

Dawn's first pink light climbed into the sky, a gift from Father Sun. The drumming began. Hy Many Blankets, regaled in the fringed buckskin shirt that identified him as the war chief, stepped the initial pattern of slow, searching steps that was the Hunting Bears Dance. The footwork of this dance was identical to the Warrior Spirit Ceremonial, except that the drumming was less syncopated. It was partly because he already knew the dance that Hy originally thought of doing the ceremony. The Old Ways spoke of thirty or more ceremonials, but he had only learned four so far. This dance, which was actually two dances, had been taught to him by old Charlie Prairie Grass when he became the war chief elect. As a boy he had learned the other two—the Corn Dance, borrowed from the

Navaho, and the wild Bride's Dance, which was sort of a fertility rite that left plenty of room for improvisation.

The stepping of the Bear Dance had to be vigorous. Each time his heel made contact with the packed earth in the back yard of his hovel, a thrill of pain shot down his legs from his still too fresh wounds, but that was the price and the honor of being a warrior—being able to look pain in the face and then disregard it. Actually, he had never imagined his wounds would hurt so much. It must be the heavy cast pulling his right arm down, stretching the tender muscles. He only needed to dance once through the ceremony, then he could stop and sing his deeds. Forty-five minutes of bone wracking pain was nothing—certainly less than nothing compared to the sacrifice of the heroic grizzly who had given his life so that the tribe could live. He danced to the Great Bear Spirit and as he stomped through the bruin-like footwork in this part of the Ceremonial, he felt himself lifted above the pettiness and continual heartbreak of being a Native American nigger in this white man's cycle. Brother Bear was returning to the tribe, he could feel it, to guide them back to health and sobriety. The wind of change was in the air, throbbing with the drumbeat. Hy Many Blankets was one with nature, so deeply into the dance that he didn't notice the first raindrops falling on his upturned face. The big, wet drops fell all around him, imploding in the dry dirt like a miniature meteor shower. The drumming continued, building to a killing frenzy. Sensibly, the women scattered to cover their cooking fires, pulling tarpaulins over spindly aspen teepee frames. Another ceremonial spoiled by the treacherous weather of Willow Mesa, where nothing went right. The women muttered; but at least, their cooking fires would be safe this time. They had taken warning from the sky. Evening gray and morning red, pours down rain on the hunter's head. Even though the Channel 4 news had said it would be a fine day, they all knew about Willow Mesa. A Ceremonial in this arid place always drew the rain. They stood under the protective tarps by the warm fires, watching that fool Hy Many Blankets. Already his moccasins were picking up heavy mud clots. Soon the other men would join him, sloshing up a sea of mud in Bettita's back yard. At least tonight most of them would refrain from drinking whiskey. They would be tired and feeling good from the dancing and the rich bear meat, and maybe some of them would even feel like fooling around.

Hy Many Blankets continued dancing. He was aware of the rain now, and the mud clinging to his feet. The longer he danced the odd, lurching gait, the more he felt like Brother Bear stomping through a boggy willow swamp with his long muzzle lifted up to smell something—something good that was coming, if only he could persevere through this quagmire.

Sri Rainy wasn't real happy to hear the rain drops pattering on the canopy of pine boughs. After a hearty breakfast, he and the yetis had been walking steadily northward since dawn. Rainy was hopeful that they were nearing the meeting place. Although he felt remarkably fit this morning, not troubled in the least by pneumonia symptoms, it didn't seem reasonable that Montclief would want him to walk farther than two days. But this rain..!

"Will the meeting be in a cave?" he asked hopefully, holding his hand out to catch a raindrop.

"Metawonga," Montclief replied, sourly. "Many small caves." He seemed somehow displeased about either the word Metawonga, whatever that was, or about the small caves.

Actually, Rainy had found himself growing annoyed with his friend's sullenness. He had never seen the yeti in so gruff a mood before. Well, that wasn't true exactly, he was always serious; it was just that Rainy could always go home to the monastery when he'd had enough heaviness. The surprising part of this trip was that he was enjoying Yolanda's company immensely. He'd always thought of her as tense and bitchy, but she wasn't at all. The opposite was true, in fact. The way she and the lad interacted was delightful. It was touching how tender they were; but strangely, that seemed to tick Montclief off. Well, he was probably under a lot of pressure. Bringing a human along must put him on the line. If the tables were reversed, I'd be wondering if a yeti would act right at an ecumenical council. Of course, at a council of Seekers, it wouldn't much matter how a yeti acted. Wrong. It would matter very much. I wouldn't want him to make even one extra wave, by himself, just him being there would cause plenty of turbulence. But, surely Montclief knows that he doesn't need to worry about me causing extra commotion. After I explain to a bunch of non-English speaking yetis what nuclear waste is all about, I'll just sit quietly and observe their discussions.

He pulled his hood up and kept walking, knowing he'd be soaked within a few minutes. A rain poncho was another item he'd neglected to pack. A poncho, of course, could have doubled as a ground cloth, and a ground cloth as a poncho. But why be a cry baby about it? He obviously had everything he needed, or else he would have remembered the two things any boy scout packs first. Think positively. He certainly wouldn't need a bath, and wouldn't need to wash his robe either. Fine.

If he had bothered to pay as much attention to his surroundings as to his thoughts, he might have seen the wrist-sized tree limb that reached out and clonked him on the head, showering his cosmic awareness with dazzling blue and white stars.

It's strange that the collective consciousness of a small town can get so stoked over a nothing, a rumor. A rumor that probably isn't going to happen at all, and certainly isn't going to happen until the studies and committee reports and lobbying is completed.

The town of Pike's Grove was split on the issue, naturally; but since most folks felt that they were stuck up against the economic wall on this mountain, the split was something like seventy/thirty in favor of poisoning the rocks and glens of their township far, far into the foreseeable future.

No other topic of conversation was heard, not even the weather, for the entire rainy day following the Co-op meeting. Land values doubled overnight, causing the normally placid Willard Jacks to start scheming on how to re:double his little nest egg. It seemed pretty evident that if he bought some more land right away, it too would double or triple. And the nearer he could buy to the actual site of the repository, the better off he would be. Although he didn't actually know, and nobody knew one damned actual fact about the project, Willard put two and two together and came up with high ground. The bear mauling had taken place way up there, and those two geologists hadn't hiked through that rough terrain for kicks. The problem was that most of the high ground was either owned by conglomerates who speculated decades into the future, or by the State. The only high ground parcels that conceivably would come up for sale were Asa Peters' place up in Mudslide Pass, or the hippie Retreat. It seemed like it might be worth his time to drop in at the Spruce Lane Lodge and chat awhile with hot little Lotti. She might know some secret about the location that she wasn't sharing.

Although Lotti acted light on smarts, she was cunning, and she seemed to know more about the site plan than anyone else. Besides, screwing her hadn't been as humdrum as he'd thought at the time. It had been pretty good, in fact. If he could get her to loosen up a little, it might even be damned good.

*

Mary McCardle was vitally interested in the rumor mill surrounding the repository, but from the opposite angle. All her talk and prodding about tourism at the Co-op meeting had been a feint. What Mary wanted, and what her mind was cranking on like a rusty windmill in a storm, was the possibility of unloading this albatross of a hotel. She was sure that nobody, not even the Atom Bomb people, would seriously consider coming to this mountain. Some problem would arise at the last minute and the project would go elsewhere. This town was jinxed, and she wanted out—and she especially wanted out if the pit *was* dug. Hard-boiled Mary didn't want to be within a thousand miles. God no! It gave her the willies to think of living on top of all that crawly-wiggly stuff, like the green guck that made watches glow at night. No, not her.

Nothing good had happened to her up here. In fact, nothing good had happened since Phil left her stranded, the prick. Nope, the first decent offer she got, she and the brat were bailing out. No living next door to mutant, slavering werewolves for Mary McCardle! No thanks! People up here were strange enough already. She sure wasn't sticking around to watch them start glowing and doing unspeakable atrocities to each other. She felt sorry for all these poor saps, thinking they were going to get an easy life from now on, thanks to the government dole. Fat fricking chance—not in Pike Township.

Her mind never stopped cranking while she checked a short, beaky guest in a safari jacket into the Lodge and installed him in Room 12. Usually, she would have pumped a new guest for information about his ancestors and news from the outside world; but this guy looked like such a geeky fly fisherman that she didn't bother to pump him. And the sleeves of his jacket were slightly frayed, indicating that he wasn't a prospect for buying the Lodge.

*

If Mary had asked, Lute Sims would have been glad to tell her all about himself. He found he always got enough towels and a decent bed, if the hotel management thought he might write something about them. But as the lady hadn't asked, he didn't tell. That was also a rule of his. He let the vibes of a situation develop naturally, without imposing his will on it. To be totally incognito allowed him to noodle around for his story without signing autographs, which was sometimes better than having enough towels. Not that he'd have to worry about autographs up here. From the appearance of the people he'd seen, he doubted if anybody could read.

The fact that the keen nose of a famous science fiction writer like Sims had caught wind of the happenings on this particular obscure mountain wasn't nearly as strange as it might seem. He'd been on the cutting edge of weird stories for many years. His nose seemed to sniff them out of mid-air, and since traveling around to get honest local color in his stories could be taken off his taxes, he found himself holed up in some pretty odd locales for months at a time. This particular trip was more than a coincidence however. Some Podunk mailman had sent him a letter offering his Podunk town as a setting for a Lute Sims novel. And on the very same day that he'd gotten the letter, his son, Jack, had called with a belated birthday greeting, and casually mentioned that he'd been on a bear hunt with the Governor of Colorado within a few miles of the same Podunk town that the mailman lived in. That was yesterday. Within the hour, Lute had made a reservation from Kennedy Airport; and now he was in Pike's Grove, having no idea what was going on, but being damned sure that something was.

Lute stashed his portable computer in a dresser drawer and his socks and underwear in another, then went back downstairs to search for a coffee shop. He normally found that waitresses were much more talkative, and what they said was more germane than any bartender he'd ever met. The reason being, he supposed, that bartenders were so tired of listening to drunks that they didn't bother to listen to anybody, thus as sources of information they were kind of zilch.

Coming down the stairs, Lute Sims knew he'd made the right decision again. The story goddess was still smiling on him. A uniformed mailman was standing beside the registration desk chatting with the dried-up proprietress.

When Willard looked up and saw his hero, Lute Sims, his mouth fell open in a parody of a goldfish. He was boggled. "You're Lute Sims!" he blurted. He had just made a killing in real estate, and now this. It was unbelievable! "I'm the mailman that just wrote you a letter."

"Uh, yes," said Lute. He smiled as he remembered the mnemonic for the mailman's name, and scuttled across the scrubbed board floor to shake hands. "You must be Mr. Jacks. Very interesting possibilities in your note. Thought I'd come up and take a look." They shook hands warmly. The mnemonic was "cracks". Cracks Jacks. This referencing to sex was a little cheap, but it worked.

Coincidences like this happened so frequently when his keen nose was leading him down a hot track, that Lute almost expected them. He was perfectly content to change any preconceived plan at a moment's notice, when the story goddess brought him a fresh contact. If the nose was onto something good, the inevitability factor was staggering.

Mary McCardle watched this passion play taking place before her eyes with grim equanimity. She expected nothing unusual from Willy Jacks. He was the mailman. But she did feel a twinge of impatience toward herself for not interviewing this beaky guest more closely.

"I can't believe it," Willard burbled, succumbing to an advanced case of hero worship. "I've read every one of your books."

"Why don't we go somewhere and get a cup of coffee?" the writer invited. "I'm sure we must have a lot to talk about."

Willard nodded his head agreeably. Since there was no coffee shop in town, he had to make a quick decision whether to take Lute Sims to his cabin or to the post office. Technically, he wasn't off duty yet, in fact the mail wasn't all delivered; but maybe it could wait today. This was hardly a normal situation. To further add to the confusion, Lotti came clacking down the stairs in a sky blue tank top, white short shorts, black hose and red leather pumps with a strap across the arch.

"Hi, Willard," she called out, going directly to the kitchen to pour herself a glass of milk.

Willard responded as if he'd been ham strung. He had to talk to Lotti right away—and he had to talk to Lute Sims. And of course, he had to deliver the rest of the town route. Not delivering it would wither his self respect. What a pickle.

Stepping into the awkward gap, Mary McCardle turned to her new Room 12 and asked, "Are you and Willard old friends? Why didn't you say so? I thought you was just passing through."

"In a matter of speaking, I am passing through, in the sense that we're all passing from Point A to Point B," the small man said with a charming, toothy smile. "And in the same sense, I suppose you could say that Mr. Jacks and I are friends."

"I see," Mary replied, not sure that she did see, but unwilling to start trouble about it with a paying guest. Nobody but weirdoes ever came up here. She was taking the first reasonable offer she got and moving to someplace where people were normal.

Lotti came swishing into the lobby with her glass of milk and a handful of Oreo cookies. Both sets of male eyes swiveled toward her rather obviously. Anyone who had ever read a Lute Sims book knew that Lute had an eye for the ladies. There was always an exotic female in distress featured prominently in the plot. That was one reason Willard liked the books.

"Are you a guest here, Miss?" Lute inquired,

seeming both harmless and interested.

"She's my daughter," Mary snapped.

"Ah, I thought I recognized a family resemblance," Lute Sims, the wily cocksman replied, without missing a beat. "Your husband must be Greek or perhaps Southern Italian?"

"Hardly," Mary replied. "I have no husband."

"Unusual," Sims commented, mostly to himself. He certainly didn't want to have a scene with his humorless boarding house lady. Humorless people were his #1 pet peeve. Lack of humor seemed to go hand in hand with mental slowness, and neither one added up to book sales. "Well, nice to meet you, Miss."

Lotti had poised herself on the first step of the staircase with her long sexy right leg extended up to the second stair, thereby putting a strain on her round buttock muscle and the short shorts covering it. Willard Jacks, while dull, was still a potential ride to Hollywood. She didn't know who this other shrimp was, but his jacket and shoes were expensive. From the way he was ogling her, he would be an easy mark if he turned out to be somebody useful.

"What room are you in?" she asked, coyly.

"Mr. Sims is a friend of Willy's," Mary interjected. "Don't be bothering him."

"Are you from the mine?" Lotti asked, disregarding her mother as if she wasn't in the room.

Willard couldn't stand it. This lack of respect to a national treasure like Lute Sims was intolerable. It was bad enough that they didn't know who he was, but they didn't even ask. "Mr. Sims is a very famous writer," he said, blasting them with the truth. "He's probably the most famous person who's ever been in this town."

"Oh, really?" Mary and Lotti answered in unison.

"I'm not all that well known," Lute replied, soft pedaling his success like he always did. Although as a science fiction writer he was far from being a media darling, his books had sold over sixteen million copies world wide, and because of that he was rather well-heeled. He often wondered about this lack of critical success. It seemed to him that his books were as thoughtful as those of supposedly "serious" writers. Oh well. He tried never to let it bother him on the way to the bank.

Willard stepped closer to the stairwell. "Could I see you later tonight," he asked Lotti in a very low voice, moving his lips hardly at all. To the other people in the room, Willard looked like an imitation of a bad ventriloquist, frogging the words up from his Adam's apple. Willard, naturally, didn't realize this behavior was juvenile and ridiculous. This low voice had always worked on the farm wives he was trying to get next to. Actually, he was pretty sure that no matter how low he talked, Mary would be able to eavesdrop on him; but he continued on in the frog whisper since he'd already committed himself. "I have to get a coffee with Mr. Sims for a couple of hours, but then I really need to talk to you."

"Are you going to Clinton for coffee?" Lotti asked in her normal voice, maybe even a little louder than normal. She knew where the nearest coffee shop was. "I'd love to ride over to Clinton with you, so I could check on Yatesy." Checking on Yatesy would give her something new to talk about at the Co-op meeting.

"No," Willard said stiffly in his normal voice, since the little twat had blown his secrecy. Served him right for sucking up to a shit-for-brains teeny-bopper. "We're just going to grab some coffee at the post office."

"How far is this Clinton place?" Lute Sims interjected. It seemed that fate had presented him with two interviewees, one a delicious young trollop who he wanted to investigate fully. And Clinton was the town that Jackie, his son, had mentioned.

"It's not that far," Lotti pouted. "They have the cutest little coffee shop."

"That would be fine with me, Willard," he said, beaming at the mailman. "Don't worry, you and I will have plenty of time to chew the fat alone. My son is planning to meet me up here in a day or two, so I'll be staying the better part of a week. Plenty of time to see this cute little coffee shop if that's all right with you."

"Sure, I guess so," Willard agreed. It didn't make sense to bicker over where they'd have coffee. Hell, anyplace that Lute wanted to go was fine with him. "We'll just zip though my mail route, then we'll head on over to Clinton. You gonna be warm enough?"

"Is it cold out?" Lute asked, testing the fabric of his brush jacket between his thumb and finger.

"The jeep gets a little drafty," Willard admitted. "And it might rain again."

"Maybe I'd better get a sweater, then."

"Good idea, Simsy," Lotti sang out. "I'll change my clothes, too, while you're doing that." She sprang up the stairs like an antelope on her flaming red spike heels.

The nurse on duty was the same black girl, who had been there the last time. If Lotti had lived in Clinton, instead of dull Pike's Grove, she could have gotten a glamorous job like this girl. Deciding on a no nonsense approach, Lotti asked firmly for Dr. Yates' room number. The nurse got such a sad look that Lotti was afraid Yatsey had died.

"He's not dead, is he..?" Lotti moaned. "I'm his sister!"

"Didn't they tell you?" Wilma Dexter asked, incredulously. "They moved him to Mary land early this morning."

"Mary land..?" Where the hell was Mary Land? Was this nurse being tactful because Yatsey had died? Instead of Heaven, she called it Mary Land?

"They moved him to that Walter Reed Hospital for government folks in Bethesda, Mary land."

"Oh, my God! Is he getting better?"

"I'm sorry, but I don't think so. I heard they wanted to take him to a specialist back there. Your mother and father went along."

"I just came in from California," Lotti lied, not remembering her previous lie had been Des Moines. She didn't even wonder why she was lying. It just seemed like the right thing to say.

"You poor thing," Wilma commiserated, thinking Lotti must be an airline stewardess. "Do you know where this Bethesda is? It must be close to Washington, D.C., I guess."

"Yes," Lotti said. "Well, back to the airport."

"I'm sorry," Wilma said, sympathetically. Lotti turned and left the hospital, with much clacking of her high heels on the institutional tile floor. She'd have to think of another reason to come to this hospital lobby. It was a perfect place to practice her dramatic exits for Hollywood.

As the afternoon wore on, the rain at the higher altitudes turned to snow. Big wet flakes stuck to bushes and pine trees, but the rocky ground was still warm enough to melt them. Sri Rainy was pretty thoroughly miserable. Winter was not supposed to come on this early, even though it did every year. One minute it was Indian Summer, and the next minute winter was here to stay in the high country. He hoped most of the potatoes were in, or at least rowed up. It wasn't much fun to dig them out of frozen ground like the students had to last year.

The red woolen long johns that he had remembered to pack were now sodden underneath his robe, but at least the itchy wool kept in some of his body heat, even when the fabric was wet. Actually, he must have been crazy to come along on this expedition.

The snow didn't affect the yetis at all, seemingly. In fact, the colder it got, the happier they were. Small wonder. Summer must be hell with all that fur. Rainy had never thought of that before. Disgusting, but he was concerned mainly with his own comfort, always had been. It was true. Living on the mountain was no deprivation to him. The poverty vows had never strained him either, not with a garden and virtual slave labor to work it. And if the garden ever failed, his relatively wealthy students weren't about to let him starve. No, he'd had an easy life, no matter what outside people thought. Pitiful, really. He'd sought a life of austerity, but what a fake it was compared to a yeti's' life. All three yetis came on this trip with nothing whatsoever, except themselves. And they were thriving. Were they less holy than he, just because getting sopping wet made him suffer? Hardly.

"Nice day for a walk," he called out to Montclief, mustering his last ounce of cheeriness. Actually, the cold was really starting to affect him. Hypothermia was right around the corner. Had to be. He certainly had no body fat to prop up his heat level. How cold did a guy get before he started to hallucinate that he was warm as toast? Isn't that what happens? Obviously, he wasn't that cold yet, because he was still cold as Hades. And his head still throbbed dully from the bump on the head. Looking down at his hand, he noticed that his fingernails were turning blue.

Montclief waited for Rainy to catch up with him. The truth was that wet snow and rain didn't particularly fill him with joy. He didn't allow himself to feel cold as long as there was enough meat to fuel his inner furnace; but after an hour or so in the rain, his fur got saturated and heavy. He was probably lugging thirty extra pounds right now, but then so was everybody else. Tough shit. Rain and snow happens. "Come on, old friend," he said, putting his huge arm protectively around Rainy. "Walk up front with me. Let the boy and his mother come behind us."

And so, they topped a small rise into Metawonga, The Meeting Bowl. The gathered congregation of wild yetis caught their first glimpse of Sri Rainy in the place of honor, side by side with Montclief, coming to their Council Meeting to clue them in to the facts of the real world.

Set in a deep limestone bowl honeycombed with caves and surrounded by tall cedar trees, Metawonga must have been a charming and friendly meeting place in good weather. But in the drizzling snow, fifty or so yetis stood outside their caves, looking none too pleased. A number of small springs gurgled down the rocks to join in a deep pool at the bottom of the meteor crater. That's what had made the bowl shaped depression, Rainy surmised—a smallish meteor strike at sometime in the distant past. The structure and rock formation weren't like the blow-cone of a volcano.

In most of the occupied caves cheery fires were flickering. Obviously, the yetis thought themselves to be safe in this spot. And probably were. Rainy, who was not a novice in the woods, had no idea where he was. He didn't think Montclief had tried to confuse him, there had simply been too many switch backs, stream fordings and irregular ascents and descents to keep track of where he was exactly. Which wasn't to say he was entirely lost. Following almost any stream would eventually take him down the mountain to civilization, no matter which mountain it was. If a flock of yetis felt secure, this was certain to be remote, probably a Federally controlled wild area, or maybe reservation land. Ute territory had some pretty inaccessible places; but he didn't think they had trekked that far west.

As for the yetis, they really didn't look too friendly. Many sets of cautious black eyes set in grey furry faces watched his progress down into the bowl. Several of them looked angry, but all of them looked warm. Rainy couldn't wait to get inside one of those cosy caves, so he could dry out.

Although acting stern, Montclief was very annoyed. All of the tribe had come, as they always did when the summons went out; but where was the central fire with an elk or deer roasting on a communal spit? That's the way it should be unless there was a major rift that didn't allow the disagreeing parties to share food. Balls. They were against him. Rainy would witness an explosive few days, instead of the productive talks that Montclief had hoped for.

He led his party down the old path toward the hard-packed space near the lake. There he stopped beside a ring of ancient, fire blackened rocks. The others stopped around him. No yeti called to greet him in the Old Way. One by one, they turned their backs and went into the caves. So that was it, then. He was isolated. They had heard he was bringing a yrt, and no one believed it was a good idea to hear from the enemy. Well, that was one of the possibilities he had foreseen. Tough shit. Just like the fact that it was snowing. He might be unable to sway an unanimous majority so that the talks could begin, but he would try.

Lifting his face, he peered around the bowl at the backs of his life-time friends. He opened his mouth and shouted in his stentorial voice. "Greetings, friends! I bring with me two newcomers. One is my young son, Chava, who has never been here." He motioned for Chava to stand in front of him. "He is a yeti who is being taught the Old Ways, but who will live to see the new days."

Chava looked down in embarrassment at being singled out. Montclief was well pleased with his son, although he himself hadn't been embarrassed when his father had introduced him. But those were different days. The mountains then had not been totally encroached by white skins.

"And I break tradition to bring a friend," Montclief shouted, even louder. "This old one of the white star men has told me many interesting things that are not in conflict with our beliefs, and he brings word of a thing that is coming to change life very much for us. He is my friend, Rainy, who I have known for ten winters, since after the time that Darla was killed saving a white skin."

No one shouted a greeting, no one moved forward

from the cave mouths. Montclief nonchalantly scratched a serrated X mark in the old ashes of the fire pit with the nails of his right foot. "Build the central fire here, please," he said to Yolanda.

CHAPTER 18

CULTIVATE BUT NOT TO HARVEST

A broadchested dark yeti stalked from one of the smaller caves and stood glaring down at the soggy foursome as they dragged wet wood to make their fire. At length he took several paces forward and bared his teeth.

Yolanda shivered. She watched him from the corner of her eye while whirling her fire stick in a nest of tinder fluff. Alienated. She hated it. Even her family was staying inside their cave mouth, watching, but making no move to welcome her or to bring a flaming stick from their fire. Did they think this was her fault? Montclief had had the dream, not her. She was just coming to the Council to introduce their son, like every mother did. What was she supposed to do, walk away from Montclief so they'd talk to her? Impossible. At least the resiny cedar would be easy to start, then she would look for sweet hardwood to bank the fire.

Sri Rainy, too, sensed the hostility. He was by no means prepared for this welcome. Were his vibes so bad that a tribe of yetis thought he was an evil person? Impossible. The same Spirit moved in all of them, yetis and humans. He was positive of that. Maybe these meat eaters were too crude to see it. Certainly he had been scoffed at by low-life rabble in cities when as a young monk he insisted on wearing his robes. Could this be the same mindless red-neck scenario?

Had Montclief and Yolanda somehow mutated far beyond these others? He'd never thought of that. Would Montclief fight for him if a bully attacked? Probably, but what good would it do? There were far too many of the dullards.

"Greetings to my brother, Chava!" the massive, dark yeti bellowed. His abrasive voice caromed around the sides of the bowl, seeming to knock the snow off the hanging cedar boughs. Chava looked up at the snarling face, and smiled. "And greetings to my father and his new wife!" the dark yeti added, as an afterthought.

Rainy heard this as unintelligible gnashing and booming sounds. He knew there were words in it, but his message center couldn't sort them out.

"Greetings to my son, Nuk," Montclief snarled back, slowly, so that Rainy could understand. "Come down and talk beside the warm fire." A little smoke curled up from Yolanda's tinder. "Speak slowly. My friend hears our words, but slowly. He is intelligent, but then he is only a yrt."

Yrt was the derogatory word for man. Rainy heard that clearly. It meant something like, "skin like a slimy slug." Judging from the low laugh that shook his belly, Montclief had made a joke.

"Nuk is not cold," the dark yeti answered, haughtily. "Stone men live the Old Way. Stone men have no dealings with yrts that can be talked about in the presence of the enemy. This council will have no talk. Next time come without your yrt." Nuk turned his back and stomped into his cave. There was not a murmur of protest about so young a yeti as Nuk speaking on behalf of the rest. He was known as a serious, conservative yeti, as both his deceased grandfathers had been.

"We will talk," Montclief contradicted. "The Old Ways teach us to be intelligent, my son, not stupid as you have become." He waited for hisses that would tell him they were unalterably against him, but again there was silence. A father may talk thus to his son, if he is prepared to meet the challenge.

"If a new animal comes to the snow fields and forests," he continued, addressing all the caves under the guise of talking to Nuk, "we want to know what animal this is. Is it good to eat, we ask?

"Well, a new animal has come. And it brings a poison sting that will make our children cripples, and the grandchildren will waste away until we are all gone. I dreamed this on the dark of the moon and my yrt friend confirmed the new poison animal. We who live in the mountain clouds could not know this because we have isolated ourselves from most dangers with the Old Ways. But the new time has come unbidden again, even as it did when the mountains rose and the seas washed over the low lands. So again we must be intelligent, as the Old Ways say, and change. This I have dreamed."

Montclief stopped. If that didn't interest them, they could all die of the slow poison. "Bring your mother more firewood, then see if you can find us food," he said gently to Chava. "A young deer would be fine. I have to stay here with Rainy. Don't worry, these relatives of yours will be friendly soon."

"Yes, father," the wet young yeti said, loping off into the forest.

"Unwrap your hooks and line," Montclief said to Rainy. "Big trout swim in this lake, but it is somewhat sacred. We will go downstream to catch your food, while Yolanda stays by the fire. Don't boil your disgusting rice until they know you better. They are a very cautious people. I feel they will come around when the females start wondering if their babies will sicken with the poison; but if not, you will have seen their narrow side, which has also helped us to survive."

The rain continued to fall on Willow Mesa Camp as the sun set behind the mountain. Hy Many Blankets' back yard had become a churned up swamp, but he didn't mind that. The winter freezes and thaws would level it again. At this moment, Hy Many Blankets was unconcerned about the million and one things he normally worried about. Euphoria swam in his brain and through his tired muscles as he chewed a lump of greasy bear meat and washed it down with a slow, thoughtful sip of the rich broth. He had already eaten his cube of bear heart and the ceremonial was gloriously completed. It had been too long since he had felt at harmony with that which was. He felt it now, strongly.

The tribe would survive, he could feel its strength flowing in his blood along with Brother Bear. The white man's ways were transitory, no worse than a long, long drought that decimated the buffalo, and made the tribe weak from hunger. Someday the wide prairie and mountains would be free again, alive with game, and the Kiowa Nation would still be here on the free land because they had faithfully kept the old ways. In the meantime, the trials of one or two generations or ten was no great matter. They would hunt and fish and survive. And this time next year, Hy Many Blankets would be living in a skin tepee, perhaps with that willowy young woman who had sat in the rain watching him dance. And he would keep the Ways and set an example for the young men to follow. Maybe he would even make a bow to hunt with, if he could find a grandfather to show him. He had heard that the Jicarilla Apache still knew bowmaking. Of course, if he missed with the bow and arrow, he and his new wife would probably starve to death; so maybe he'd better keep his Winchester in case of emergency. Big Luke had dropped by the hospital to say he'd picked the rifle up. Now, there was a good white man. If it wasn't for Big Luke he'd be dead now, instead of at peace with the world. Luke said he found the rifle fifty or sixty yards away from the bear. How about that? What a powerful bear that one was.

The Wildwood Cafe was owned by an ex-hippie with insomnia, who believed he could tailor his work place to his life-style; and thus Clinton had an all-night coffee shop with the Beatles and Stones on the juke box. No self respecting citizen of Clinton stayed out after nine PM, and those who weren't respectable drank beer, not coffee. So the Wildwood was rather deserted after the supper rush, which suited Willard and Lute Sims, but was a little short of the mark for Lotti. There was no one to appreciate how nice she looked in her tights and Scotch plaid mini, except one sourpuss waitress.

On the other hand, Willard and Famous Lute seemed to appreciate her outfit. Lute even said he found her to be a very interesting young woman and wanted to hear her opinions on any old thing. Actually, she was a little sorry that Willard was with them. All he could talk about was how famous, Famous Lute was, then reel off a bunch of titles of books like just saying the names put him in orbit. Really boring. If Willard wasn't with them, she thought she could maneuver Famous Lute into about any position she cared to have him in. But of course, Willard was driving. And he kept asking these really strange questions to her, in between chanting off a string of titles or character's names. Questions like, where had the geologist said the mine shaft would be located, as if she'd had time to get every little secret out of Yatsey and that handsome, dead other one, Charley. Jeese, if she'd had two or three nights, maybe she'd know more. Did Willard think she kept going to the hospital because she liked the smell of Lysol so much?

It was just like a magic act for Lute Sims. All he needed to do was make one little prod in any direction, and both admiring informants spilled their guts. In a one hour period, at the cost of two cups of coffee and two pieces of pie (one apple and one blackberry a la mode,) he had a pretty good idea what was transpiring on this busy little crag. It was kind of interesting, too. If he turned the story into a book, maybe he would let the mining crew uncover a hidden colony of green aliens living in the heart of the mountain. Perfect. It's not even a mountain at all, just protective camouflage to hide the giant space ship that they've been trying to repair since before Columbus arrived with his band of hell soldiers. As always, Lute was amazed at how fast a story clicked into place when he had the right local color to spice it up. And it didn't look like the girl, Lotti, would present any real difficulty at bed time. The particulars of avoiding her grim mother would add a fillip of real life spice to the sexy heroine character in the new book. He definitely loved the concept—a quaint mailman and an innkeeper's daughter save the world from aliens. He would start writing next week, after he secured the go ahead from his publisher, of course. That was one thing that Lute Sims was very practical about. No use spending all that time on a book, unless it was going to be published. There were lots of stories, and only time for the ones his editors were enthusiastic about. And the only sure way to tell if they were enthusiastic was to deposit their check. If it cleared his bank, they were hot for the book. Not that Lute Sims thought of himself as mercenary. Far from it. He was prudent, that was all. Prudent, and very experienced.

Chava had been gone, hunting, for over an hour. Montclief insisted that the rest of them stay outside beside the lake in the quietly falling snow to cook their meal. Sri Rainy counted twelve empty caves where they could have been dry. It was a fascinating display of stubbornness.

And the visual effect of clouds of steam rising from the wet yetis' pelts as they stood near the fire was also quite wonderfully bizarre. He supposed that the same billows of steam were rising from his robes, but he was too close to see. At least, the fire was hot and his body temperature was climbing back to normal. His old skin inside the red long johns was bathed in moisture, and would be until he could get out of the wet clothes and dry them. Yes, indeed. Warm and wet, a lovely invitation to any kind of galloping bug or virus that was hanging around with these yetis.

The sleeping bag, too, was sopping wet. He had it hanging loosely on a couple of forked sticks near the fire; but of course, snow continued to fall on the bag, melting as it landed, keeping the insulation from ever drying out.

On the plus side, he and Montclief had caught a dozen nice trout in the brook below the lake, in no time. The reason being they used Montclief's astounding fishing method. Like a gray cloud, the huge yeti slid under water into a deep pool below a riffle and started pitching trout onto the bank for Rainy to bonk on the head. Each fish had a spear mark on one flank, presumably from the yeti's finger nail. Rainy was quite simply astounded by this display, having always considered himself the better fisherman. When Montclief had caught enough fish, he took time to explain that the only way to deal with the Council was to wait them out. Then he strung the trout on a willow switch and back they went to the fire.

The trout were now spitted on sticks over the coals, crisping and sputtering. That would soon solve the problem of Rainy's empty stomach; but the wetness factor wouldn't abate until he could get himself installed in one of those caves with a cheery little fire. He realized that Montclief was making a stand at this central fire pit; but truthfully, Rainy was now more concerned with surviving this trip than with establishing himself as a yeti friend. If they didn't want him and his pitiful knowledge, which wouldn't help them much in any case, why should he force himself on them? No, after dinner he'd make for one of the smaller caves, and let Montclief and Yolanda settle their family problems. And tomorrow he'd start back, if relations hadn't thawed. Perhaps Montclief would let Chava guide him, or if not he'd go alone.

A sly whistle sounded from the lip of the bowl and Chava appeared out of the snowy darkness with the carcass of a spike horn buck over his shoulder. Rainy heard an approving murmur coming from the caves, as Chava laid the buck near the fire and proceeded to shove a heavy stick through both of its back Achilles tendons. The deer was already field dressed and bled. Rainy wondered how the boy had accomplished that feat without a knife. Then he wondered why the yetis eschewed tools, when it was perfectly obvious that they could have developed and used them at any time they wanted to. In fact, in their cave, Yolanda had used a full set of dishes and implements. But they hunted bare handed, and during this entire trip they had used only the tools that could be found or fashioned on-site. Survivalists, pure and simple. But why?

Rainy watched closely as Montclief helped the lad hoist the deer into the air, suspending the splayed carcass over a stub limb of a nearby cedar. Then with the index fingernails on their right hands, they proceeded to skin the deer. Apparently, that fingernail was sharpened, but Rainy had never noticed such a deformity of Montclief's finger. Another demonstration of his lack of observation. Montclief had almost certainly used the same tool to spear the trout. When he got dry and filled his belly, presumably Sri Rainy would be able to put a suitable explanation on all this, but right now it seemed superhuman.

After the hide was stripped professionally down over the head, Montclief grabbed the spike antlers, and while Yolanda and Chava steadied the carcass, he twisted the deer's head sharply. Voila, the head and pelt came off clearly. As nice a cleaning job as any slaughter house could do in about half the time. Then they set about quartering the buck. A short while later four huge roasts were rotating on a hand-turned rotisserie which Yolanda had rigged from a green ash sapling between two cairns of rocks.

Montclief called out to the caves that his son had provided meat for anyone who was hungry; then the four of them set to on the flaky white trout flesh. Rainy was positive that he'd never eaten anything so delicious. As the venison turned on the spit, dripping liquid fat onto the coals, he thought that it might be a smart idea to break his meatless fast of nearly sixty years. When in Rome, etc. And besides that, a little fat for his system to burn would surely help him combat the cold night. One thing for sure, it would take a strong-willed yeti to resist the incredible aroma that was drifting on the greasy smoke to all the caves inside the bowl.

*

Lute Sims' bedroom was dark, except for the light of a single streetlight out on Spruce Lane which cast a glow through the wet window pane. Lotti was modeling several articles from her extensive collection of lingerie. Simsy was so interested in everything about her, that she didn't see any harm in showing him a few special items. He was so worldly.

He'd paid for their pie and coffee with a hundred dollar bill, after the restaurant wouldn't take his gold credit card. That was pretty impressive. Nobody around here had either a hundred dollar bill or a gold card, except maybe that creep Billy Bad Boy Drummond, and he wasn't really from here. He was from Creepsville.

Lotti didn't conceive of getting turned-on herself

from modeling the undies. This was acting practice. She didn't buy the stuff to be a rebel, or because it aroused her. Naturally not. She bought it with every cent she could find because it was stylish. A woman had to keep current or she might as well forget about having any decent friends, let alone admirers. And just about the only man she'd ever met who understood that simple premise was Lute Sims. There he was, sitting on the bed fully clothed, being a perfect gentleman. He'd even suggested that she turn out the night stand lamp, so she wouldn't be too exposed as she changed from one outfit to another.

Lotti felt truly accepted for the first time in her life, and the things Simsy said were so interesting. Stand a little straighter, he encouraged. Accentuate your hip thrust. He didn't even act like he wanted to make love with her. Later on, if he wanted to, then she'd do it. Fair exchange for the acting lessons. It would probably make him sleep better. For herself, she slept like a baby with or without sex. Tomorrow she would show him the Frederick's of Hollywood catalogues, and together they could pick out a few things that would do her justice. She really valued his opinion.

For Lute Sims, it was like shooting fish in a barrel. Ages ago, he'd taken stock of his not very impressive looks and decided that since he liked to sleep with beautiful women, he'd have to find out what made them tick, if he was to be successful at the bedding game. His long nose wasn't going to help him, and neither would his bank account at the time. So he took the time to study these rare creatures with the curves and nuances that interested him so much, and he came up with two rules of the hunt. First, they loved to be flattered. No compliment about their beauty was too outrageous to be believed instantly. Even if they didn't believe it, they were positively eager to believe that he believed it. And second, they loved to talk about themselves and about their friends and ideas, but mainly about themselves.

Males, generally speaking, are so self-consumed

that all they talk about is their grandiose plans. Lute found most of those plans boring; but women allow men to talk, so they can flutter their eyes and act interested. In spite of currently being the dominant sex, the only reason that men are necessary in modern society is biological. Young women are keen on reproducing; but socially, Lute had discovered, they like to talk about their clothes, their make-up, their babies and their concerns with being pretty in spite of aging. And occasionally one will want to talk about her political views or her ideas on literature or aerobics. But they want to do the talking. As soon as Lute Sims grasped that concept and learned to act interested in everything that passed through their pretty teeth, the soft and mysterious goodies that he sought flounced into his bed night after night. Rather than getting bored with the ease of his conquests, Lute looked at the parade of young heroines as pure research. After all, every single one of these beauties had some special quality that was innately her own. By linking any dozen of his conquests, the female characters in his books virtually sang with realism.

Lute kept a good selection of the finest, thinnest condoms that money could purchase, and insisted on using them to prevent pregnancy. Being actually rather intelligent and knowing just how many different women he screwed, he classified himself as on the high risk list for sexually transmitted disease. Since he didn't want to be a statistic, he insisted on the condom. He had learned to be so charming about letting the ladies pick out the kind they wanted to use (ribbed, fluted, black, red, yellow, beaded) that he seldom had a refusal. And if an occasional bedfellow did balk at using the protection, he simply admitted with just the right element of embarrassment that he had a rubber fetish and couldn't get off without the feel of rubber or latex. Then they would invariably do it with him. Women love proof of weakness, and fetishes too, if they are properly presented.

*

Up at the Retreat, Sister Angie was determined to get a piece of Billy Drummond for her memory bank, and she was willing to offer any of her orifices to accomplish the mission. Anything that might intrigue him. She knew that her clumsy attempts to find out what turned him on were making her a laughing stock in the kitchen, but damnit, she just didn't care. All her life she'd put up with sniggering behind her back, and she wasn't going to let that stop her now.

The first minute she had seen Billy, eleven years ago, a hot empty space had awakened in her belly; and when he had gone away to Los Angeles, she felt sure that she would die. For some inexplicable reason, she hadn't died. Now that he was finally back, she couldn't afford to waste the chance that might satisfy her forever. With all this talk about the nuclear blitz, the Retreat might be closing soon, and she'd never see him again. Sure, she could go to concerts and try to worm her way through the gaggle of teeny-boppers, but he was here now! And what was the use of trying to act like a lady, if what she wanted was slipping away? Sri Rainy had taught her that. Go for the throat, he was always advising. True, he wasn't referring to getting laid, but it was the same thing, wasn't it? She lived in her body, didn't she? Getting split wide open by Billy's big prong certainly wouldn't make her receptacle any less holy. It was a natural act, after all, and her desires were perfectly natural, too. She was a natural woman, completely without artifice. A vessel waiting to be filled with purity.

Like a hunting puma, this natural woman was stalking down the hallway to Billy's tiny private room carrying a tray of his favorite homemade tollhouse cookies and hot cocoa. She had made the cookies while the kitchen crew was cleaning up for the night. Cleverly, cleverly, she had doled out two of the hot cookies to each of the helpers, pretending she had made them as a treat, then with a deft movement she had squirreled the rest of the batch into a tea tin. Now the remaining eight cookies lay on a napkin on the Retreat's best red lacquered serving tray. The cocoa was in a mug also on the tray, and Sister Angie's tawny hair was out of the babushka and brushed to a sheen. She had even gone to the trouble of plucking out a dozen or so long white strands, not that Billy would care about that. And she had carefully swished her mouth out with cranberry juice, which she had extravagantly ordered with the food order on the pretext of using it in a recipe. Licking her lips after swallowing the juice, gave them a delicate red color.

There was the door to Billy's cubicle. Closed. Well, naturally it would be closed. There was a nasty draft in this corridor. And no light was leaking out under the crack. He was asleep! No, not necessarily. He could have a throw rug stuffed in the crack. She often did that herself, not that drafts affected her, but they were cold and she always slept naked. Did Billy? Probably. It was much more healthful.

Holding the tray in one trembling hand, Angie tapped on the homemade plywood door, tapping as lightly as a brushing moth wing.

"Billy," she whispered, urgently. Answer the door, she begged silently. She would die of shame if anybody discovered her out in this hallway. Once they were in bed together, it didn't matter if the whole monastery knew, but not with a cookie bribe. "Billy..!" she whispered again, tapping a little louder.

Inside the damp, dark cell, Billy Bad Boy Drummond shuddered. This was going to be sticky. Why wouldn't the battle axe go away gracefully? Would she force him to answer the door? Beneath him Alice Tookey, currently from Spokane, Washington, started to giggle.

"So that's why she baked the cookies," Alice whispered, shaking with high energy spasms of mirth. "I can smell them out in the hallway." Alice Tookey was famous for her sense of smell, which she believed privately to be one of the aspects of Buddhahood. "She's bringing you cookies and milk! Aren't you going to answer the door?"

"Quiet," Billy whispered back. "She'll go away in a minute."

"Billy..!" Sister Angie hissed, frantically. "Are you asleep?"

*

With sizzling fish protein warming him from the inside and the smoky cooking fire baking his tired old body alternately on the front and then on the back as he turned, Sri Rainy started to entertain serious thoughts about sleeping.

"I'd like to build a fire in one of those caves, so my sleeping bag will dry out," he suggested to Montclief.

"The Rule is that those who want to talk stay beside this fire until everybody agrees," Montclief replied, rather inflexibly.

"Fine. But I'm not a yeti, and my sleeping bag won't dry out if it keeps getting snowed on."

"I know that."

"Then it makes sense for me to go to a cave. Maybe your friends will come down to eat, if I'm not here."

"I don't think that's possible," Montclief replied, dourly. "You're one of my party. It would be a surrender if you went away. They'll come around in day or two."

"I can't sleep in a wet bag."

"Yes, we won't sleep. That's how it's done. They're not sleeping in there either."

"They're not sleeping..?"

"No. It would be disrespectful to the one who wants talk. They may get grumpy, but nobody sleeps. And nobody hunts, except the party who wants talk. So they will come out before the four days go by. Of course, they may decide to starve rather than talk; but we won't starve. Chava is a good hunter for his age. This is a proud time for him."

"We'll just stand here in the weather for four days, then?"

"Yes. But I hope it won't take that long."

"And if I just start talking?" Rainy asked. "If they're not asleep, they'll hear me. All I want is to tell them the little I know about the danger."

"Yes, you could. But I won't translate. That is not the Way, and I will lose face if you do."

"You might have explained these rules, before you bought me out here," Rainy groused.

"Are you unhappy to be here, seeing things that no man ever has?"

"Very clever of you to draw that to my attention," the old man said, smirking at the yeti. "What if I fall asleep? I feel very tired."

"You won't," Montclief answered. "I wouldn't have invited you, if I thought we would fail."

CHAPTER 19

SOFT AS COTTON— HARD AS STEEL

The first batch of letters was sorted according to destination, and boxed so as to cause the local post office no problems. Most of them were going to D.C., but a few hundred were off to influential people and possible contributors in other states. Instead of delegating authority, Billy drove the mail down to the post office himself. He wanted to make sure that everything was in order, even though he was undoubtedly needed back at the funny farm to orchestrate the madness.

Last night had been uncomfortably close to disaster. Inviting Alice Tookey to his room had been a lame brain thing to do; but cripes, she was so darned sexy. Every time he saw her in that designer robe, which she had evidently picked up before arriving at the Retreat to help with the letters, her eyes had fluttered so many soothing nothings. Finally, he had succumbed.

Well worth the risk, one part of him hummed as he drove through Pike's Grove toward the post office. Another less libertine part was shocked. Sheesh, just like any other two-bit charlatan holy man, using his office to get all the innocent nooky in the nunnery. Or not so innocent, as was the case with Alice Tookey. She had screwed him every which way but sideways—just like the old days. Actually, it was fabulous, and he was well pleased with himself. Even the blundering of Sister Angie had added to the excitement. What a character she was, bringing cookies and hot chocolate to his room. He had found the tray outside his door when Alice sneaked away before dawn. After the marathon tantra session, he had needed some food to get his blood sugar back to normal, so he had eaten the snack and thought kindly of Sister Angie. Munching the cookies and cold cocoa didn't commit him to any indiscretions with the tubby cook, but still the cookies had been delicious.

Parking outside the post office, Billy unloaded a box of letters and carried them inside. After his third trip from the 4X4 to the mail counter, the postmaster got up from behind his desk to help the counter woman lift the boxes.

"What's all this?" Willard Jacks inquired, chattily. Mail in this volume looked good for the sub-station, of course. The accountants down at State kept track of stuff like total volume, total stamp sale, total incoming, all kinds of stuff. Then they determined whether to keep the various township branches open, or merge them. Whether to increase staffs or cut them. All the computer crap that accountants think they're so good at, but which usually balls everything up. So Willard and Jolie were glad to see the unexpected mountain of mail. And since it was pre-sorted, it wouldn't even be much extra work.

"A few letters we're sending off from the Retreat," Billy said pleasantly, answering Willard's question.

"Is that so..?" Willard asked, blandly. It wasn't his job to pry. He glanced at several addresses. All to the Senate. Old Mortimer must be lobbying for something. Why would he do that? The only thing that was going on around here was—the nuke dump! Was Mortimer for or against it? If he was against, maybe he'd sell out to a friendly buyer. Cripes, he had a lot of land up there. What would a reasonable offer be?

"And I guess I'll need about two hundred more dollars of first class stamps. On the roll, if you've got them yet." Billy smiled a friendly smile. He'd bought all the rolls in the post office yesterday. Roll stamps weren't a big item in Pike's Grove.

"Out of rolls," Willard said. "I could pick some up when I take this batch down to Clinton. If you can wait a few hours, I could deliver them up there with your mail." Which would add to his stamp volume and also give him a chance to look the Retreat over from close range. Those old buildings couldn't be worth much could they? He'd never actually been inside.

"Sure, that would be great. About what time will you be delivering?" Billy had gotten heavily into scheduling, so the volunteers wouldn't sit around picking their noses while Sri was away. They were starting to call him "Slave driver", but he wasn't here to win popularity contests, was he?

"Oh, about three o'clock, I'd guess."

"Great," said Billy, handing his last two hundred dollars over the counter. He could hit the money machine down in Clinton. Actually, he could pick up the stamps in Clinton, since he had to go there for the fliers; but why waste the time if the mailman wanted to deliver them. "Another thing, we're going to send out a flyer for a rock concert we're producing. I'd love to not spend the money for 1st class on those, if I can avoid it."

Willard retrieved a set of schedule cards from his desk and passed on the information as to size, folding restrictions and the nonsealing policy that qualified advertising for bulk rate mailing. "How many you think you'll be sending?"

"Quite a few. I ordered two thousand from the print shop."

"Yeah, I see what you mean." He feigned neutrality, but hot damn! This would make the request for the new jeep slip through like a greased pig. Maybe even get him another temp for Christmas. He was readying a friendly quip about what kind of musical instrument Mortimer Snerd would be playing at the concert, when he saw Lute Sims and Lotti walk through the front door, arm in arm.

"Ready for breakfast, Willard?" Lute asked, cheerfully, as if it was the most natural thing in the world for a postmaster to take a break at 9:30 for breakfast.

Lotti was done up like a China doll hooker, with lots of white powder on her face, accented with bright cheek rouge and carmine lipstick. Her body was covered with a baggy lounging pajama thing in lime green with white chrysanthemum decorations. "Hi, Willy. Hi, Jolie," she said. Then her voice chilled as she said, "Hello, William," to Billy Bad Boy Drummond.

Billy swiveled his head to look at her, not quite believing her outfit. She would have turned heads on Sunset Boulevard, but up here, the girl was as sublimely out of place as a space alien. Then something about her companion caught his memory. "I know you from somewhere, sir," he said, just as his recovering druggie's mind flashed on a name. "You're Lute Sims!" He held out his hand. "Billy Drummond," he said. "We were guests together on The Larry King Show, a couple of years ago. Remember?"

"By God," Lute Sims exclaimed. This was exciting. Another layer was about to unfold, he suspected. "The mad rock and roller. Foul Boy, or something like that. What brings you up here?"

The geeky writer had messed up his name, but Billy just smiled. Here was a possible source of postage revenue. Lute Sims was rich as a bed bug, and a card carrying liberal if one could judge from his books. And it looked like he'd latched onto bitchy little Lotti.

"You're Billy Bad Boy Drummond?!" Willard gulped, in spite of his new resolution to quit gulping at everything. Lotti had pointed out the gulping defect yesterday over their pie and coffee. "I didn't recognize you."

"That's alright," Billy said. "No big deal."

"Well, no wonder you're giving a concert!

"I told you," Jolie Spalding piped up. Billy and his band had given a mini-concert at Edison Rural Consolidated High School which she and Willard had both attended. It was unlikely that any of the girls in her class would ever forget who Billy was. She, herself, had every record he'd ever released. And after seeing him these last few days, she'd been thinking seriously about enrolling in a few night classes, or whatever they called whatever they did, up at the Retreat. She didn't think her husband would appreciate that too much, but what he didn't know, wouldn't hurt him.

"You didn't tell me, Jolie," Willard laughed. "You never mentioned a word about it."

"Yes, I did. The other day. You never listen."

"You must have whispered."

"No. You were busy being a real estate tycoon."

"So Billy, you're going to give a concert," Willard said, paying no more attention to Jolie. "I remember the time you came over to our high school assembly. That was great! Really great."

"I remember it better than you do," Jolie chimed. Why did she always have to be so slow and embarrassed? She should have talked to Billy the first time he came in, when she was alone, instead of waiting to chirp up like a twit, now. God, if she could only crawl all over him, her life would be complete. Forever. She'd never ask for one other thing as long as she lived. "We girls were crazy about you."

"I seriously doubt that," Willard responded, with a sharp glance at his subordinate.

Lotti glowered, attaching herself firmly to Lute's elbow. She had spent a long time dressing and making-up, and didn't appreciate not being the center of attention one little bit. Why would anyone make such a fuss over a degenerate like "Foul Boy"? That was a perfect name for him. Lute was so smart.

"You seriously doubt that I was crazy about him?" Jolie yelled, amazed that her obsession was being questioned. "Well, you're wrong, Willard. I was, and I still am!"

"Jeese," Willard hissed. "I only meant, I doubt if you remember that assembly better than I do. Don't you have some work to do sorting those letters?"

Billy chuckled, indulgently. He hadn't expected a fan club calamity in the post office, of all places. "They're already sorted," he restated, then turned back to Lute Sims. "That's the price of past glory," he said, apologetically.

"You're giving a concert up here?" Lute asked, opening a fact finding discussion. It seemed very strange to find a world famous rock star in this tiny community. Did he live here? If so what was he escaping from? Maybe that was the story. Or was it another layer to the story he was already piecing together? Billy had been pretty drugged out the last time he'd seen him. Damned unpleasant, actually. But he seemed better now. Fame does play nasty tricks to those it chooses to love. Lute was half-glad he'd never made bright-light celebrity status.

"To tell the truth, we're having a little flap up on this mountain," Billy said, preliminary to hitting Sims for a donation. "If you've got a few minutes, I'll tell you about it."

"Right now, Lotti and I only have time for breakfast with our favorite postman." He smiled over at his China doll. "Why don't you join us, Billy? Is that alright with you, Willard?"

"With me? Sure." What the hell, Willard had to go

to Clinton anyway. Why not have some breakfast with two of his favorite celebrities? Mickey Mantle and Dolly Parton would probably be at the Wildwood Cafe waiting for them. The mail route could wait for an hour or so. Normal people ate breakfast, why shouldn't he? "You want to go over to the Wildwood again?"

"Can't we find someplace a little more exciting?" Lotti whined.

"I thought you liked the Wildwood?" Willard said, with a pressured smile. Lotti was going to be here after Lute had gone away to his glamorous life in New York. No use letting her get too uppity.

"I used to," she said, sweetly. "But the food isn't as good as it was. Couldn't we go to the Pancake House, instead?"

"I have to go to Clinton anyway," Billy stated somewhat officiously. "Wherever you decide to eat is fine with me."

Rather than squabble with Lotti, they decided on the Pancake House. Jolie, of course, was the odd man out. Somebody had to take care of business. She waved wistfully as the foursome walked out into the bright autumn sunshine.

Montclief had remained standing beside the fire all night. Shortly after dawn, the snow had stopped. Then the sun came out and it turned into a gorgeous morning. Chava and Yolanda went back and forth to the woods. Hunting and wood gathering was considered a reasonable excuse for leaving the circle as long as someone stayed behind to tend the fire.

Rather than hang around the fire doing nothing, Rainy had slipped off for a few hours of superb, contemplative angling. He stood on the stream bank letting the morning sun warm him. Standing also prevented him from falling asleep. He had a strong urge to meditate, but realized the inherent dangers in the sitting posture. Many times in his life when overtired like this, he had fallen fast asleep while meditating. Admitting that shortcoming wasn't particularly painful to his ego, it was one of the hazards of the religious trade; but rather than risk breaking Montclief's sleeping taboo, he went back to the camp with his stringer of trout.

No sooner had he cleaned the fish and set them to broiling, than Chava returned with a fat yearling mule deer buck over one shoulder and a half grown razor back piglet under his arm. The boy grinned happily and asked his father if that would be enough meat for the day. He wiped a smear of blood off his soft fur with some leaves.

"We'll see," Montclief answered. He began dressing the meat. Rainy set about spreading his sleeping bag on a sunny ledge to dry. After propping several forked sticks inside so that air would circulate freely, he went back to watch Montclief.

"Do you eat pig?" the yeti inquired, hopefully.

"No," Rainy answered, thinking of the Christmas ham and New Year's Day pork roast his mother always cooked.

"Neither do we, unless it can be roasted. Something about a pig is evil."

"Trichinosis," answered Rainy, informatively. This wasn't a true wild pig, but a descendent of some domestic strain gone wild. These razorback hogs were usually found in swampy county. He'd never heard of them being in the high lands, and of course, the true wild peccary and javelina were found much further south toward Mexico. Had they gone south, instead of west like he thought?

"Trichinosis..?" Montclief asked, cutting neatly through meat and sinew with his fingernail, then popping the exposed joints free.

"Little worms that live in the muscles of an infected pig. Thorough cooking kills them."

"Oh," the yeti said quietly, evidently pleased to

learn of it. "You will explain this when the others come down to talk."

Shortly after Yolanda had set the piglet to roasting, three yetis came out of a cave. By their fur color, Rainy assumed that two of them were greybeards, a male and a female, with a younger female, probably their offspring. The young female wore a necklace of tiny sea shells around her neck. Walking briskly down the path from their cave, they all hugged Yolanda warmly and made a big fuss over Chava, pulling at him and jabbering so rapidly that Rainy couldn't make out any of the words, except that they were all obviously delighted to see the lad.

"Those are my wife's parents, Mamuk and Shanni, and her sister, Hanni," Montclief explained. "I expected them to be with us last night, but old Mamuk had to make a show to satisfy the others."

"Out of curiosity, why do you and Yolanda have yrt sounding names, but the other yeti names are more natural?" Rainy asked.

"Simple. Montclief and Yolanda aren't our real names. I found them in a book and started using them to make it easier for you."

Rainy smiled. Those names were bizarre choices from all the alternatives. He watched the three new yetis starting to gorge themselves on the venison, which was very well cooked by this time. "What are your real names?" he asked.

*

Mamuk had not planned to be the first to end the boycott, but listening to Shanni's constant yammering about how hungry she was had gotten on his nerves. She had been much hungrier than this countless times during the deep snow freeze days when hunting was impossibly treacherous. No, she wanted to get the girl married. Sitting in the warm cave wasn't accomplishing her purpose in coming to the Council.

The marriage of his second daughter was certainly not something he personally longed for. It would leave him alone with Shanni, and that was one woman who loved to talk endlessly about every little thing. But she was determined to find Hanni a mate this year, so after his ears couldn't stand it any longer, he had come out of the cave. He had meant to come out eventually, of course. What good was a Council if nobody talked? And he was curious to see this yrt. What kind of creatures were these star men, really? Breeding like flies was about all they were good for, wasn't it? He had dispatched several when they encroached his canyon looking for the yellow pebbles; but that had been years ago, when he was younger and angrier. This one that Naka had fetched didn't look like he could fly, and he was certainly too old to breed, so maybe they could have a peaceable pow-wow and find out about Naka's dream. Young Naka had never seemed like the unbalanced type before. He had always stressed the Old Ways at previous Councils. But you never know, he could have fallen off a slippery log and cracked his head. The boy, Chava, certainly looked fit and well trained, so did Zuwi, his oldest daughter. It was nice that she'd finally given him a grandson. He would go hunting with the lad and teach him some real woodsmanship. It would probably be another day before the stone-heads came out. Yep. Going hunting with a grandson would be a real fine thing to do.

Shanni was sure that her oldest daughter looked peaked, in spite of the good show of wifery she was putting on. She couldn't exactly classify Naka as a brute, although most males had a tendency toward brutishness. All the same, she had wanted a more manageable mate for her darling first girl. Zuwi had been such a playful, happy little cub and now she seemed to have put those happy qualities aside. Maybe it was just the stress of having a disgusting yrt here, or of having her husband at odds with everybody, but Shanni didn't think so.

"This deer meat is delicious, Zuwi," Shanni exclaimed loudly, although the meat was cooked to a flavorless leather consistency. "Your darling Chava is such a handsome boy and such a good hunter!" Raving about the meat would get those fur-balls out of their caves and down here, so everybody could sleep and party. Her other daughter, Hanni, took the cue and loudly joined in the praise. Truly, the yeti ways were so stupid sometimes. That old yrt looks so frail he can barely stand up? What threat can he be? Let's get on with it. An accident can always be arranged if he proves too troublesome, even if Naka vouches for him. Who can say how accidents happen?

"Oh, and look at this succulent pig," she said, smacking her lips enthusiastically. "How white and juicy the meat is! When will it be ready to eat, Zuwi dear?"

"When the sun stands straight in the sky, we will sample it, Mother," Yolanda said quietly, as was her role. She heartily disliked this stupid ritual, but of course, it had to be played out. Thank goodness her mother had finally convinced Daddy to come out. She smiled, thinking how her father hated being dinged at. He was such a good-hearted male. She would broach the subject of an extended visit with them to further Chava's education. A boy should learn from his grandfather, and Montclief's father was dead. If Hanni was wedded after the Council, there would be no problem about a visit. She looked so pretty.

Yolanda turned the rotisserie duty over to her mother and embraced her sister, feeling glad to see her. If only Hanni knew what a drag married life could be, she wouldn't be so eager to spit curl her forelocks and singe her eyebrows.

Meanwhile Yoli noticed that several of the younger males were standing in the mouths of their caves, watching hungrily. It wouldn't be long now, judging by their impatient glances back toward their elders.

"Do you think we have enough meat?" Yolanda wondered aloud to her father and Chava.

"Try not to overcook the good meat that me and this whipper-snapper bring in," Mamuk said, munching happily on a haunch of venison. He jabbed Chava playfully on the shoulder, a blow that would have broken a deer's neck.

Chava smiled shyly.

"Nobody forced you to stay in the cave all night," Yolanda chided. "The meat was perfect. We all ate so much we were stuffed, but some yetis weren't hungry, so they let the good meat get burned. Maybe soon they'll be hungry at the correct time." Her father grinned and set off into the forest, with Chava tagging along like a proud puppy.

"I have a taste for some real meat," the old man rumbled. Real meat to him meant either wapiti or wood's buffalo. Yolanda hadn't eaten buffalo hump in a long time and hoped her father would find one. There were no buffalo near the yrt settlements where she had to live. Eating that rich red meat always made her so affectionate—well horny, really. Maybe it would have the same effect on Montclief. But if not now, then during the visit to her family she would taste buffalo again.

*

On the ride over to Clinton, Lotti had made it very clear to Simsy that he'd made a mistake by inviting Billy Drummond to breakfast with them. Leaning forward between the jeep seats, she thoroughly slurred the rock star's character without giving away specific facts. Willard didn't like her interruptions. He was trying to warm Lute Sims up to a serious literary discussion. With a final spiteful sally, she suggested that Lute might consult her as a character witness before inviting other of the local dead-beats to spend time with them.

Lute smiled benevolently at her and swore he would. Then he began a discussion of perfume versus cologne and body splashes with Lotti. Willard thought he might go insane at the idiocy of wasting Lute Sims' time on such mundane topics, even though he was surprised at how much Lute knew about perfume. Finally arriving at the Pancake House, he was shocked to see Billy's red 4X4 parked in the parking lot, and Billy himself leaning on a fender smoking a cigarette. How the hell had Drummond beat him? A lifetime of driving had convinced him that there was only one road to Clinton, and the 4X4 hadn't passed him on the way. Damned mystifying.

Climbing out of the jeep, he held the door open for Lotti, then whispered to the China doll as she stepped daintily over one of the mud holes that pockmarked the gravel parking lot. "Try not to monopolize the conversation in here," he whispered. "These are important people."

Lotti iced him with her best frozen stare and, light as a feather, glommed onto Lute's elbow.

"Hey, how the heck did you get here before me?" Willard yelled at Billy.

Billy grinned. There's a reason for a person getting to the top of the heap in any given field, and it usually isn't luck. For instance, there was a quirk in Billy's nature that hated to be a second place finisher, therefore he took the trouble to scope out the fastest side streets wherever he was. The route he had taken from the post office to the main highway had one stop sign and two alleys. True, he goosed the Bronco a touch on the highway, but what the hell, that's what a rented car was for. He nonchalantly flicked his butt into a mud puddle, and still grinning said, "You must have taken the scenic route."

"Maybe so," Willard agreed, leading the group into the restaurant.

The Pancake House in Clinton wasn't part of a

chain, but it made an effort to be like one, even down to the four kinds of syrup on each table and fifty kinds of pancakes on the menu. They found a booth under a rustic Pancake House window and ordered pancakes.

"So Lute, how's the story coming?" Willard blurted as soon as the waitress had gone away. He didn't want to take a chance on Lotti going on about earrings or something.

"Tumbling and bubbling," Lute Sims replied genially. He looked over at Bad Boy Drummond. "Do you have a home up here? It's a wonderful place for a summer home, isn't it?"

"It's a fabulous mountain," Billy agreed. "Very spiritual. In fact, you'd probably be interested in the reason I'm here."

Lute nodded responsively. Unknown to Billy or Willard, Lotti was teasing him by running her long fingernails up his thigh under the table in a gesture from the Kama Sutra called the "Lioness Swirl", which Lute had taught her last night. "The Swirl" was making him responsive to almost anything.

"The Federal government is proposing to poison this whole area with nuclear waste," Billy said, choosing his words carefully to give the maximum punch. "Those fat-heads won't be satisfied until they ruin everything beautiful in this country."

"I doubt if that's a fair assessment," Willard interrupted. "Just where exactly are they planning to sink the main shaft?"

Billy, of course, didn't know the answer to that. Forced to confront the question directly, he realized that Sri Rainy had been a little hazy on the location. For that matter, the entire project was shrouded in haze. He'd been spending his energy on the assumption that his teacher knew a clear and present menace. Willard had asked a damned good question. Billy would have to seek clarification from Sri when he got back.

"That's not it at all," Lotti said, forcefully. "They're trying to develop this area economically. God knows, it needs some new life breathed into it." Her Lioness

Swirling nails dug a little too deeply into Lute's tender inner thigh.

"Ouch," he said, pulling his leg away from her claws.

"If you think nuclear waste is a breath of life, you're sadly mistaken," Billy rebutted, rather more harshly than he wanted to.

"How the hell do you know so much about it?" Willard retorted. "Don't act like you're as concerned as a resident."

"That's right!" Lotti shouted. She suddenly felt very close to Willard. They saw things the same way. After all, they were the locals.

"That reminds me of a cute breakfast story I heard," Lute broke in, deciding to keep peace at the table. "Bacon and eggs, right? A normal breakfast, right? Well, the chicken is involved, but the pig is committed."

Lotti looked blank as an egg. Lute Sims' biggest fan, Willard Jacks, roared with laughter—a little faky, but laughter none the less.

Billy smiled and nodded sagely. "Which one are you, Mr. Sims? Involved or committed? Either way, we could use a little donation to help us protect the mountain."

"We..?" Lute Sims asked. It seemed it might cost him five bucks to find out why Billy Drummond was up in these sticks begging for money. Well worth the price. He had a feeling that this was the heart of any story he might write.

"Actually, I'm committed to Sri Rainy at the Seekers of Light Retreat. Ever been up there?"

"No, he hasn't," Lotti spat, insolently. "And he doesn't want to. They're just a bunch of kooks and sex fiends, Lutie. Nobody around here has anything to do with them."

"Sex fiends?" Lute asked. His interest was perking up. "Is it a tantric order, Bill?"

"Well, no. Not actually." Remembering last night's escapade, he wasn't so sure he could pass a lie detector test on that point.

"I have rather a fondness for some forms of tantra," Lute replied. "A woman I dated was involved in Buddhism."

"Well, the main issue here is that somebody's trying to nuke this mountain, and we're getting set to resist them."

"Then I guess Mortimer wouldn't be interested in selling the Retreat just yet?" Willard asked, letting his greed shoot him right past Tantric Buddhism.

"Sell it?" Billy asked in amazement. "Who's saying anything about Sri selling the Retreat?"

"Oh, people are buying and selling right and left in Pike's Grove," China Lotti reported innocently. "It's going to be a boom town. We're very lucky to have a mountain made of granite at this critical time."

The waitress arrived on cue with platters of steaming pancakes.

"Pass the maple syrup, would you please, Willard?" Lute asked, politely. "Have you heard there's going to be a shortage of maple syrup in Vermont this year? Something to do with acid rain or bugs or something. The Iroquois up there are quite concerned about it."

"Gosh, no," Willard gulped. "I haven't heard a word about that. How bad's it going to be?" He decided to buy a couple of quarts of syrup from L.L. Bean before the price went up.

*

Since the Retreat probably wouldn't come up for sale, Willard Jacks decided he'd better make an offer to Asa Peters up in Mudslide Pass. With that in mind, he foisted Lute and Lotti off on Billy Drummond for the ride back to Pike's Grove, and set off to Mudslide Pass by himself. Willard didn't realize he'd made a huge mistake until he had trudged halfway across the overgrown meadow in front of Asa's dilapidated log cabin way back from the road where nobody ever went.

Crazy old Asa had logged off all his land before Willard was born. He had cleared the stumps and had a go at big time potato farming on about a hundred acres of hillside. But the ground up there was just too poor, even for spuds; and after his wife died, Asa let everything go to hell and became a mountain hermit, paranoid of dealings with people. The only mail he ever got was the L.L. Beans' catalogue, a letter from the State Tax Board once a year, political mail-outs and junk mail. Willard faithfully delivered everything into the rusty mailbox that was propped on a slumping cairn of stones; but the only thing that Asa ever picked up was the Beans' catalogue. The rest of the junk mail accumulated in the mailbox getting soggy until Willard picked it up again after two weeks or so had passed. He knew Asa was alive and that he checked the mailbox, although the postman had never seen him, because there was a worn foot path leading from the cabin to the mailbox. The rusty flag was always turned down the next time he drove past. When there was something new to deliver, the Beans' stuff was always missing. Willard returned the disdained tax statements to sender and used Asa's junk mail for fire starters in the post office Franklin stove.

Asa owned the farm outright. Willard had checked on that, so there would be no bank encumbrances if the old man accepted his offer. But what about those tax bills? The State must have a terrific lean on the farm by now. It was a wonder they didn't come out and kick Asa off the land. Willard was a little hazy on state tax law. There must be some loop hole. He'd have to bone up on that kind of stuff now that he was a landowner. Speaking of which, he'd have to pay taxes, himself. Cripes, he hoped that mine shaft got started before a year passed and he had to pay. How much were the taxes, anyway?

He was yakking away to himself about the unfairness of the tax laws, when a spume of dirt kicked up at his feet. An instant later he heard the report of a high powered rifle. Christ almighty, Crazy Asa was shooting at him from somewhere up in the rocks! That crazy old fool!

Waving his arms in the air, he yelled, "Don't shoot, Mr. Peters! It's me, the mailman..! Willard Jacks! Don't shoot!!"

Another bullet thunked into a scrub aspen off to his left, severing a branch and careening across the field in a high pitched whine.

"Fuck that crazy bastard," Willard muttered, unclearly. He'd never been shot at before and didn't know what to do. The scrubby trees growing in the former potato field offered no real cover, and good old Asa had dragged all the boulders to the edge of the fields to make fences with. Since the nearest cover he could see was the broken down cabin, he took off running toward it. Running toward the cabin was a mistake. It heightened the old man's paranoia.

Somebody in a grey uniform was attacking his cabin, Asa perceived, dimly. Who was it? A tax man? Or worse, maybe it was a damned revenuer coming to smash his still. Hells bells, couldn't a man even have a little potato whiskey if he wanted it? Well, nobody was going to smash his still! Not while he had something to say about it. Jacking another shell into the ancient Model 94 Winchester, Asa took careful aim on the revenuer bastid. He was intending to put one through the bastid's leg, so he could crawl back where he'd come from and tell all the other bastids that Asa Peters was nobody to mess with. But his old eyes weren't what they once were. Twenty solitary years of drinking potato home brew had left him partially blind and had sent him well down the path to insanity. His rotting brain cells served testimony on the potency of his brew.

Asa squeezed the trigger. A 150 grain bullet sang across the overgrown meadow and whacked into the middle of Willard's chest, passing through the right ventricle of his heart and sending his body into shock as it cartwheeled backwards like a rag puppet.

Willard didn't feel much pain at all. He was already

dead before his body came to rest against a grey birch sapling.

After climbing down from the rocky lookout ledge and walking into his front field, Crazy Asa Peters was real sorry to see that the bastid he'd shot wasn't really a bastid at all, but a mailman. He wondered idly if this meant that his Beans' catalogue would stop coming now. Then he realized that the smart move would be to get rid of the evidence. If they found out he'd shot the mailman by mistake, they were sure to go poking around, and sure as shit they'd find his still. Then where would he be? No whiskey and no Beans' catalogue. Hell, that would be a sorry-ass day. Wouldn't be hardly nothing to live for if both the things he liked best was took away from him. Course, he could still hunt and fish and plow his little patch of taters, but hell.

So after figuring it out, he hauled the heavy mailman way up into Box Canyon, where he'd buried those other couple of snoopy bastids. Box Canyon was about as far away from the still as he could logically go and still be on his own property, but it was a lot harder this time. His old mule, Old Flop Ear, had died last week, so the mailman had to be drug by hand. Asa said a little prayer over the damned snoopy mailman and covered him over, tamping the rocky soil that wasn't fit to raise a crop in.

It was dark by the time he snuck back down the hill to deal with the jeep. He was still a pretty crafty old fellow, he chuckled to himself, even if he was getting a little long in the tooth. Nobody screwed with Asa Peters, and if they did, they'd be damned sorry about it.

Starting the jeep, he drove it all the way down to Toby Berlinheimer's place with the lights out, and parked it beside the mailbox, then he hiked back up the mountain. Toby was a good old boy. He'd figure out what to do with the jeep when he found it. Maybe he could use an extra vehicle.

But on the strength of Willard's cash deposit, Toby Berlinheimer had sold his remaining few sheep and had gone to Fort Collins to visit his daughter. Or to be more accurate, old Toby was quite enamored of a widow lady named Mandy Tice who lived down the street from Sally and her kids. Now that he no longer had the sheep to worry about, it seemed logical to cozy up to the widow Tice. The holidays were coming, and she made a tasty anise cookie, the hard kind that he liked to gum on.

Chuck and Bert Stedley happened to be driving up Mudslide Pass later that night, working as usual. Their autumn and winter occupation was jacklighting deer who were trusting enough to come out on the roads. The deer meat was sold to Harold's Meat Locker down in Clinton, who in turn passed the venison on in the form of "ground beef" to various fast food chains. Chuck and Bert thought it would be a good joke on Willard to move his jeep across the county line. It seemed like a harmless prank. Willard wouldn't be stranded or anything. Old man Berlinheimer would drive him back to town, and the Logan County cops would report the jeep soon enough. Chuck and Bert figured they could kid Willard for years to come over that one.

➛ ➚

CHAPTER 20

SUBSTANTIAL AND INSUBSTANTIAL

By nightfall, all the yetis had left their caves and had come down to the circle, as Montclief had predicted. The last to give in, scowling and holding back, was Nuk, the dark one. Finally when he reached the fireside, he seemed to decide on total participation and embraced his father. After that, the group became very congenial and integrated. All the others had already been introduced to Rainy, and were eating vast quantities of meat. Chava and the old grandfather had returned earlier lugging a young bull elk, and seeing that their hungry relatives needed feeding, immediately dressed the meat and put steaks and haunches on to roast.

The whole deal was very interesting to the monk. He hadn't visited a foreign country for a very long while; and consequently had mostly forgotten how to converse without words. Only Montclief made communication with the yetis possible. Sri Rainy knew a few key phrases and that was it. He had no idea what Montclief was going to propose to his people—they hadn't discussed it. That in itself was lunacy of a certain kind, and yet Rainy was fascinated with what he was seeing. Once the stand-off was finished, the whole encampment of fifty-six yetis acted just like this was a family picnic. It felt extremely similar to the picnics the Raisenbe clan—aunts, uncles, cousins, in-laws and kids—used to have every summer at that little park on Staten Island.

His own childhood had been rather tragically dull and normal. After highschool he'd gone to New York University. His father expected him to take over the produce market after he graduated, but he fooled everybody. On a whim, he took a comparative religions class, and somehow that innocent beginning had led him to this conclave of the yetis, seventy years later. Another picnic in the park; but this family seemed far less bored or boring than the Raisenbes had always been.

Maybe it was just that he couldn't understand the language. Probably what they were saying as they flirted and sparred around was just as mundane as any comparable number of human country bumpkins, or college professors for that matter, but maybe it wasn't. All Rainy could do was read the body movements, and that was why he was fascinated. Most of his life had been spent trying to get his students to move and act freely, without being completely bound up with tension. He had failed miserably, but these yetis had exactly the quality that he'd been trying to teach all those years. Complete naturalness. It was the damnedest thing. And although they were all jabbering their heads off to each other, he could barely hear the words. Something about their language made the sound disappear into the trees and rocks. Strange.

Montclief was currently trying to herd all these energetic giants to one side of the fire pit, so that discussions could begin before the young ones started pairing off and the older ones went to sleep. At least, that's what he told Rainy he was doing. The herding process wasn't going very well. Then as if on a prearranged signal, they all started drifting over to sit on the banked side of the bowl behind the fire. Probably someone in authority had given a command that Rainy hadn't understood, but he couldn't tell who the leading figure was. Within a minute or two every yeti was sitting, waiting silently for Montclief to speak.

Standing in front of them, Montclief formally introduced Sri Rainy, then said he was going to tell the yetis his dream without translating, since Rainy already knew it; but he would translate the gist of the discussion that followed. Then he launched into his reason for calling the meeting. Fifty-five pairs of eyes watched him unwaveringly. Rainy, who made the fifty-sixth, observed the whole scenario. It was an impressive display. If he had students such as these, there was no telling what he could have accomplished. Oh well, here he was with a completely endangered race, who he thought might be better prepared to survive in their environment than anybody he'd ever met; and deep in his heart, he knew they were on the edge of extinction.

While Montclief continued speaking, Rainy wondered at Nature's Plan. It had been so elegant, and it seemed to be coming to an end. Would the other races really push this one past the limit? Why exactly was that a good idea? But maybe Nature had not been overwhelmed. If not, wouldn't she react eventually? Surely there would come a time when Mother Nature would want to protect some pet species from extinction. Maybe she loved a particular little blue and green bird enough to swat the heartless machine that threatened it. Or maybe she wanted this whole planet denuded for reasons of her own. Who knew? One thing for sure, no matter what this superb group of yetis decided, Rainy couldn't imagine them having the power to guide their future against the forces of "progress".

Montclief spoke rather briefly, then turned to the monk. "I have told my dream, and the problem that I see. Now, we will decide on the path to follow until the next Council. May the Spirit guide us, because I don't see the answer. I told them that, too."

Before any discussion could begin, old Mamuk stood. "I and the boy will go make more meat," he growled. "Talking is hungry work. If the vote comes while I am gone, I give my nod to my wife, who thinks she is smarter than I am anyway." Chuckling, he pulled Chava to his feet, and they jogged into the trees.

Translating for Rainy, Montclief found that he would have been better pleased if Chava had stayed to listen; but it was certainly a grandfather's prerogative to hunt with his grandson. His own father had hunted long with Nuk before his death. And Nuk had become a dark one. Montclief's father had been a very conservative person. The reactionary teachings had evidently found a home with his first son. And Darla's death with the yrt hadn't helped much. Nuk had been with her, and had carried her broken body home. After that he darkened perceptibly, and Montclief had been too grief-stricken to help much. So it surprised Montclief when Nuk bounced to his feet and announced that he, too, would hunt with his little brother. More surprisingly, he gave his proxy to Montclief, then loped off to follow Mamuk. Montclief's chest swelled at the unexpected vote of confidence from his son. He didn't understand what had caused the sudden change after yesterday's chilly reception, but he was so pleased that he smiled briefly in Yolanda's direction.

The discussion of Montclief's dream began, and eventually someone called for the yrt to speak. So

Rainy found himself center stage in front of the fire, with Montclief standing near him to translate.

*

The Co-op meeting was in full swing. For the first time in history, the minutes had been approved without being read. Tim Waters had phoned his old high school history teacher over at Edison Rural Consolidated to find out the procedure for skipping the minutes. He shocked Esther by saying that in light of the important guest speaker from the Governor's office, who had come to shed some light on the current situation, he would entertain a motion to suspend the minutes so they could get down to new business. Two of his cronies from the pool hall jumped up to make the motion and second it.

Esther had spent most of the day typing the minutes, so they would be easy to read. She'd even bought throat lozenges at Kim Wong's Liquor in case her throat went out, but what could she do? Her starring role had been upped by parliamentary procedure.

But when that rascal Tim Waters opened the meeting to new business, a loud hubbub of "Where's the mail?" drowned out several attempts to introduce the Governor's toady.

Jolie Spalding felt it was her patriotic duty to take the heat, so she timidly stood up to announce that Willard hadn't come back from the run to the main post office in Clinton. She apologized and said the jeep must have broken down again. Not knowing whether to report it to the sheriff, she'd come over to the meeting. Looking around the room, her eyes lighted on Dink Moran, the deputy sheriff, who was the ranking officer in Pike Township.

Dink was a large, homegrown boy, who had joined the Sheriff's Department after his stint in the Marines.

The County Sheriff lived in Clinton, naturally. That was where the votes were; but Dink knew all the weirdos up in Pike Township, and presumably could keep order, so he'd been assigned up there under three successive sheriffs. He had a fondness for beer, but who didn't, reasoned the three sheriffs. Hoisting his huge beer belly out of the chair, Deputy Dink Moran stood up. Turning around in the tight aisle, he looked at the postmistress and said, "You should have called me, Jolie."

"We're getting a new jeep in January," Jolie responded, hopefully.

In the back of the room, Lute Sims found this new development very interesting. "The Case of the Missing Mailman." Quite possibly Willard had stumbled upon a hostile colony of space aliens, and was being held for questioning. Lute liked it. If he couldn't hang a story on that plot line, he was a monkey's uncle. His fingers suddenly felt itchy to get to his computer. He might have left the meeting forthwith, if he hadn't needed to listen to the drivel these mountain people were going to fill the night with. He needed to get drenched in the rustic rhythms of their speech pattern so that authenticity would flow into the book. And he was sure the Governor's man would impart a large dose of drivel. An author just can't get enough authentic political hogwash. It adds such an aroma to the printed page.

*

Under the cold sliver of moon, the three yetis were having a high old time slipping through the shadowy woods. Hunting, to a yeti, was the best time a guy could have without breaking a taboo. They'd already cached a fat white-tail doe to pick up on their way back. Nuk was proud of his little brother's skill. Chava was such a nice little guy, never bragging, seemingly eager to learn anything that he or Mamuk could teach him. And deadly when the prey was in view.

"I want real meat," Mamuk said again. He'd relayed his feelings on the subject several times already. He meant bison, which was fine with Nuk, but woods bison were hard to kill. There were lots of the wooly blackbeards in the north where Nuk lived, but he seldom bothered with them. A calf now and then, but the bulls and cows were too big for a solitary yeti to transport, and besides they were hard to bring down unless one resorted to a trap or pit, which Nuk also disapproved of.

Mamuk thought buffalo were hard to kill also, but Shanni had mentioned that a buffalo robe would be a nice dowry item for the girl, and since he had some good help with him, it seemed like a perfect time to take a large bull.

He and Chava had seen a few tracks during the day, but woods bison were more wary then their plains cousins had been, which was the main reason they'd survived the yrt hunters, while the remaining plains bison had been reduced to the status of shaggy domestic cattle.

Circling a wooded ridge, the three yetis swept what would have been an impossibly wide swath to a human hunter. Of all the predators, their senses were the most perfectly balanced. Superb day or night vision, ears sharp as a rabbit's. Sense of smell that put the great bears to shame and delicate movement sensors in their furry feet that detected the stepping of large game animals a hundred yards away. And besides that, they possessed the keen intelligence that put all these signals together to come up with a yes or no answer.

A large dark shape moved silently through an aspen thicket off to Nuk's left. A cow moose was attempting to sneak away. This was more like it. Moose meat was tasty and the actual killing was far easier than bison. True, if cornered a moose's sharp hooves were formidable weapons, but Nuk had no intention of backing the cow into a tight place. Just the opposite. He would drive her into a meadow, where one of them, preferably himself since Chava was too young, would leap on her back and break her neck. But he had to check with Mamuk first to see if moose meat was wanted. Before he had a chance to do so, he heard Chava hiss, then an answering night owl call from the grandfather. It was good to hunt as a team again, he thought. Very good. It made a game out of the hunt. He had missed the fun part of the chase very much. The People believed he sought isolation for its own sake, and he had led them to think that. But it was not true. Nuk had a dark secret that only the far north range would protect. It was strange, he thought for the billionth time, that his blood line should be so determined to break the taboos of the Old Ways. It had all started with his mother, surely. But then his father had gotten infected. Naka, at least, had the courage to bring the strangeness forward; while he, himself, lacking such bravery, hid his secret behind gruffness. But Naka had far less to lose than he did.

Coming together in a glade-like hemlock grove, all three of them pointed in the direction the moose had gone. The comraderie was so heady that Nuk could scarcely stop himself from screaming his joy. Quickly, they formed a plan to drive the cow toward a hillside that had burned several years earlier in an lightening storm. It was an unhurried operation. They didn't want her to spook, but their plan was laid a little too carefully. She balked at the pursuit, and instead of trotting into the meadow, the wily old cow plunged down a side hill toward an abandoned beaver pond and the safety of knee deep water. She stood there, the picture of woodland majesty in the moonlit shadows of drowned pines and cedars, turning her head to catch the scent of her pursuers. Ordinarily, Nuk and Mamuk would have abandoned the hunt at this point. A moose can stay in a swamp for hours, days even if he feels like it. The pond had plenty of moose moss to graze on and water to drink. But from their vantage point at the brushy edge of the pond, Chava asked his kinsmen how they would take the moose if they were starving and no other meat was available. A probing question like that from a young hunter is hard to disregard. Unless you feel like boxing the youngster's ears for speaking out of turn, an answer has to be found.

"Well, since there's three of us," Mamuk said, "I suppose the youngest would sneak around to the opposite side and swim underwater until he came to the beaver lodge. Then he'd surface behind the lodge and screech once like a goshawk to let us know he was ready. Think you could do that?"

Chava nodded. Of course, he could do that. He could swim right up to the moose, if he wanted to.

"Okay, then you jump up on top of the lodge, wave your arms around and roar like you're really angry. Got that..?"

Chava nodded.

"The cow will be so scared, she'd jump straight up in the air and run over to us. Something like that..."

"Should I do it, then?" Chava asked, eager to show his prowess.

"If you feel like taking a swim," his grandfather replied, with a kindly smile. "But be mighty careful. If the cow charges you, you'll be in a fix. A moose can fight a whole lot better in the water than we can. You'll be all waterlogged. And what have you learned about a moose's hooves?"

"Well, Father told me they were like a swivel socket, but I never saw them in action."

"And you don't want to," Mamuk said. "Mind you don't let her get close enough to club you. She can split a black bear's skull open with those hooves, and you know how hard a bear's head is."

"Not really," Chava replied, honestly.

"A lot harder than yours," Nuk advised. "Swim like hell, if she attacks."

So Chava disappeared into the forest, and in a few minutes his hunting mates heard a goshawk's screech. They relaxed their muscles, getting ready for anything to happen.

Chava knew that the abandoned beaver lodge would very likely hold his weight. His father had investigated many beaver ponds with him. He knew that the tree gnawers lived in a hollow chamber inside the dome of sticks and mud, and that their constructions were very solid. Last winter when the ice was on, Father had insisted that he break into an old lodge like this one, to shelter from a blizzard. It had taken a long time to break a hole. The flat-tailed gnawers were excellent builders. This spring he had watched a family of beavers at work for several weeks, constructing a dam across a small brook; then as the pond grew, building their lodge in deep water. It was beautiful how they could do all that building with no hands, just using their teeth and clever little paws. But this lodge had been abandoned for several years. The beaver smell was weak, the dam was in disrepair and some willows were starting to grow back around the pond. That meant that the lodge could have weak spots, so he was cautious as he climbed the back side of the structure. But it seemed solid.

Testing for footholds, he readied himself to spring up and scare the moose. How would his uncle and grandfather make the kill? Jump onto the old cow's back as she lurched out of the pond? That was how he'd do it. Then a bite to the back of the head where the soft part connected to the hard bone. That would be the best. Or maybe a blow to knock her senseless. Soon he would know. Tensing his legs, he leaped into the air, screaming his most blood curdling yell.

The old cow calmly turned her head from sixty yards away, looking at him levelly with her bored, mean eyes. She hooked her webbed rack at him once to prove that she meant business; then she lifted her tail with ultimate disdain and excavated a few balls of manure.

Sensing failure, Chava bounced on the branches of the lodge, waving his arms wildly, and emitted a series of hideous shrieks. The cow turned her head slowly away from him, choosing to gaze instead at the two yetis on the far bank who were doubled over, convulsing with laughter.

Chava stopped bouncing. He grinned sheepishly, knowing he'd been tricked.

Later, on the way back to the Meeting Bowl with the whitetail doe over his shoulder, Chava was less than enthralled to hear his hunting partners still chortling about the beaver pond. It seemed pretty likely that he'd be hearing that escapade repeated around the campfire—about a hundred percent likely.

Since they were no longer hunting, they walked single file along a game trail. Uncle Nuk carried a willow stringer with four large trout that Chava had harvested from the pond on his return swim. Grandfather held a bushel-sized birch bark cone full of red currents that he said Grandmother and the girls liked. Grandfather and Uncle Nuk seemed to like them, too. They both had crammed their faces with the little sour wild grapes, while Chava had filled the cone. Chava preferred berries to currents, but since the berries were gone for the year, he had eaten several pounds of the fruit after the cone was full. Now, they were almost back to the camp and he was curious to know what was going on there. They'd been gone several hours, and he hoped the old man hadn't talked yet. He like that old one, even though he was as weak as a baby. In spite of being taught from infancy to be wary of yrts as if they were worse than poisonous snakes, he didn't see the harm in this one. What was the taboo all about, anyway? He needed to know about that. Probably the Council was shedding light on all his questions, while he was out hunting.

Up ahead, the flickering from the Council fire seeped through the thick cedar boughs. Chava thought it was strange that the light didn't carry farther in the dark woods. Only a few steps back, he hadn't been able to see the firelight at all, although he had been orienting himself on the cooking meat smell for almost a mile. Suddenly, Uncle Nuk stiffened. Chava and Mamuk immediately froze behind him.

*

What had started out tense as a witch trial in front of the Grand Inquisition soon turned into an easy, animated discussion. The minute Sri Rainy finished enlightening them on one topic, another yeti would stand up, introduce him or herself, and pose another question. The subject of nuclear waste and nuclear energy had been exhausted rather early on, partly because Sri Rainy was far from an expert in that field. But during the last two hours, the questions were aimed directly toward practical and moral issues that related to human beings, or star men as the yetis always referred to them. Star man was apparently the official designation, while yrt meant something like pig with smooth skin. As one might reasonably imagine, Sri Rainy was somewhat blown away when they kept referring to him as a star man, since that tended to confirm his own private theories of the origin of the species—theories that probably would have gotten him locked in a nut ward if he went public with them.

Some of the questions already discussed were: where did the star men originally come from? Why did they come to Earth? Are they planning to destroy the planet on purpose, or just because they're stupid yrts? If you were a yeti, how would you stop them from spreading into our mountains? Rainy, as the visible representative to the star men, was forced to admit that he didn't know the answer to any of those questions.

A nursing female named Megan, with rather large, lactating breasts, then raised the issue of birth control. Specifically, why star men thought they should overbreed the existing livable land.

Sri Rainy smiled at her, surprisingly finding her breasts very attractive. "I myself have no offspring," he answered. "And as I said, it's difficult for me to speak for my race, but the sexual act is considered very pleasant."

"Of course. It's pleasant for us, too," Megan said, shyly. Most of the younger females tittered in agreement and the males nodded their heads. "But with rare exceptions, we limit ourselves to one offspring per parent."

"Which explains why you haven't overrun the planet," Rainy replied, seriously. "But zero population growth doesn't leave much of a surplus in case of disease or natural disaster. If your policy had been more like the yrts, you would have had a considerable population when we yrts originally came. You would have perhaps been in a dominant position instead of being forced to hide on the mountain tops."

Montclief translated, then added, "I don't believe we were ever forced to hide on the mountains. We chose to do so. The Old Ones suggested that this was the best course for us. Thus we have survived the floods that twice destroyed all but a few of the star men. That is what the Ancestors say." There was a murmur of approval as he translated his comments back to his kinsmen.

"You are in actual communication with your ancestors?" Rainy asked in astonishment.

"Naturally. As you are. I have seen you sitting crosslegged many times, deep in talk with the Ancient Ones."

"Ah, meditation..? Do you talk to supernatural beings in a trance state?"

"With the Ancestors," Montclief said firmly, then translated for the others. A commotion on the edge of the bowl stopped his growling words. All the yetis leaped to a defensive posture.

Rainy looked up to see the large black yeti, Nuk, stepping through the cedar trees carrying the dangling form of Norman Ungerer, the student who had disappeared, clad in a filthy white Seekers robe. Sri Rainy was shocked to see the boy.

"What have we here?" Nuk shouted, holding the former cook at arm's length. Nuk seemed wild with outrage. Norman was smiling beatifically, unaware that disemboweling was the penalty for witnessing a yeti conclave.

"Ungerer..!" exclaimed Sri Rainy. He hastily explained to Montclief that the boy was one of his students and couldn't possibly mean any harm. "He must have followed us!"

"No," Montclief replied, gruffly. "Nobody followed me." He canted his head toward Yolanda as if seeking confirmation.

Yoli shook her head in negation. "Nobody followed," she agreed gutturally in Yetiese.

But there didn't seem to be another explanation. Rainy remembered that Ungerer had run off somewhere after the horrible incident with the bear and bicycle. He must have followed them from wherever he had been hiding. How else could he have gotten here?

Montclief motioned for Nuk to put the disheveled monk down.

"No harm is done," old Shanni said, peaceably. "We can always accident them in the ripeness of time. For now, what the old one is saying pertains to the Council. Let him say on." Nods of agreement bobbed around the semi-circle. Montclief translated, leaving the part out about the "accidents".

"Hello, Sri Rainy," Norman said, ecstatically. "Isn't this something!"

"How did you get here, Ungerer?" the old man asked, quietly. "Did you follow us?"

Montclief translated almost inaudibly, while Yolanda stood up and took the deer from Chava. She patted him on his wooly head and told him to wash up.

"I've been walking for days, sir," Norman answered. "It just seemed like I had to get to someplace. It was the most important thing I ever did, like the reason I was born. I can't even explain it, but when I saw the firelight, I knew this was the place I had to be. Then I looked through the trees and there you were! It's uncanny, isn't it?"

"Very," Sri Rainy replied. He turned to the yetis. "This is Norbert Ungerer, one of my students. He says he was guided here by destiny or the Great Spirit, or something..."

The yetis murmured among themselves as Montclief translated.

"Norman," Norman corrected.

"What..?"

"My name is Norman, sir. You said Norbert. No big deal. If you're changing my name to Norbert, that's fine. I just wasn't sure if that was what you were doing."

"His name is Norman Ungerer," Rainy corrected himself. Montclief didn't bother to translate.

"What are these magnificent creatures, Sri Rainy? Did you see the way that black one lifted me straight up in the air with only one hand?"

"They're Rocky Mountain yetis," Rainy bluffed. He didn't know if that was technically correct or not, but since Montclief was translating he would shortly be finding out. Anyway, since he was the first man to see them, he could name them that if he wanted to. Or maybe he should name them Rainy's Yetis. Why not?

"Sit down, Mr. Ungerer, and be quiet," he said to the boy. Something was very disturbing about Ungerer. Any normal person would be scared blue in this situation, but he didn't seem frightened in the least. Maybe there would be time soon to interview this lad, at length. Could it be that he'd skipped all eight of the Cardinal Steps and really had landed in a permanently enlightened state? What a thing that would be. I could perform the Master's Ceremony right here. Obviously, these people love ritual.

"What's a Rocky Mountain yeti, Sri Rainy?" Ungerer asked, calmly sitting at his master's feet. His voice had none of the snivelling moron quality that he was famous for. He genuinely wanted to know.

"Quiet," Rainy whispered, gently. "It's like a Himalayan yeti. Are you hungry?"

"Not really. I've been finding nuts and little sour berries."

Rainy nodded. "I'll catch some fish for us later. Just follow along with the flow. My friend is translating into English." He nodded to Montclief. Norman locked his lips and crossed his legs in a full lotus position.

But the yetis all seemed hesitant to speak in the presence of an extra yrt. After what seemed like an eternity, Nuk stepped forward from the shadows of the cedars where he had been prowling around, looking for other interlopers. He made what seemed to Rainy like a "warding-off of evil" gesture with his left hand.

"Why the Old Ways speak of taboo between stone man and star man?" he asked gruffly in broken English.

Eyes widened around the campfire, especially Montclief's, but he translated Nuk's words off-handedly. Then he asked, "How is it that you know yrt language, my son? I did not teach you."

"No, you did not. But you know it and I know it, which means we both break the taboo, unless I don't understand what the ancestors say."

Montclief looked around the ring of surprised faces, waiting for someone to speak. Finally he remembered to translate for Rainy.

"What is the taboo?" the old man asked. "I saw Nuk make a warding-off sign." Norman Ungerer's eyes were alert and peaceful in the firelight as he followed the conversation. "And who are the stone men that he spoke of?" Rainy added.

"This is the beginning of what I called the Council for," Montclief said, speaking slowly in the yeti language. It seemed as if he was searching for the correct words. "It did not seem correct to me that I could be the only stone man who was attracted to the star men. Now, I know I was not alone. My heart feels big in my chest for my son, Nuk." He patted his massive chest. "Who would explain the taboo to our visitors from the stars?" He looked around the circle of glowing eyes again, hoping someone from a different family would take up the story. But no one did.

Finally, Old Mamuk spoke. "You tell the taboo, Young Naka," he said.

"You tell it, Mamuk, and I will translate," Montclief offered deferentially, although he was nearly as old as Mamuk.

"I will tell the taboo story, if all agree," a strong but wizened yeti named Og spoke from the center of the group. A wide swath of old scar tissue ran down his neck and over his right shoulder. Og was Darla's uncle, and he loved to talk at Council Meetings. Montclief counted on fairness from old Og.

"Yes, you tell it, Og," Mamuk rumbled, agreeably.

Old Og rose to his feet and set them firmly on the ground, then clearing his throat, he began. "First there were two peoples living in harmony—the Stone People of the mountains and the Grass People of the plains. They met in Council and honored the Ancestors together.

"But when the first Star Wanderers came, the Grass People disregarded the Ancestors' warnings and joined with the Star Wanderers to build the great stone and mud cities. And they broke the taboo of interbreeding, and eventually they forgot their Stone brothers and the Old Ways.

"Then the little moon broke apart and there was great sorrow on the world. Mountains rose and fell. The ocean wave covered the land and the ice came. When after long seasons of birth and death, the ice was rolled back, the Stone People sought the Grass People, and they were gone. We fasted and asked the Ancestors, did the breaking of the taboos cause the sorrow? But the Ancestors did not answer. It seemed they had spoken once on the taboos and would not speak again. So we remembered the original words."

Og paused to look around. Rainy was enthralled.

Ungerer, sitting beside him, was practically levitating as Montclief finished speaking the English words. Why hadn't this boy shown any early signs of progress? Hadn't he been dull as a brick? Yes, he had. But he certainly wasn't dull now. He was vibrating with baraka. Rainy could feel his strong emanations and they were very good. He seemed to be totally awakened.

On the other hand, a few of the older yetis were nodding off. That was presumably why Og had paused. Rainy had employed the same technique many times before a sleeping audience.

The scarred old yeti resumed his tale. "Then when the ice melted and game was plentiful again, the Star Wanderers returned in their flying bowls. This time the Star Wanderers weren't so strange looking and we called them Star Men. In time, Red and White and Black and Yellow came, but all men from the stars. No Grass Men were alive to join with them. Once again we kept the Old Ways and the taboos, and only watched while they built their cities. Then the terrible booming-fire wars came and the cities were destroyed and all but the red skin Star Men were driven away. Then there was peace. But a huge roaring came from the sky, and darkness and falling stones. The mountains heaved and a thunder wave of water ate the land, killing and smashing everything. And the ice came again.

"When the ice went back again to the north, only the stone people remained. We fasted and asked the Ancestors what had caused the wars of sorrow, and how we should continue; but again there was no answer, for if the Ancestors knew, they did not answer.

"In time, a wandering people came from the south. They looked like the Red Star Men, but the cities they built were of bison skins stretched on tree poles, or of mud, and they had no fire weapons. It was a time of peace, and meat was plentiful. And we kept the Old Ways.

"And then, Star Man," Og said, looking directly at Sri Rainy, "after many generations of Ancestors, the

Whites and Blacks came back from the East to make war again on the Reds. This time they rode on horses, not on flying bowls.

"Now, for sixty winters the wars have stopped. We believe the White Star Men have won because they multiply like maggots from the black fly, while the Reds and Blacks do not. But lately we have seen the Yellows, too, moving up the mountain. Since you are here, tell us this story from your eyes. Tell us why you kill the others of your kind, but not even for meat. What is the reason for this thing? The Ancestors do not know, and we have thought long on this, but we do not know." Og stopped talking and sat back down.

The fire was burning low. Montclief walked over to a pile of logs which had been gathered. He picked up a long birch limb. "Do we talk on through the night, or are there some here who would sleep?"

Restlessness rustled through the yetis, while Montclief held the limb unmoving. Finally, a greybeard stood. "I am Shih," he said. "I would eat again before we sleep, but before even my stomach is filled, my ears would hear the story of this Star Man." He sat back down, prepared to listen.

Montclief placed the birch log on the fire and nodded to Rainy.

Sri Rainy stood. He had been hoping that the decision for sleep would carry the day, but since it hadn't, he tried to arrange his thoughts. "Your story of the long history was good for my ear to hear. Those of us called yrts have forgotten that we came from the stars, so our story is very short compared to yours. We do not remember the ice. Only by studying the mountains and the plains do we read the signs of this history. Many of us have a longing for the stars, but none of us knows why. We believe that the four races, black, yellow, red and white are descended from a common ancestor. By studying the land to find our story, we have discovered the bones of ancient people—maybe the Grass People of your story. We believe that all yrts are children of these old ones. And we explain the differences in our physiology with the weak theory of selective breeding."

Many of the yetis smiled at the foolishness of that speculation.

"Since I have never fully believed that theory, I am glad you say a different history from ours," Rainy went on. "As far as killing and war, we are aware that we are the only large species on this planet which often kills its own kind. We do not easily explain this to ourselves. In some isolated communities, yrts even kill other yrts for meat, even though other food is readily available. We do not explain this practice either, but most yrt societies have a taboo against eating the flesh of their own kind. As to your real question, I do not know why we kill. We say we do it to protect our territory, but other mammals seldom kill for that reason. The stronger male might drive the weaker away, or not let him breed, but they seldom kill."

"If the weaker will not go away, sometimes the stronger is forced to kill," Mamuk said, softly.

"As you say," Sri Rainy answered. "But you have witnessed that we star men also have wars, where we kill many and destroy cities. No one knows why we do that either. We say it is to protect an idea of freedom, or to force another to our way of living. Perhaps sometimes we kill for plain greed, lusting after another man's possessions or females. Or maybe just in fear. Then, when the killing is over, we are sorry and no longer sure why we did this terrible thing. We act like we could never do it again, until something makes us angry once more. Then suddenly another killing cycle starts."

Rainy looked reflectively around the circle of furry faces. "I would say that your Ancestors were wise to make the taboo against becoming friends with my people. But I don't know how the Ancestors could have known that."

"The Ancestors are very wise," Montclief reflected.

"Yes, but wise or not, your territory will soon be overrun with star men you cannot hide from. Their numbers are too many, and if you make them angry, they will hunt you to extinction. I cannot stop this from happening, I do not believe anybody can stop it."

Montclief translated, then added, "Like they did to Sigmoid." Many of the yetis nodded their heads in agreement.

"Who is Sigmoid?" Rainy asked, thinking a yeti had been killed. Surely he would have heard about that; but perhaps not. The yeti might have crawled off to die alone, or the hunter might have thought he killed a polar bear.

"Sigmoid is the red bear who made your people angry," Montclief said. "I thought I told you his name."

"No. If you did, I don't remember. Are your people and the bears friendly?"

"Not friends, but we share the same mountains. We sometimes name a dominant bear or a wolf leader, so we can talk about their deeds. It's not important."

"I see," Rainy replied. "Yes, your situation is exactly like the grizzly's," he said to the larger audience. "Sigmoid frightened the yrts and made them angry, and they shot him. The same will happen to you, if you decide to protect your territory. And if the poison comes to my mountain, there will be many more yrts living in the high country, therefore more danger to you."

"May I speak, Sri Rainy," Norman Ungerer asked, urgently.

Rainy looked down at the young man sitting at his feet, then spoke to the yetis. "This young star man, my student, claims he was called to this spot. Perhaps the Great Spirit called him, or perhaps your Ancestors did. I don't know what did, but something definitely called him—or else why would he be here? I believe you should let him speak."

Heads nodded agreement around the Council fire. "Speak," Montclief said to Norman Ungerer.

Looking like a string bean in a dirty robe, Norman struggled to his feet. His legs were both asleep from sitting crosslegged so long. That often happened to him when he was meditating or playing the drone. He kept asking people what he was doing wrong, but nobody seemed to think it was very important, so he hadn't found a way to sit like that without killing his legs.

"My legs are asleep," he said, sheepishly explaining why he had to clutch onto Sri Rainy for support.

"I'll teach you to sit right tomorrow," Rainy said.

"Thank you," Norman answered. He turned to address the yetis. "While I was listening to your legends, an idea came to me. It may sound foolish, but I think it might be a reasonable solution to some of your problems. Sri Rainy has a monastery where several hundred people can live. I count your number to be fifty-six. No one comes to the monastery except people who Sri Rainy allows. If many new workers come to the mountains, you could put on our robes and live with us. I am sure you would look like the other students. All of our men could grow beards and long hair. You would be safe there, if we organized it correctly. Then when the workers leave the mountain, as they surely will someday, since living at the high altitude is unpleasant for our kind, you could go back to your old ways. Or whatever you want to do. In the meantime, you could learn our ways. Anyway, that was the thought that came to me." Norman sat back down.

The yetis stirred, but no one spoke.

Sri Rainy watched them. It was clear that Ungerer had been called precisely to deliver that message. It was inspired. Rainy himself, would never have thought of that solution. It was perfectly simple, and it would work. Although certainly far from the freedom that the yetis now enjoyed, it definitely would keep them safe through the initial repository filling period. Ungerer had suddenly become his logical heir, praise the saints and the Spirit for sending him. When he takes over the Retreat, the yetis will have a safe haven for years to come. It definitely could work. We can even buy more land from the people who will want to sell if the nuke poison comes. But won't we all be infected with escaping radiation? Not for awhile. They'll protect it for at least a hundred years while everybody is watching. Barring an accident, of course. It actually might work. Ungerer is brilliant.

"Which brings us back to the matter of the taboo," black Nuk said, standing up again. He looked cautiously around the circle, then let his eyes rest on his father. "Five winters ago, I found a red woman of the Kiowa tribe wondering lost and injured in my hunting ground. I remembered the taboos, and I remembered my mother was killed in birthing because she helped a yrt to escape an avalanche. But my heart was moved toward this red star woman, and I followed her. When she fell and did not get up, I carried her to my cave and nursed her back to health. The beauty of her spirit takes my breath away. We have two children, a boy and a girl; so the taboo has been broken. Maybe that is what brings the poison to the mountains. I sought council only from the Ancestors, but they did not speak. Our children are strong and healthy. They learn our ways and my wife's. I do not believe that all Star Men are evil." Nuk sat back down, and lifted his face to stare at the star lit sky.

Pacing around the fire, Montclief reached down and pulled the still flaming birch log to one side, so it would burn out slowly. "I think that we should sleep now," he said. "Tomorrow we will speak again." He took Yolanda's hand and they walked up the incline toward one of the caves with Chava tagging along. "Sleep in your brother's cave," Montclief said gently to his second son. Chava smiled slyly and turned his head around toward Nuk.

"What do the children look like," Old Shanni asked brashly, grabbing Nuk by the elbow. Her daughters and the other young women sucked in their breath, and all eyes turned back to Nuk.

"They look like furry red star men," he answered with a grim smile. "Come, little brother. You hunted well today, even though an old cow moose wasn't frightened of you. Tomorrow I will teach you to be more ferocious."

The boy's grandfather roared with laughter. He'd been waiting all evening to tell the tale of the beaver pond. It was at least as important as the dull history they'd been discussing. "You should have seen young Chava," he began, but all the yetis were dispersing to their caves.

Shanni jerked his gnarled hand. "Come to bed, old grandfather," she scolded. "Leave the the young ones to talk and get acquainted." She pulled Mamuk up the hill with one hand, and with the other shoved her daughter, Hanni, toward an eligible young bachelor.

CHAPTER 21

HIDE THE STROKE IN THE SLEEVE OF THE GOWN

Some months later, a shaggy grizzly bear rug complete with the huge taxidermied head frozen in a snarl, arrived at Melton Pinkle's office at the Nuclear Regulatory Commission, a gift from the good people of Colorado. Pinkle and Dewitt Gefflerhagen chuckled over the preposterous gift for a ten full minutes, arranging it here and there around the foyer and calling in various secretaries to see what effect it had on them. Then Pinkle called a custodian and had him cart the hideous thing down to the archives where it would be permanently mothballed.

With that taken care of, he sent off a letter of effusive thanks to Colorado's sorry Governor, who seemed to be doing rather poorly in the pre-election polls. Melton failed to inform Governor Potts of the inquiries he'd received from a substantial number of legislators regarding the Pike's Folly site. He also forgot to mention that the Colorado site had been indefinitely shelved because of the Congressional nosiness. As a parting remark, he offered his congratulations on the new Pike Township Federal Wilderness Park that had passed the House of Representatives as an addendum to a housing bill the other day.

Then he got down to the heady business of making his final decision on which of the two salt dome sites to approve first. One was in Nevada, the other was near Four Corners, New Mexico. He leaned slightly toward New Mexico, although both governors had assured him that choosing their state would see him immortalized. They promised to name the hole after him. The Melton C. Pinkle Nuclear Waste Repository. He loved the sound of it, and couldn't wait to attend the inaugural ribbon cutting ceremony.

*

Billy hung around the Retreat, keeping up the pressure on the legislators. He felt very much like a mosquito trying to bother an elephant. He gave two concerts with his old band, both of which were recorded live and turned into albums, but they weren't enough to restart the stalled wagon train of big time success. Well, truthfully, the new songs in the set weren't his. The other guys in the band had been writing and wanted to air their new material. Billy had agreed, even though he was only lukewarm about the songs. His own new songs hadn't happened. He hadn't found time to write them.

The concerts, naturally, raised enough money to buy stamps, and sparked a little interest in his old albums, but... But one day, Sri met with a handful of his older students and suggested that it would be a good idea for them to start the next phase of their personal work. He thought it would be interesting for them to move to the monastery in Trinidad. Carlo Sentori had written, extending an invitation to a few senior students to take part in an in-depth seminar he was planning to give on the creative use of spiritual energy. The suggestion stuck a harmonic chord in Billy. Trinidad, calypso music, steel drums. Yes, maybe he could find something fresh there. A rebirth of sorts.

Later in the day he asked for a private audience with Sri, and after talking briefly about the dwindling letter writing campaign, he said that Trinidad sounded like a good idea.

Sri was thoughtful for a few minutes, then advised him to go freely to Trinidad. The seminar might be useful to him. The old man got a sly look on his face. "What would you think of traveling incognito?" he asked. "You could change your name and get a haircut. Maybe grow a beard. I think it would be very useful for you to be, well, a normal Seeker for awhile, with no special favors shown." He nodded his old head and smiled meaningfully. "What do you think?"

Billy didn't know about that. Had he been shown favoritism at some time? His sleeping cell was as cold as anyone else's. But maybe Sri was right. It might be interesting not to have his reputation proceed him. At least for a few weeks. He could always let it slip in Trinidad who he was, if he needed to work on his music. After a pause, he told Sri that he'd think about a new identity, and stood up to go.

"I can arrange for you to be, uh, Clarence Dibbs. How does that sound?" Sri asked. "You can fly down by yourself, get there a month before the others arrive. Just be this Clarence Dibbs from Los Angeles, and nobody will be the wiser."

"Won't our people know?" Billy asked.

"I can practically guarantee that nobody from here will catch onto a thing," the old geezer said, with a twinkle in his eye. "Come back in a few years, if the time gets ripe for you. Ungerer will be here, I expect, overseeing a new project. He may need a music director. And Sister Angie may have a better recipe for tollhouse cookies by then." He winked at Billy.

Billy grinned and shook his head in amazement. How did Sri know every little detail that happened at the Retreat? It was mind boggling.

*

That winter was a rather awful time for Lotti McCardle. The news of Willard's disappearance swept back and forth across the township in waves of gossip. Finally after Christmas, the Steadly boys fessed up to moving the jeep for a joke. They thought Willard had been visiting with old man Berlinheimer.

Dink Moran, the deputy sheriff, now had a location for the vanishing act. At last, he could sink his teeth into an investigation. Old man Berlinheimer proved conclusively to have been Christmasing in Fort Collins at the time, and that left the only other resident of Mudslide Pass, the old crazy coot, Asa Peters, as the prime suspect for foul play.

Dink saw no useful purpose in bogging down a search party in Mudslide Pass during the severe winter snows; but come the spring melt-off, he and four deputies from Clinton paid a surprise visit to Asa Peters' potato spread. What they found was Asa and his mule both inside the cabin, both frozen to death, or starved to death and then frozen to death. Either way the facts seemed clear, Asa and the mule were dead. The mule seemed deader than Asa. Part of him was eaten.

After sampling a bottle of Asa's homebrew, a thorough search of the farm was made in hopes of finding the legendary still, where a few more bottles were likely to be stashed. In the process, the shallow grave of Willard Jacks was discovered.

Lotti was shattered. Much more shattered than she'd imagined she would be, since her other prospective rides to Hollywood had evaporated. She had held out the slim hope that Willard would reappear with some story of amnesia or a trip to Tahiti, but now he never would. Her grief was boundless. And her letters to Lute Sims went unanswered, week after week. She even sought consolation with Billy Drummond up at the Retreat, but he'd sold his cute red 4X4, or it had been repossessed or something. Just like the creep to be no help at all in her hour of need. Mortimer, of course, never had a car, so he was no help either. All that summer and into the fall she moped around town, sometimes not even bothering to change clothes more than twice a day. She was desolate. The mine had closed before it was even opened, and hopelessness hung over her like a leaden cloud.

About the only good thing that happened was that one day around Labor Day a package arrived from New York. In it was Lute Sims' new book entitled Martians on the Mountain. Lute enclosed a note and a small vial of expensive perfume from Saks 5th Avenue.

The note read:

Dear Lotti,

Hope you like the book. I enjoyed meeting you. Give my regards to your mother.

Lute

Sure that the slim novel would be her ticket to fame and fortune, the girl hurried upstairs and changed into her reading outfit. Hollywood would be clamoring for her shortly. Why not? Real life heroines of a book were in high demand for game shows and appearances on Opra. But as she read the first few pages of the goddamned book, she realized that Lute had it all wrong! She was nothing like this tramp, Dora Castro. Dora Castro?! What a stupid name! How could he do that to her? She couldn't call up Opra and say she was a bitch like Dora Castro.

Everybody else in the book was just like real life, but not goddamned Dora! Why didn't he put in all the good things she did? Here she was, practically the saint of Pike's Grove, and he made Dora into a vile slut! It was so unfair!

*

The two day hike back to the Retreat had been extremely wonderful for Norman Ungerer. Walking beside Sri Rainy and Montclief, having far-ranging discussions with them about the deep nature of everything, had sent Norman to the moon. Sri Rainy knew so much and shared it freely, now that Norman had a new name. Baba Norman Ungerer. The Shepherd. That's what the name meant. Baba. And his job would be to care for the yetis, to see that no harm befell them.

In a firelight ceremony at the Meeting Bowl, he had received the new name and his life task, and the pledge from all those magnificent yetis to be his friend. Sri Rainy had been solemn, stern even, as he recited a long list of promises that Norman was honored to agree to. The next morning, they had started back to the Retreat, stopping along the way to fish and cook the rice that Sri Rainy had had the foresight to bring.

Back at the Retreat, Sri made everyone assemble in the dining hall, and announced to them that Baba Norman was his successor and that his lineage of Seekers would now continue unbroken. Norman sat on the raised dias to the right of Sri. It was quite an honor; but the deferential way that everybody treated him after the meeting was a little disconcerting at first. Even Sister Angie was suddenly sweet as sugar.

The Plan that he and Sri Rainy discussed and agreed to was to let the colony of Seekers dwindle of its own accord, and then to further reduce the number by other means that Sri had in mind, until the only people left behind could be trusted with the secret of the yetis. By early autumn of the following year, this was accomplished and Montclief, with six other yetis, arrived at the Retreat one moonless night. It was Baba Norman's brainstorm to dress them as lumberjacks, and give out the cover story that they were harvesting and replanting some timber on the extra acreage that the Retreat had purchased. And by golly, in the wool jackets and baggy wool pants, they did look exactly like hairy Swedish loggers, or at least close enough that nobody in Pike's Grove seemed to pay any attention when he accompanied one or two of them to town. It was great! He was almost sure that his life work would proceed with no major hassles. And when Sri Rainy finished the Book of Yetis, which he was working on daily,they would get it published quietly when the time was auspicious. The royalties from the book would fund the little community blissfully into the foreseeable future.

*

With the coming of fresh snow, Lotti's hope took a surge. A logging operation or something had evidently started up on the mountain near the Retreat. Every now and then she'd see burly loggers coming into town with that Norman Ungerer boy. From her desolate balcony window, she watched them carefully, making no overt move. That had been her problem before, she decided. Too eager. Real women played hard to get for real men. And these were obviously real men. Strong and silent and heavily bearded. True, they were a little too old for her. Their beards were gray and shaggy, but their wool shirts were bursting at the seams with heavy muscles. What they needed was a real woman's touch to spiff them up a bit. Bachelor loggers were always pretty scruffy; but after working all winter in the woods, they'd have money to burn.

And loggers always had wheels, that was a well known fact. They had to. Moving around looking for new trees to cut required wheels. They'd be putty in her hands. When spring came, these huge, virile loggers would bring their trucks to town, and then she would play hard to get in just the right way.

The future very definitely was brightening. Lotti sprawled across her bed and filled out an order to Frederick's of Hollywood for the very latest black see-through teddy. If she couldn't catch a logger with that, she would be very, very surprised.

But wait a minute..! The post office was putting Willard's old jeep up for sale at the auction over in Clinton. If there was any fairness at all, she should get that jeep, since she was practically Willard's widow. If he had lived another month or two, she would be his widow. She should, at least, get first crack at buying it. Mother, dear, would probably give her the down payment. Lord knows, they needed a vehicle for the Lodge. How had they survived all these years without one? Even her mother would understand the simple arithmetic of going to Food City in Clinton for groceries instead of to Wong's. Without waiting for second thoughts, she ran downstairs, threw on her parka and snow boots and set out to see Jolie Spalding. Jolie would get her that old jeep if anybody could. Jolie understood that jeeps from Pike's Grove should stay in Pike's Grove. Perfect. Then once she got it paid for, she was out of here. Hello Hollywood!

Wait a minute! Maybe Jolie would give her Willard's old job delivering the mail. Why not? Then she could get the new jeep, just like Willard would have. Wouldn't that be slick—driving down Sunset Boulevard into the MGM Studios in a brand new jeep? Eyes would turn that day. Walking lightly over the deep snowdrifts, Lotti planned her wardrobe. Eyeballs would definitely turn, that was for sure.

ORDER INFORMATION

Telephone Orders: Call (310) 829-2752.
Have your credit card ready.
Postal Orders:

Synapse—Centurion
225 Santa Monica Blvd. Suite 1204B
Santa Monica, California 90401

Please send the following books.
I understand that I may return any book in new condition for a full refund—no questions asked.

The Bride's Book
by Rev. Bill Smith $6.95

The Devil's Drainpipe
by Keith Kirts $10.95

Space Sex by Keith Kirts
- coming 1994

Acupuncture & Fishing
by Stephen Rosenblatt, M.D., Acc.
& Keith Kirts
- coming in 1994

Shipping Charge:
Book Rate: $2.00 for the first book and 75 cents for each additional book.
Air Mail: $3.50 per book.
Sales Tax: California residents add 8.25%

• Discover • Mastercard • Visa • AMEX